LOST SOULS

AT THE

Neptune Inn

ALSO BY BETSY CARTER

LOST SOULS
AT THE
Neptune Inn

A NOVEL

BETSY CARTER

GRAND CENTRAL
PUBLISHING

NEW YORK   BOSTON

Copyright © 2020 by Betsy Carter

Cover design by Joanne O'Neill
Cover copyright © 2020 by Hachette Book Group, Inc.

Grand Central Publishing
Hachette Book Group
1290 Avenue of the Americas, New York, NY 10104
grandcentralpublishing.com
twitter.com/grandcentralpub

First Edition: August 2020

Grand Central Publishing is a division of Hachette Book Group, Inc. The Grand Central Publishing name and logo is a trademark of Hachette Book Group, Inc.

The publisher is not responsible for websites (or their content) that are not owned by the publisher.

The Hachette Speakers Bureau provides a wide range of authors for speaking events. To find out more, go to www.hachettespeakersbureau.com or call (866) 376-6591.

Print book interior design by Abby Reilly

Library of Congress Cataloging-in-Publication Data

Names: Carter, Betsy, 1945- author.
Title: Lost souls at the Neptune Inn : a novel / Betsy Carter.
Description: First Edition. | New York : Grand Central Publishing, 2020. |
Identifiers: LCCN 2020008871 | ISBN 9781538763919 (hardcover) | ISBN 9781538763902 (ebook)
Subjects: GSAFD: Love stories. | Mystery fiction.
Classification: LCC PS3603.A7768 L67 2020 | DDC 813/.6--dc23
LC record available at https://lccn.loc.gov/2020008871

ISBNs: 978-1-5387-6391-9 (hardcover), 978-1-5387-6390-2 (ebook)

Printed in the United States of America

LSC-C

10 9 8 7 6 5 4 3 2 1

For Susan Kamil

But home was a dream
One I'd never seen till you came along.

—Jason Isbell

"Cover Me Up"

LOST SOULS
AT THE
Neptune Inn

PART 1

Like a piece of shattered glass, New Rochelle slips into New York with its jagged southern coastline butting against the Long Island Sound. The winters are colorless and cold, and the Sound turns a discouraging metallic green. But in springtime, cherry blossoms and lilacs perfume the air. The Sound becomes a tropical blue, hospitable to the sailboats that pour into its waters. On land, the flouncy three-story Queen Annes and plainspoken Cape Cods come alive with the sounds of lawn mowers and the smells of fried chicken.

In this congenial suburb, Geraldine and Earle Wingo ran the bakery founded by her parents, Shore Cakes, the oldest bakery in town. The smell of melting butter and cinnamon oozed from its whitewashed façade, strawberry shortcakes and chocolate cookies filled the shelves, and its walls were covered by photographs of New Rochelle sunsets and various shots of a humpback whale that once swam so far inland that the *New York Times* even sent a photographer.

Both her parents were gone now, but Geraldine still had her mother's Italian looks: olive complexion, midnight black hair and dark whirlpool eyes. With her feisty nature, she was the opposite of soft-spoken Earle, whose pale blue eyes played like chimes against his milk-white skin and wavy blond hair.

The young Wingos' story seemed a happy one in a happy place, hardly worth telling, until, on an early March afternoon in 1929, as the sky turned black and a hollow wind blew through town, Geraldine gave birth to a girl baby.

Geraldine was in labor for three hours, easy as these things go.

After that, "easy" went the way of the wind.

Chapter 1

It was Earle who wanted a baby.

At twenty, Geraldine wasn't ready to give herself up to a child.

Once the prom queen of New Rochelle High, she tended to herself with the fastidiousness of a cat. Each day, she massaged Pond's cold cream into her skin and dabbed 4711 cologne onto her wrists and neck. She brushed her hair with one hundred strokes and spread Vaseline over her fire-red lipstick. With her curvy figure, held in place by a girdle, Geraldine enjoyed the way men's eyes blanketed her with something more than admiration, and she blushed when they told her that she smelled like gardenias. Why on earth would she give all that up for a child? In her vanity and wanton thoughts, she defied God and the Catholic Church.

Earle was an Episcopalian. He found it funny the way Geraldine crossed herself before having sex, and the clatter she'd make rubbing her fingers over those old beads of hers. Did she really think all that confessing would make God overlook the silk stockings and garters she wore?

She told Earle and her priest that her reasons for not wanting a child were practical. "The bakery's starting to make money, and we've just bought our first house. Let's not rock the boat."

But in the late twenties, a childless woman was considered as odd as an unmarried man in his thirties. Geraldine saw how the ladies patted down their hair and ran their tongues over their teeth before speaking to Earle—beautiful Earle. She knew he had other choices. So, grudgingly, she allowed herself to get pregnant, and in 1929, just before the country slid into a depression, Geraldine gave birth. Earle wanted to name their daughter Shirley Mae, after his mother. But Geraldine insisted on Emilia, her grandmother's name. They compromised and called her Emilia Mae.

During the first two months of her life, Emilia Mae howled in colicky pain for hours each day. Earle spent his time at the bakery, leaving Geraldine to wash, feed, diaper, and try to console the inconsolable baby. Geraldine tried everything—rocking chair, castor oil rubs, singing lullabies—but nothing quieted Emilia Mae. Sleep-deprived and desperate, Geraldine took the baby's screams as an affront. Often, she'd run out the door as if her house were ablaze with her daughter's shrieks. No one had told her how a baby would claw at her, body and mind, how she would be lucky if she had time for a shower, much less to run a brush through her hair once or twice.

Earle would come home from work by six thirty. He'd sit with Emilia Mae writhing in his arms and sing to her in his sweet high-pitched voice. She was a chunky baby with light strawberry hair and narrow chestnut eyes that defied you to look away from her. He'd kiss her ample tummy, and nibble on her ears. He'd tell her what a precious girl she was and how her tiny ears smelled like butter cookies straight from the oven. Because he loved her so much, he said, he would try not to eat them. *Of course she smells like butter cookies fresh from the oven,* Geraldine thought. *I spent the last hour cleaning up Emilia Mae's vomit and bathing her. Earle can afford to be all goo-goo-eyed over this baby. If I saw Emilia Mae only two or three hours a day, slept seven hours a night, and had normal days of talking with real people, I could be damned goo-goo-eyed as well.*

By June, whatever hormonal gumbo had kept Geraldine afloat had been sucked dry by the baby's constant wailing. Before Earle even took his jacket off at night, Geraldine would shove the baby at him and demand: "You take her. I've had enough."

Emilia Mae was two months and twelve days old when Earle and Geraldine sat across from each other one Saturday morning. Earle had just looked in on Emilia Mae. "She's sleeping like an angel."

"An angel, *pph*." Geraldine made a spitting noise.

"Let me ask you a question," he said.

One of the things that attracted Geraldine to Earle was his lack of guile. What he said was what he meant, and mostly what he meant was as uncomplicated and well intentioned as a priest's sermon on Christmas Eve. So it never occurred to her that with this question, Earle was about to wheel in a heap of trouble that would sit between them for years.

He put his elbows on the table and leaned toward her. "You do love this baby, don't you?"

It was a rhetorical question, and Geraldine could have nodded or said "Mmm hmm" and left it at that. But she'd been up half the night with Emilia Mae. Her hair was dirty, and her eyes were tiny as apple seeds. She wore her lavender robe, the one with calla lilies embroidered on it, the one that was so sexy and fluid against her skin that Earle hadn't been able to keep his hands off her whenever she wore it. Now it was stained with breast milk and crusts of spit-up, and Earle hadn't laid a finger on it or her since Geraldine's belly was big enough to bend the calla lilies out of shape. In short, Geraldine, who had enough guile for both of them, didn't bother to phrase her answer in order to please Earle. Instead, she spoke what she felt. "I would love this baby if she didn't make me feel like a monster, or if for one moment, I felt she loved me back and didn't bawl her eyes out every time I came near her. If she let me sleep through the night or gave me a moment to shower or fix my hair, that would be nice." Her voice was harsh as the sound of raked rocks. "I know she's your precious lamb. That's because by the time you get here, she's exhausted herself from carrying on all day with me. Then she lies in your arms like a rag doll, and you go all moony. You get to go to work, put on clean clothes, talk to other grown-ups—the things normal people do." She stood up in front of him and outlined her body with her hands. "*This* is how I look on a good day. *This* is not normal."

Earle spoke quietly. "C'mon honey, give it time. She'll grow out of whatever this is. Everyone has trouble adjusting in the beginning."

But time was running out. Earle could tell that whatever initial love Geraldine might have felt for her daughter was drying up. In a desperate attempt to cure the colic, Earle began adding Pepto-Bismol to Emilia Mae's bottles when Geraldine wasn't looking—a drop or two here and there.

Late one afternoon, after Emilia Mae had been wailing for two hours and filled three diapers with inky liquid diarrhea, Geraldine scooped her out of the crib and held her overhead like a trophy. The gesture only made Emilia Mae scream louder. That's when

Geraldine noticed her tongue. She dumped Emilia Mae back into her crib and ran to the living room, where she telephoned Earle at the bakery: "Come home immediately," she shouted, her voice panicked.

"Is everything all right? The baby? Did something happen?"

"The baby is alive. But no, everything is not all right. Nothing I care to discuss on the telephone. Please, come home now."

Earle ran the ten blocks home and threw the door open. "What's wrong?" Geraldine thrust Emilia Mae into his arms and pried open her mouth. "That," she said, pointing to the baby's tongue. "That's what's wrong!"

"What am I looking at?" asked Earle. "I don't see anything."

"Are you blind? Do you not see the color of her tongue? Look again!"

Earle lifted Emilia Mae so she was facing him. "Oh, it's black. I see it now. I'm sure it's completely normal."

"*Normal?* Are you crazy? A baby with a black tongue is not *normal*." Her voice rose with each sentence. "You know who has a black tongue, don't you?"

"I have no idea," said Earle.

"The devil, that's who."

"Oh Geraldine, you don't really believe that, do you?"

"I most certainly do. How else can you explain it?"

"I'm guessing there are at least twenty other explanations, none of them having to do with the devil. Jeez, Geraldine, you take this church stuff too seriously."

"You don't know a Goddamn thing about my church stuff. But I'm telling you, we are seeing the work of the devil in our child."

Emilia Mae was sobbing now, a low, sorrowful wail different from her colicky screams. Her mother's voice was shrill, and her father was holding her too tight. It was as if she knew she was swaddled in trouble.

"Tell you what," said Earle, trying to keep his voice calm. "I'll take her to Dr. Rogan just to make sure everything's okay. Why don't you stay here and get some rest?"

"That old guy won't know any more than we do," said Geraldine.

"I'll take my chances," said Earle, as he bundled up the baby.

Dr. Rogan examined Emilia Mae while Earle told him how Geraldine saw the devil's work in the baby's black tongue. Dr. Rogan waved his hand as if sweeping away cigarette smoke. "Bah, she'll be fine."

He asked Earle what they fed her. "Have you added anything to her formula? Juice, medicine, anything like that?" Earle thought for a moment and mentioned the Pepto-Bismol. He told Dr. Rogan how he'd given Emilia Mae a spoonful now and again to quiet her colic.

Dr. Rogan had a pale, wide face with squinty gray eyes. His lips were always pressed together, as if he was trying to puzzle something out. It was startling when he opened his mouth wide enough for Earle to see his bridgework and let out a guffaw. "There's your devil. I'm afraid the culprit is the Pepto-Bismol." When he pulled himself together, he told Earle that Pepto-Bismol contained a chemical that, when combined with sulfur in saliva, formed a black compound called bismuth sulfide. "You tell that wife of yours that the devil, in this case, is her own husband." He laughed again. "Next time Emilia Mae goes colicky, try a hot water bottle on her stomach. The colic should go away within a month. Pepto-Bismol! The devil! Honestly, I thought I'd heard everything."

When Earle came home, he told Geraldine that he'd been feeding the baby small doses of Pepto-Bismol. "Dr. Rogan says that stuff can turn a tongue black. He had a good laugh about the whole devil thing."

"Well, Dr. Rogan may think that's hilarious, but he doesn't live with this child."

"Oh, Geraldine. Come now, she'll be fine. Dr. Rogan says it will just last a few more weeks."

Geraldine's body went slack. "All that screaming, it's gotten to me. I can't seem to do anything right with her. Why didn't you tell me about the Pepto-Bismol?" She started to cry. "Really, I'm at my wit's end."

"I know, honey," said Earle, wrapping his arms around his wife. "I'm sorry. I was only trying to help."

"I'm trying too, Earle, I really am."

"I know you are. She's an infant. Her tummy hurts. She wants us to make it go away. But she can't tell us, she can only cry. That's what babies do when they hurt. She needs your love."

"I love her, I do. I just don't like her very much."

"You're a good mother, you really are. Remember, only a few more weeks."

"A few weeks seem like forever," said Geraldine, wiping her nose on Earle's jacket. "Anyway, no more Pepto-Bismol, okay?"

"Deal," said Earle. "Can we just love this child and go back to being Mr. and Mrs. Earle Wingo?"

Geraldine leaned her head on his shoulder. "I'd like that." She smiled. "I'll do my best."

Chapter 2

Geraldine tried.

She sang to Emilia Mae, songs her mother used to sing to her.

She went back to brushing her hair more than one hundred times a day, but it never got back the gloss of its youth.

She dressed Emilia Mae in lacy bonnets and hand-knit sweaters.

She worked for years to lose the weight she'd put on while pregnant.

She took Emilia Mae to the park each day and pushed her back and forth on the swing.

She tried a fashionable up-do hairstyle, but it made her Romanesque nose jump out of her face.

At night, she read stories to Emilia Mae.

She dabbed on Guerlain, Joy, and Evening in Paris, but no one told her she smelled of gardenias.

She'd read that getting angry made you furrow your brow and cause permanent wrinkles. She tried not to furrow her brow.

Geraldine was older now, old enough for men to pay her no heed other than in a polite way.

She tried to love her daughter, and in a familial way, she did. But she still couldn't forgive Emilia Mae for stealing the part of her that had turned heads and run wild. Even her own husband, who used to come at her with renewed hunger every time they made love, seemed to have lost his appetite for her since Emilia Mae's birth. Emilia Mae had made Geraldine a mother, and for all the poetic things said and written about mothers, no one seemed to think they were sexy.

The next years lurched by like that, with Geraldine intermittently resentful of her daughter and trying to be a mother whose daughter actually liked her. When Emilia Mae was in fifth grade, *The Wizard of Oz* came out. The first time Earle took Emilia Mae to see it, she gasped when the movie blasted into Technicolor after Dorothy opened the door to Munchkinland. The second time, she went with her friend—really, her only friend—Nina Tyler, and grabbed her arm every time the green Wicked Witch of the West alighted. The third time, she went back with Earle and was thunderstruck by the Scarecrow, Tin Man, and Cowardly Lion. It was like the time she walked by the Touch Up Salon near the bakery and saw herself reflected in their storefront glass, hunched over, a big girl trying to shrink herself. The Scarecrow, Tin Man, and Cowardly Lion took up residence in her imagination as the Oz brothers as she became their leader, Dorothy. At night, Emilia Mae would lie in bed and envision them sitting next to her. They'd have conversations about the day, about school, and how she would speak out in class and bring cupcakes from the bakery to school and make friends with other kids. Although words were never spoken, she always felt that they were cheering her on, and in the morning, she could swear she saw the indentations on her blanket of where the Oz brothers had been sitting.

Not long after, Geraldine came home from the bakery one night and said to Emilia Mae, "I have a surprise for you." She handed her an illustrated copy of *The Wonderful Wizard of Oz*. "I know how much you like the movie, so I thought you ought to read the book. The pictures are beautiful, take a look."

Emilia Mae couldn't remember a time when her mother gave her a present when it wasn't her birthday or Christmas. The Cowardly Lion, Tin Man, and Scarecrow agreed with her that this was a sign that her strong Dorothy personality was working. She ran her hand over the cover and slowly turned the thick gilded pages to pictures of lions, dogs, and scarecrows. The book was heavy and smelled like paste and wood. She clutched it to her chest and said: "This will always be my favorite book."

She thought to throw her arms around Geraldine and say, "Thank you, Mommy," but instead she mumbled, "Thank you, Mother."

More than anything, Emilia Mae wanted to call Geraldine Mommy. She wanted to love her mother. *If she loved me, I know I could love her*, she thought. But with Geraldine's severity and disapproval, Emilia Mae could never find a way in. When she was sick or scared or lonely, she'd think, "I want my mommy." But there was never a mommy there, just a perfectly coiffed trim woman with red lipstick whose hard eyes reflected back to Emilia Mae what she thought her mother saw: a chubby girl, with unkempt curly hair and her father's pallor.

Emilia Mae longed to have her mother stroke her cheek, touch her in the soothing way that mothers touched their children, but Geraldine didn't seem interested in those things. Emilia Mae thought her mother was pretty. She knew how to get things done. She could be funny. People noticed her. She was all those things, but she wasn't a mommy. Emilia Mae took *The Wonderful Wizard of Oz* to her room and learned more about Dorothy, who lived on the sun-bleached prairies of Kansas with her Uncle Henry and Aunt Em. Aunt Em, she read, had once been a young pretty wife, but the sun and wind "had taken the sparkle from her eyes and left them a sober gray; they had taken the red from her cheeks and lips, and they were gray also. She was thin and gaunt, and never smiled, now."

That night, she discussed it with the Oz brothers. Maybe Aunt Em was sad. New Rochelle wasn't sun-bleached, but the Tin Man said that there were other things that could take away a person's sparkle and glow. Emilia Mae thought about this for a long time. Maybe her mother was sad, too, because she had a daughter who was boring, who never really said very much. The Scarecrow suggested she could change all that. How she could talk up more, be braver. The Cowardly Lion said that if Dorothy was brave enough to face the Wicked Witch of the West, surely Emilia Mae could try harder to make a good impression. To be noticed. Emilia Mae agreed. Her mother would like to have a daughter who got noticed.

Earle always tried to give Emilia Mae enough love for both him and Geraldine, but by the time she was a teenager, the girl had taken her sadness inside and locked the door. On weekends, she helped Geraldine and Earle out at Shore Cakes. She unloaded deliveries, swept up, and carried pans of cakes and rolls from the baking room to the store. One morning a little girl pointed to a butterscotch square behind the glass shelf and started crying that she wanted it. The girl's mother took out her purse and counted out her change. She didn't have enough money. The girl cried harder. Geraldine must have seen what happened. She went over to the mother and said, "We've just started making those squares, and I'd love to know how children like them. Mind if I use your daughter as a guinea pig?"

Geraldine handed the girl a butterscotch square and said, "I hope you like this, sweetheart, I made it just for you."

Emilia Mae had never heard her mother use that tone of voice with her. Geraldine had never called her own daughter "sweetheart." It made Emilia Mae want to shake her mother and cry out, "I'm a sweetheart, too!" She had noticed how her mother elongated her neck and batted her eyes at the male customers and spoke in a sweet, condescending voice to the women. The only way she could think of to punish her was to act just the opposite. "All that stupid small talk, 'how are you,' 'you look pretty today,'" she told her mother. "It gets you nowhere. If someone wants an apple pie, I'm happy to tell them everything about the apple pie but I don't see why I have to also discuss the weather or their new shoes."

Geraldine rubbed her neck. "You know, Emilia Mae, we're selling more than cakes and bread here, we're selling at-mos-phere, a happy, welcoming at-mos-phere."

Emilia Mae rolled up her sleeves. "You've got the good looks and personality, so you handle the at-mos-phere," she said. "I'll take care of the cakes and bread."

Geraldine smiled at her daughter. "Holy moly," she said. "You're starting to sound like me."

Emilia Mae and the Oz brothers took that as a sign that she was making inroads.

After the first semester of ninth grade, Emilia Mae's English teacher wrote on her report card: *Emilia Mae is an excellent student, but she keeps to herself. She seems to be an unhappy child. May I schedule a conference with the school social worker?*

Geraldine tried to hold back her anger when she read those words but could feel her brow furrowing. "I'm going to tell that Mrs. Morris a thing or two," she told Earle.

"What can you say?" he asked. "At least she's an excellent student, but right now, Emilia Mae *is* an unhappy child. There's no denying that. It's a phase. Let it be."

"Earle, Emilia Mae is not just an unhappy girl. She's a loner who's carrying around an extra ten pounds on her body. She doesn't need a social worker; she needs to quit eating and make some friends. This is about discipline, not some fancy social worker."

When he'd first met Geraldine, Earle had found her fieriness and passion exciting. She was so different from everyone else he knew. It never dawned on him that someday "fiery and passionate" would scorch his marriage and family. He'd thought they'd have a big family, three or four kids, but after Emilia Mae, he knew there'd be no more. By now, her anger and disappointment had worn him down, and he began stretching his hours at the bakery, leaving Emilia Mae and Geraldine to themselves.

"Alright, suit yourself," he said. "Go see her teacher, but I'm telling you, it's going to amount to nothing."

The next afternoon, Geraldine marched into Mrs. Morris's empty classroom. "You absolutely may *not* schedule a conference with the school social worker," she insisted. "Emilia Mae is *not* an unhappy girl. She comes from a happy, churchgoing family. Unfortunately, she was born with a difficult nature. Nothing a social worker can do about that. Nature is nature and comes with the package. My husband, Earle, has an outgoing nature. I myself am a people person by nature."

Was that surprise she saw in Mrs. Morris's eyes?

15

★ ★ ★

School and the bakery: that was Emilia Mae's life until, one day in December of her fifteenth year, the first thing resembling a miracle blew her way.

Sam Bostwick, the owner of the Neptune Inn, the oldest—and only—inn in the area, walked into Shore Cakes and pulled Geraldine aside. "I have a favor to ask. I'm looking for a charwoman for the inn, someone to clean the rooms, help serve the meals, and keep the place in order, an able-bodied young girl. I'm getting a little long in the tooth to do this by myself. I'll pay handsomely and provide free room and board. If you happen to know somebody, I'd be much obliged if you'd pass along her name to me."

Geraldine covered her mouth with her forefinger and *hmmmmmed* (*Thank you, God*), pretending to think about it. She let a respectable amount of time pass before shooting her finger in the air. "Wait a minute . . . I do happen to know somebody who might fit the bill: my daughter, Emilia Mae. A hard worker, that one, sturdy and capable of anything she puts her mind to." Geraldine believed in truth telling and convinced herself that what she'd told Sam was correct in every sense of the word. Emilia Mae was a hard worker, and Lord knew she was able-bodied. She continued: "This sounds like a wonderful opportunity for her to learn about the real world and get some working experience at the same time. I'd allow her to leave school for a while should she fit the bill."

"I've seen her around here, but don't really know her," said Sam. "Keeps to herself, that one, doesn't she?"

Worried that Sam, like everyone else in town, knew how withdrawn Emilia Mae could be, Geraldine quickly added: "She's grown into quite a young lady, smart and sturdy as a mule. You ought to get to know her."

"Okeydoke, I'll do that," he said. "Will she be here this weekend?"

"Come by Saturday. She'll be here all day."

Geraldine was proud of herself. This was perfect: She was solving two problems at once. She was generously seizing an opportunity for her daughter's future. And boy, what a relief it would be to get Emilia Mae out of the house. God knows she'd tried with that girl. Every week in church she'd pray for guidance. For patience. For a break. Whatever she did seemed to be wrong. Everything she said came out like criticism; every gesture she made, Emilia Mae rebuffed. The last time she took her shopping and picked out a dress, Emilia Mae shook her head and said, "That's for your thinner daughter, not this one." After she took her to get her hair done in a slinky Veronica Lake style, Emilia Mae came home, brushed out her hair, and put it up in a ponytail. When Geraldine brought home a copy of *Black Beauty*, Emilia Mae smirked and said, "Guess what? I'm not ten anymore." It hurt her feelings, but she kept on trying. Geraldine bought her lotions and perfume and once a beautiful scarf made in Italy. Always Emilia Mae would thank her politely and shove the stuff to the back of her drawer. She had to face it: Her daughter didn't like her, never mind love her.

Maybe she didn't have the gift so many women had. Nothing seemed to come naturally with this child. She couldn't bring herself to hug her, call her "sweetheart" or say "I love you." Emilia Mae called her "Mother." So dry and formal. It was hard looking in the mirror every day knowing that yours was the face your daughter despised. If she sent Emilia Mae to work at the inn, no one could call her a bad mother. People would understand that a job is a job.

All she had to do was pray that Emilia Mae would act civil to Sam Bostwick when he came around.

That night, after Emilia Mae went to bed, Earle and Geraldine retired to the living room. Earle was playing one of his jazz records on the Victrola and Geraldine was smoking a cigarette. Earle leaned back in his chair and closed his eyes as Duke Ellington and his orchestra played "Mood Indigo," one of his favorites. Geraldine figured this was the perfect time to tell him about Sam's offer. Earle kept his eyes closed as she spoke. Only when she got to the part about Emilia Mae learning about the real world did Earle pop up, eyes wide open. "For Pete's sake, Geraldine, the girl is only fifteen. That's way too young for her to be living away from home."

Geraldine puffed her cheeks and made a sound like air leaking out of a balloon. "May I remind you that the Neptune Inn is about five and a half miles from here? She could ride her bike back and forth that distance."

"And what about her schoolwork?"

"Our little genius can catch up on her own. Let's face it: We could use the money. Hard work will be good for her, teach her some life lessons."

"She can learn life lessons at home," said Earle. "We can't toss her out like a stray dog. She needs to be around people her own age, not ragtag strangers from who knows where."

Geraldine ran her tongue around the inside of her cheek. "Can you honestly tell me that our home wouldn't be a happier place if she was gone?"

"I can honestly tell you that our home would be a happier place if you weren't so angry all the time." Earle got out of his chair, turned off the record player, and left the room.

Geraldine followed him. "I'll tell you what, Mr. High-and-Mighty. We'll let her choose. Sam's coming back on Saturday, he's going to talk to her directly. If she says yes, she goes; if not, she doesn't."

"No, absolutely not," said Earle. "I will not have my daughter leave school and work at some inn where absolute strangers come and go and there's no one to watch over her. That's out of the question."

Emilia's bedroom was adjacent to the living room. The walls in the Wingo house were old oak, thin enough to let everything through except a draft. Emilia Mae could hear the click of the switch when her father turned the Victrola off. When he said the part about letting her go where there was no one watching over her, she heard his words as clearly as if he were standing next to her.

The Oz brothers must have heard him too, because they immediately appeared on her bed. It was never clear exactly who suggested that Emilia Mae not wait for Mr. Bostwick to come to the bakery Saturday but that she go to the inn and seek out the man before the weekend, but the thought flowed through her as if it had been in her head all along. If she was going to go work at the Neptune Inn, it would be her choice, not her mother's. Isn't that what Dorothy would do?

On Friday after school, Emilia Mae rode her bike to the inn. With its gray wraparound porch and white slat-wood rockers, the Neptune Inn was one of Westchester County's landmarks, and Sam Bostwick one of its fixtures. She walked into the lobby and from a distance saw a little man with white foamy hair and spidery veins on his nose: Sam. She walked up to him and held out her hand. "Hello, I'm Emilia Mae Wingo. I think my mother spoke to you about me. I'm looking for work, and she said there might be a job here."

He studied her with his milky brown eyes: "Ah yes, the sturdy girl. I'll get right to the point. I'm looking for help at the inn, someone to tidy up the place, keep the rooms orderly. I can't do it on my own anymore. It would mean free room and board. It's a well-paying job, and you'd be on your own. Your mother says you might be just what the doctor ordered."

Emilia Mae couldn't imagine that her mother would ever tell anyone she was just what the doctor ordered. "What exactly did my mother say?"

He was standing close to her. Close enough for her to smell the Sen-Sen on his breath. "She said you're just the kind of gal I'm looking for, strong and capable of anything you put your mind to. What do you think?"

"My mother really said those things?"

Sam nodded. "Yes, she said all those things. Said you could leave school for a while and have a real-life experience. That's what she said. Are you interested?" He sounded impatient.

Strong and capable! Her mother really thought that. Well, she'd show her mother just how strong and capable she was, and make her proud. It took Emilia Mae but a few seconds to answer: "Yes, sir, I am interested. Very interested. When can I start?"

"How about the day after New Year's?"

"Perfect," said Emilia Mae, trying to hide her smile. A fifteen-year-old at the Neptune Inn? Yup, there's a girl who'd get noticed.

PART 2

Snow, like a bridal veil, draped the mountain peaks in winter. In spring, the braided green mountains shouldered the clouds while in summer, wild columbine set the mountains ablaze. Each sunrise renewed its vow of beauty, and when the sun set, it was as if the earth had split open to reveal its deepest colors.

Measured against any other place on earth, Skyville, North Carolina, had no peers. It was the kind of place that defined and inhabited a person no matter if they were born in it or serendipitously stumbled upon it. While they were there, it devoured them; when they weren't, they craved it. In its isolated beauty, Skyville was a place that heaven might have called a neighbor.

Or so they said.

Chapter 3

After Beau Fox's car broke down outside of Asheville, North Carolina, in 1929, he found himself a small log cabin on the edge of a town called Skyville. The cabin had two small bedrooms; a tiny kitchen with a wash basin, an icebox, and a two-burner stove; a bluestone fireplace; and, miraculously, built-in wooden bookshelves in the living room that held all of his antique musical instruments. The place was dark and small and had no land to speak of, but the price—$8 a month—suited Beau just fine. When he lit a fire, the room took on a permanent sunset glow. Beau said that glow was all he needed and bought no furniture except for a used bed.

The first time Beau brought Lily Doucet to the cabin, she threw her primrose shawl onto the dingy bed and said, "You need color; this will have to do."

Beau had met Lily at the La Salle pool hall two miles outside of town, where she was a waitress and where Beau would hang out when he wasn't on the road. He took notice of her one evening, when the song "After You've Gone" was playing on the gramophone. He saw that Lily stood in place by the kitchen door, closed her eyes, and sang along. She knew all the words and sang with brazen sadness and a wad of gum in her mouth.

After you've gone and left me crying
After you've gone, there's no denying
You'll feel blue, you'll feel sad.
You'll miss the dearest pal you've ever had.

He moved to the side of the room where the kitchen was so that when she opened her eyes, he was standing next to her. "That was pretty," he said.

"Marion Harris," she answered, without looking at him.

"That gal sings from her heart," he said. "So do you. Anyway, how in the world do you know about Marion Harris?"

Lily smiled impatiently. "Everyone who knows anything about the blues knows Marion Harris. I aim to be a blues singer like her someday."

Beau had never met a woman who'd ever heard of Marion Harris, much less knew about the blues. "I understand a thing or two about music," he said. "I'd say you haven't far to go."

"You in the record business?" she asked, tilting her perfectly square chin toward him. Her cinnamon eyes lit up as her baby lips curved into a flirtatious smile. Beau was tempted to say he was, just to see what else her mouth and eyes would do, but he knew from experience that women like this always saw through his flimsy lies.

"Nah, I'm just a guy who sells antique musical instruments. I can play a bit, but I wish I had a real ear for music."

"Well, at least you're an honest man. I like that."

"And you're a beautiful woman," he said even though he didn't think she was. Her teeth were yellowed and her knees knocked, but she had that mouth, a perfectly square chin, and a body that was generous in every way. That counted for something. Plus, she spoke her mind and had more music in her than any woman he'd ever met.

She looked him up and down. Older, much older than she was. Saw that he was short and slim and powerful, with no waste on him. He had a tiny beard like a grackle's tail, but there was truth in his blue eyes, and sweetness in his smile. So when he said, "I know a place we could go to hear real blues and drink real booze. You care to come along?" Lily did that thing with her eyes and mouth and said she could be ready by ten.

Beau took her to a place that was hidden under Pack Square. If you hadn't seen it in daylight, you'd never find it at night, just a green wooden door with windows shaded. Beau knocked several times before a gray eye appeared in the peephole in the door. "Password," said the eye, and waited for Beau to breathe the secret word.

"Dillard," whispered Beau.

"Say it again!"

"Dillard!" he shouted.

The man unlocked the door. The place was filled with smoke and smelled of stale whiskey and peanuts. People sat in chairs or parked themselves on stools; some even sat on the floor. Beau and Lily found an empty wall near the stage and leaned against it. It was hard to speak over the chatter and noise of the band. Beau motioned lifting a glass to his lips and mouthed "Gin cocktail?" to Lily.

She nodded and held up two fingers. She downed the first two quickly and didn't say no when he offered her a third. She knew all the music being played and tapped her fingers in time against the wall. She sang along softly at first, but as the gin cocktails took hold her voice got louder. She carried the tunes perfectly, and once she sang along to "I Ain't Got Nobody," Beau noticed there were tears in her eyes. The trumpet player standing to the left of them came over to Lily during the break and asked if she knew the words to "Baby Won't You Please Come Home?"

"Course I do," said Lily.

"Good, come on up and sing it with us, after the break."

She turned to Beau with a confused expression.

"Go on," he urged. "You'll knock 'em dead."

"Sure thing," Lily said to the trumpeter. "After the break."

She handed Beau her primrose shawl, took out a mirror, put on lipstick, powdered her face, and popped a Chiclet in her mouth. When the band returned, the trumpeter gestured for her to come forward. "Well, here goes," she whispered to Beau.

"Look who we have here," the trumpeter shouted into the microphone. "A special guest. What's your name, darlin'?"

"Lily. Lily Doucet from Chattanooga."

"Lily Doucet, the Chattanooga Songbird," said the trumpeter. "Give her a big hand, she's gonna join us in 'Baby Won't You Please Come Home.'"

The few people who weren't holding drinks in their hands clapped. Some hoisted their glasses. Beau let out a "Whoop!"

Lily threw herself into the song. The trumpet and clarinet players riffed along with her, and they fell into an easy rapport. When it was over, the trumpet player stepped forward, gave Lily a hug, and said to the audience, only half of whom were paying attention:

"That was Lily Doucet, the Chattanooga Songbird. You can bet your bippy you'll be hearing more from this young lady."

When Lily came back to Beau, he put his arm around her. "Told ya, you'd knock 'em dead." Her face was flushed, and her body was steamy.

"Another gin cocktail?" he asked.

"I wouldn't say no."

Later, when they went back to Beau's log cabin and sat on Lily's shawl, Beau asked her to tell him how she got from Chattanooga to around here. She put her head on his shoulder. "It's not all that interesting," she said, slurring her words a bit. She was the only girl in a family of four boys. The oldest, she was mother to those boys, bathing them, cooking for them, dressing them, and putting them to bed. When Beau asked where her mother was, she shrugged. "Mama was a bit of a socialite. She was a real beauty. People in town just loved her, and she and Daddy were always going to this party or that dinner. It didn't leave a whole lot of time for mothering, so I did what I could for those boys. They called me 'little mama.'" She smiled. "I love those boys, I really do. I always sang to them. I sang to myself. Singing was my best company. I knew I wanted to be a singer, but I kept that to myself. When the boys got older, they didn't need me so much. I decided to leave Chattanooga and come to a place that had music. Mama and Daddy were fine with me leaving home: one less mouth to feed and all that. As long as I could support myself, they gave me their blessing. I'd always heard that Asheville was beautiful and had the music. So here I am." She placed both hands firmly on the floor. "That's it. Story's over."

"You must have had a fella or two along the way," he said. "A gal doesn't up and leave home without any prospects."

Lily turned to him, her mouth a straight line. "I said, story over. Let's talk about you. How'd you get here?"

Beau told her about how he sold antique musical instruments and how his car broke down here when he was driving from his home in Orlando, and how if he never saw Orlando again—a swampy shithouse was how he described it—that would be fine with him.

Lily asked to see the antique instruments. Beau got up and removed a leather fiddle case from the shelf. He made sure to hold it close enough to Lily's nose so she could smell the leather. "It's genuine," he said, unzipping it and removing the fiddle.

"You know how to play that thing?"

"In a manner of speaking," he said.

"Okay, let's hear."

He started to play some honky-tonk number. Lily stood up and cocked her head. It was as if the music was spiraling through her. It started with her feet tapping. It wriggled up her legs, shook her abdomen, and made her breasts sway. She thrust out her arms and tossed back her head. The louder and faster Beau played, the more frenzied Lily became, until she pulled Beau into her vortex. Although now there was no music, there was Lily's body. The thrum and thrusts of it were all he needed to fall into her rhythms, dance in her spell. Lily slipped the straps of her chemise off one shoulder and then the other. She opened a few buttons, unsnapped some strategic snaps, and before you knew it, Lily Doucet and her clothes had parted company, and she and Beau found their way to the primrose shawl.

Lily Doucet did not seem to Beau like anyone's "little mama." Beau even wondered if Lily Doucet was her real name, though she wore it as if it had been sewn onto her. He didn't give a fig if she'd made up the whole story about her mama the socialite and her four little brothers. Lily Doucet was fun and sexy and tasted like peppermint Chiclets, and for the next four months, fun and sex was exactly what Beau had.

For Lily's part, she said she liked men with class and could tell that Beau was such a man. As a salesman, seeming to be a man of class was Beau's top priority. He wore a straw boater and tweed suit every day and carted his instruments in those leather cases that smelled expensive. That he was also something of a looker in his own right, with his velvety black hair, globe-blue eyes, and that feathery mustache, didn't hurt. Beau was the kind of man who became your friend at his first "howdy." He made the ladies laugh and could talk man-to-man about Jack Dempsey or the latest Lon Chaney movie.

Personally, Beau felt that *classy* was overrated, and in that regard, Lily Doucet suited him just fine.

Chapter 4

Before either of them had ever talked about any of it, Lily was pregnant. So much for courtship and marriage. Beau was forty-five, and the idea of being a father had long ago passed him by. Now, the thought of having a family intrigued him, so he asked Lily to marry him.

Lily was never one to swoon about marriage or daydream about having a kid. Quite the opposite. She'd never even had a doll. With four younger brothers to take care of, babies held no romance for her. Freedom was what she dreamed about, freedom and singing. So when Beau first asked her to marry him, she said absolutely not. What better way to stomp out a career than to get married? Lily figured no man wanted to be sung to by a gal with a ring on her finger. Better the fantasy of not knowing, the romance of possibility.

But as Lily got rounder and fatter and couldn't even bend over to tie her shoes, it dawned on her that if she had a kid by herself, she'd be trapped forever. She had no money. How would she ever get out of the house to work? To sing? Beau was a nice guy. She could tell he'd be a good father, and she guessed she liked him well enough to marry him for a while anyway. So a very pregnant Lily—"Under no circumstance will I change my name"—Doucet and a beaming Beau Fox were wed before the justice of the peace in March, two months before their son was born on May 28, 1931. They called him Dillard in honor of the password they used to get into the gin joint their first night together.

Lily's first reaction upon pulling out of the ether haze and laying eyes on her newborn son was to curl her bottom lip and say, "Oh crap, he looks more like you than me."

Beau traveled a lot in those days and did a pretty good business in the South. But on nights when Beau was home, Lily would perform at Barney's, despite the ring on her finger. One night, when Dillard was three, a man came up to Lily after she'd sung a few songs by Alberta Hunter and Sippie Wallace. He wore a brown fedora and shoes that matched his suit and pocket square. A real city slicker. He told Lily he'd been coming to Barney's for a few months and that her voice had an earthy quality to it that would play well on radio. His name was Raymond Kriss, and he worked for a record company in Nashville. He handed her a card and said: "You call me whenever you get serious about this singing business."

Raymond Kriss's card became soaked through with a peppermint Chiclet smell as Lily kept it in the zippered compartment of her pocketbook. By this time, Lily, Dillard, and Beau had become a pretty normal family. When they celebrated Dillard's fourth birthday, Lily had to pinch herself. She'd never thought she'd stick around this long. Beau and she got along fine, and Dillard—she called him Dilly—turned out to be easier to care for than any of her brothers had been. Even so, she couldn't deny this thing that burned within her. Ambition. Restlessness. Boredom. Whatever it was, it was a part of her that always yearned to break free like one of those horses bucking at a starting gate. She kept thinking she'd wait a little longer, until Dilly was older and able to hold some memories of her. Every few days she'd take Raymond Kriss's card out of her pocketbook and cup it in both hands like holy water. Then she'd sigh and go back to life as a wife and mother.

At home, she'd put Dilly on her lap and sing to him: always the same song.

Lavender blue, dilly dilly
lavender green.
If I were king, dilly, dilly.
I'd need a queen . . .

She'd sing while she chewed gum and ran her fingers through his wavy blond hair, which she always said was as soft as puppy fur. The matter of Dillard's hair, well below his shoulders by the time he was four, was at the heart of every fight between Beau and Lily. She refused to cut it. She said he was special, angelic with his flowing hair, and that Beau had no imagination. Beau argued that she was trying to fight nature: "He's not an angel, he's a little boy, there's no getting around it."

The last fight happened right after Dillard's fourth birthday. While Lily was singing at Barney's one night, Beau took scissors to Dillard's hair and told him it was time he had a big boy haircut. It would be a surprise for his mother. Dillard sat still as ice while Beau cut off so much hair that his scalp showed through. "That's more like it," said Beau when he finished. He held Lily's ivory hand mirror up to Dillard and told him to take a look. Dillard remembered not recognizing the face that shone back at him. He was all eyes now, big blue ones that scared him so much he looked away.

When Lily got home later that night, she went into Dillard's room to say good night. She kissed his cheek and got ready to run her hand through his hair. When her hand rested on a bristly scalp instead, she let out a scream.

Beau ran into Dillard's room and turned on the light. Dillard bolted upright as Lily stood up and pointed at Beau. "What the hell have you done?"

"Nothing," said Beau. "I gave him the haircut any four-year-old boy should have."

Lily walked up to Beau and stood so close that Dillard thought she might push him over. She didn't, but she did jab his chest in rhythm to the words she shouted: "What do you know about what the boy should or shouldn't have?"

"I know more than you seem to know about letting him grow up in his own way. You need to quit trying to control how he looks and what he does."

"*I'm* the one who feeds and dresses him. *I'm* the one who knows what he should and shouldn't have. Christ, I knew from the moment I met you that you were not someone a gal like me could ever take seriously. But we were having a good time, so I thought what the hell? Then we had our little accident and I did the right thing. I married you." She walked back into the living room, where she'd thrown her pocketbook on the couch. She took out Raymond Kriss's card, and while she was at it, a few Chiclets.

Back in Dillard's room, she held the card up to Beau's face and stabbed at it with her finger. "I have a real opportunity here. This man says there's an earthy quality to my singing, says it would play well on radio. If I don't take my chance now, well then Lily Doucet might as well lie herself down on the railroad tracks and wait for a train to flatten her. I'm a damn good singer. I need to make something of myself before all the stuffing gets knocked out of me."

"You're saying all this because I cut the boy's hair?"

"No, I've been thinking it for a long time." She pointed to the card again. "This man said I should call him when I get serious about my singing. Well, I'm serious. Tell you what, you take charge of how Dilly looks and what he does. You help him grow up in his own way."

Lily suddenly became aware of Dillard, lying in a fetal position, his big eyes turned on her. She lowered her voice and said, "Dilly, I'm sorry you had to be present for this ugliness. I want you to know that I'm not leaving because of you. Damn, I've liked you more than most anybody I've ever known. You'll understand someday."

Beau didn't believe Lily would really walk out. "This'll blow over." He winked at Dillard and put his arm around Lily. "She'll stay right here where she belongs." But Beau should have known better. Lily Doucet was not a woman to be persuaded by sentiment or logic. She pried Beau's hand from her shoulder: "I never did love you, Beau Fox. I swear, if I stay here any longer, I'll die."

That night, despite Beau's pleas and Dillard's tears, Lily Doucet packed up her few belongings and walked out of their lives.

Chapter 5

Emilia Mae lay in her narrow bed listening for the sound of her father's jazz records, her mother running a bath, the crazy way she'd sing to herself in a high wobbly voice, the smell of the Joy perfume she'd dab on herself after. It was Emilia's first night at the Neptune Inn, the first night she'd ever spent away from home. She was only five or six miles away, but it might as well have been a million. She tucked the blanket tightly around her and felt the presence of the Oz brothers by her side. She thought about what it was like to be cut loose. Alone. No one's child in no one's house. She supposed it would be exhilarating, no one watching what she wore or what she ate, but right now it only felt lonely. She thought her mother would be so proud of her when she landed the job at the inn, but her mother barely acknowledged it. All she'd said was, "You'll eat well over there. Just don't eat too well." Sam Bostwick had told her that her mother said she was "strong and capable." The words looped in Emilia's head before they turned on her and she realized she'd just been dealt a bad diagnosis. A betrayal. Her mother had said those things to Mr. Bostwick because she was trying to get rid of her. She could feel the Oz brothers turn away. She lay grappling with these thoughts until sheer exhaustion pushed her into sleep.

Emilia Mae's job at the Neptune Inn was to wash the floors; dust and straighten the main hall; help Xena, the cook, serve the meals; clean the guest rooms once a day; and bicycle over to Shore Bakery and pick up desserts for the inn. The rooms were dark and smelled like wet dogs, but there were definite advantages to working there. She learned things about people: the women who walked the streets at night and turned in at six in the morning, the men who shared a bed and wore matching black turtlenecks, the couples who left odd stains on the sheets. These things and the detritus that strangers left behind made her see that there was a world beyond the tiny parameters of her own. Old magazines, books, torn-up notes, empty pill and liquor bottles: They filled her mind with questions of what life outside of New Rochelle might be like. She had her own room, a sliver off the kitchen. At night the briny smell of the Sound carried her to sleep. And she'd made a new friend.

Xena had lived at the inn since the Coolidge years, and some speculated that she and Sam Bostwick had been friends in the biblical sense for just as long. A tiny woman, a little under five feet, with a crooked nose and faded freckles on her wrinkled cheeks, she let her long gray hair run wild. By now she was mostly deaf, and her arthritic fingers looked like gnarled tree trunks, yet she managed to turn out eggs and bacon every morning and a three-course meal for anyone who was around at suppertime.

Xena washed the dishes while Emilia Mae dried them. They fell into a routine of singing together over the sink—Broadway hits from musicals like *Show Boat*, old songs like "You Are My Sunshine." Xena had a surprisingly low voice for someone her size, like raindrops hitting the bottom of a barrel. When they prepared meals, they stood close to one another behind the wooden chopping block table. Xena taught Emilia Mae how to cook. "We add shredded carrots to the meatloaf for texture and color," she'd say, or "If we use buttermilk instead of cream in our mashed potatoes, it will give them a tangy lemon flavor."

Emilia Mae liked how Xena always said "we." It made her feel as if she was a part of something. Xena smelled of earth and cinnamon, and Emilia Mae found that comforting. One night, when Xena was explaining how "we" make squash soup, the conversation took a different turn. "Squash soup was Wallace's favorite. He claimed that mine was as smooth as God's ermine robe."

"What robe? Who's Wallace?" asked Emilia Mae.

"I'm not sure if God even has an ermine robe. Wallace, my ex-husband, always said things like that. I never knew if he was making stuff up. That man had a way with words." Xena shook her head. "I should've known that pretty words do not the man make. Our daughter, Frances, was stillborn. After that, Wallace would have nothing to do with me in the intimacy department, if you know what I mean. Then I discovered that he had been two-timing me with another woman since before Frances's birth. I threw him out, and he pleaded with me to take him back, but I said never. How can you trust a man like that? Terrible, terrible, the betrayal. Betrayal, Emilia Mae, that's the worst thing a person can do to another person. You're much too young to understand this, but believe me, it's true."

Emilia Mae had to bend over to shout into Xena's good ear. "My mother. She's resented me since I was born, thinks I literally have the devil in me. She told Sam Bostwick all these good things about me just so I'd get this job and she'd get me out of the house. I'd say that counts as betrayal."

"That is terrible," said Xena, cutting a radish into paper-thin slices. "What about your father? Didn't he have something to say about that?"

"My mother's a bully. My father tries to stand up to her, but she's so overpowering he gives up. I wish he were stronger."

"Sounds difficult."

"Yeah. I'm used to it." Emilia Mae looked down at the tomato she was chopping and smiled. This was normal conversation, unlike the silly chitchat that went on at the bakery, one of many advantages of working at the Neptune Inn. Food here was plentiful. Other than Xena, food had become Emilia Mae's main companion. She knew she ate more than she needed. Xena was no help, always pushing leftover banana bread or cherry cobbler her way. "Go on," she'd say. "It puts a shine in your eye like nothing else."

Eventually, other things put a shine in her eye. Men started paying attention to her. An old man, at least fifty, asked Emilia Mae if he could touch her hair. She shrugged. The man closed his eyes and wove strands of it in and out of his fingers like sand. "So soft," he muttered, his breath coming faster. She didn't mind one bit.

Forgive me, Father, for I have sinned, she said in confession. *It made me feel special.*

Father Daley, her priest at St. Bernadette's, made her say seven Our Fathers.

Another man, pale as Swiss cheese, told her that her hips were beautiful: "Ripe for childbearing." He fondled them in a way she knew was wrong, but his hands against her body made her tremble, so she let him.

Bless me Father, for I have sinned. But it felt good.

Father Daley warned her: "God does not forgive all transgressions" and made her perform penance for three days.

Emilia Mae wasn't a looker, but she was eye-catching. By sixteen, she was big-bosomed and statuesque. Her baby fat was more sexy than flabby. Her auburn hair fell nearly to her waist. Against her pale skin, her chestnut eyes gave off an orange glow, as if they'd been baked into her head. She still thought of herself as plump, but more than that, she enjoyed being noticed.

The men who came through—lost souls, most of them—noticed her. They noticed how she batted her eyes and elongated her neck when she talked to them. A couple of them said she was the prettiest girl they'd seen in a long time. Some were wounded and coming back from the war overseas, so she probably was the *only* girl they'd seen in a long time. One fellow was missing teeth; another had a wild stare. Emilia Mae figured most girls would never pay them any mind. But she did. When the men touched and held her, she imagined she was getting the warmth and love she craved from her mother. At confession, she told Father Daley: "I've never fought in a war, but I understand how it feels to be alone, and these men are as alone as it's possible to be. I listen to their stories. I offer whatever advice and encouragement I can. Sometimes, I even make them laugh." Father Daley remained stone-faced. "Leave the encouragement to God." Three more days of penance.

One man told Emilia Mae he'd enlisted at eighteen. "My father was an officer in World War I. The only way I could prove to him that I was a man was by becoming military. But I'm not the man he was. Sometimes I cried in front of the other soldiers because I was so scared. One time, a land mine went off not fifty feet from where I was standing." He turned away from Emilia Mae. "I was so terrified, I messed myself. That's when I got stuck with the nickname Shit Pants. Shit Pants? If my father ever found out he'd kill me."

Emilia Mae understood how disgrace could have no mercy. She told the man he was brave to have stayed. "If it were me, I'd have run away, and I'd be Shit Pants for the rest of my life."

Another young man, who had studied to be an army chaplain at nearby Fort Slocum, admitted how he didn't feel he had any godliness in him. "Just the opposite, truth be told. I've done every sinful thing it's possible for a man to do and still be alive. Things I could never tell anyone. I was hoping religion would absolve me, but deep down, I'm bad to the core."

"My mother always says I was born with the devil in me," she said. "Who knows, maybe I was. So what are people like us supposed to do, sit around and watch our souls rot? At least you're trying."

Emilia Mae gave these men carnal comfort when they asked for it. Until she came to the Neptune Inn, all Emilia Mae had known about sex was what she'd read in *Tropic of Cancer* and *Lady Chatterley's Lover*. Sex was messy and complicated. It was also considered a mortal sin by the Roman Catholic Church. Turned out, she liked it. Liked the warm shiver of how it felt, the ease with which her body responded to it. Mostly, the men came at her like a drill. They pushed and grunted as if trying to make a point, and from the noises they made they seemed to enjoy it. She never lost complete control, but their hunger made her feel desired and powerful.

"If it weren't for those men, the Germans would have taken over the world, or something like that," she told Father Daley. "Allowing them my body is the least I can do for my country."

Father Daley shook his head but said nothing. That was around the time that the Oz brothers took their leave.

Then, on a rainy day in August 1947, a real estate broker from Albany showed up. He seemed to be in his late twenties, with mud-brown eyes and wavy dark hair. He was a little shorter than her and stocky in build. He wore black and white wingtips with taps that tick-tocked against the wooden floors. The way he pursed his lips, it looked as if he might break into a whistle at any time. Because it was a Wednesday, he was the only guest at the inn. Emilia Mae served him dinner. He asked if she'd join him. "Why not?" she said and sat down at his table. His name was John. He told her that the Neptune Inn was cheaper and cleaner than any place in New York City. "I'll be going back and forth a lot," he said, giving her a sidelong glance.

"It's a good thing you have such nice shoes," she said. "I mean, with all that back-and-forthing, you'll need them."

John stared at his feet with a puzzled expression, before realizing she was making a joke.

Emilia Mae asked about his work. "The suburbs in this area are sprawling like fungus. Here in particular. And you know who is planning to get in on the ground floor of this development." He pointed both thumbs toward his chest and smiled. That's when Emilia Mae noticed the wide gap between his two front teeth, wide enough to run a train through. "And you?" he asked, still smiling. "Are you planning to remain in the hotel business?"

Emilia Mae laughed. "I'm hardly in the hotel business. I just clean and dust around it. My family owns Shore Cakes; it's the only bakery in town. I guess that puts me in the baking business. Speaking of... the blueberry pie here is really delicious, it's from our bakery. You should try some."

As they finished their pie and last sips of coffee, John leaned across the table and grabbed Emilia Mae by the wrists. "A fella can get lonely on business trips," he said. "Particularly on rainy nights like this one. I'd really like it if you would keep me company." He smiled a purple-toothed smile.

"I am keeping you company." Her smile was as purple as his.

"That's not the kind of company I meant," he said in a hoarse voice. "I'm talking about company in the pit of night when you're alone in a strange bed in a strange town and even the moon is hidden behind the clouds. *That* kind of company."

Emilia Mae was flattered that a man like John would want her company. He was a grown-up in a suit and tie, and handsome in a professional way.

"Yeah, I get that," she said. "Middle-of-the-night company. Why not?"

He studied her as she cleared the table, set their dishes in the sink and turned out the lights. In the darkness, he took her by the hand and led her to his room. He didn't say anything but pinned her against the wall and kissed her hard after he closed the door. In bed, he held her so tightly that she thought he might have dislocated her shoulder, and when he came, he made noises as if he were crying. After he left, she found bubble-sized bruises on her arms. Unlike with the others, sex with him had made her lose her way and want more. After that, she didn't bother to go to confession.

By October, Emilia Mae had been with John four or five times. He didn't wear a wedding ring, but something about the way his shirts were always neatly pressed and the inside of his suitcase smelled of lavender soap—not the kind a man would use—told her there was a wife in the picture.

Emilia Mae didn't care. She liked the way John talked to her about the world: things like movies, books, Manhattan, and a lot about the New York Yankees—they'd won the pennant that year and were playing the Brooklyn Dodgers in the World Series. She told him she knew nothing about baseball, and he said: "A night game at Yankee Stadium is something to see. Maybe you and I can go sometime." She felt giddy, buoyed by the promise of a night game at Yankee Stadium. That was something to look forward to. He was something to look forward to. When he was gone, she could lose herself in the recounting of their lovemaking and the wanting and waiting that came with it.

· By November, Emilia Mae discovered that her weight had shot up ten pounds, to 158. It only rounded her already curvy figure and didn't concern her much until the night she was awakened by an unsettled stomach. Over the next two weeks, the unsettled feeling continued, and her sleep became more fitful. No amount of Pepto-Bismol could stem the heartburn and nausea that coursed through her.

Emilia Mae knew how babies were made. Whenever she'd ride her bike to pick up desserts for the inn, she'd watch the pregnant women at the bakery. They rubbed their bellies like fortune-tellers warming up crystal balls. They looked flushed and pleased in a way that was different from when they selected petit fours. She was definitely not one of them. *I'm eighteen and not even out of high school,* she thought. *God knows I have nothing to be pleased about. I'm not pregnant like they are. Mother is right: Natures are natures, and maybe mine does have the devil in it. Maybe that's what this is all about. It will go away soon.*

But it didn't go away. Emilia Mae was scared and tired and had trouble keeping food down. She needed her mother. Or a mother. Someone to comfort her, tell her she'd be okay. On her trips to the bakery during the week and sitting next to her mother at church on Sundays, she waited for Geraldine to notice. Surely, she would see her belly, the dark circles under her eyes, and ask what was wrong. As she grew out of her clothes, she wore the same overalls and large oxford shirt every day. She became careless about stains on the shirt and how often she washed her hair. She walked with the slumped demeanor of fatigue. The men who visited the Neptune Inn stopped noticing her. Still, her mother said nothing, and her father greeted her warmly as if nothing were amiss.

It was Xena who noticed her friend's weight gain and stains on her shirt. She figured she was going through some sort of teenage moodiness and kept Emilia Mae in her prayers. One afternoon, as they were preparing a meatloaf, she asked Emilia Mae if she was a churchgoing girl.

"Not by choice. My mother makes me go with her to St. Bernadette's on Sundays, but I'd just as soon clean dead mice out of the basement. I hate the priest over there. He's cold and mean and has an oily voice."

"Well, that doesn't sound like enough reason to hate the man."

"Yeah, well he does these creepy sermons like he's trying to scare us into believing."

Xena nodded as she worked the meat with her hands. "A lot of them do that. What does he say?"

"The other day he talked about how a sinful soul could corrupt the flesh. Believe me, I wasn't the only one who was secretly study-ing the skin on my arms. He's always telling us that impure thoughts could make for a soiled life. He makes me feel dirty inside. His stories about fallen women who have improper intimacy with men are horrifying. The women always end up dying, but not before they suffer baseball-sized tumors in their throats or pus-filled sores up and down their legs."

"What about the men?" asked Xena.

"He never says what happens to them. I assume they go off to play golf or hunt down little birds. Anyway, one time, Father Daley told us that demons could take over a person's body if that person is evil. That's when my mother poked me in the ribs as if to say, 'There you have it.' So, yeah, I hate the priest over there."

"Do you really think demons have taken over your body?" Xena sounded incredulous.

Emilia Mae laughed. "I kind of do. If you count unkind thoughts as evil, I've got a tribe of demons living in me."

Xena looked up from the meat she was kneading. "Wash your hands and help me with this. What kind of evil thoughts are you talking about?"

The cold meat squished through her fingers as Emilia Mae gave voice to her secret thoughts. "My mother. No matter what I do, I can't make her like me. Sometimes I wish I had another mother. I don't much like New Rochelle. The rich are too rich and the poor too poor here. I hate all those stores my mother's always swooning about. Sometimes I wish a fire would burn the whole place down. How's that for evil thoughts?"

Xena rinsed her hands and wiped them on a towel. "I will say, your priest sounds a bit severe. I can tell you this, not all houses of worship are that harsh. It's not my business to meddle, but it troubles me the way you seem not to be caring for yourself. You can ignore what I'm about to say and tell yourself that Xena's just

45

being an old busybody, but I spoke to the reverend at my church about you—it's the First Baptist Church across town. I told him how you were living on your own, and he said you'd be as welcome at our church as any other member of his congregation. His name is Aloysius Klepper, and I think you'd find him to be a gentle man. His services are joyful, nothing like what you described. I could sure use the company if you'd care to join me some Sunday."

"But I'm Catholic."

"Reverend Klepper always says that the Lord only sees our hearts and doesn't much care about the rest of us. He says that anyone who passes through our doors is welcomed to be loved, not judged."

Emilia Mae liked the idea of not being judged. Even more, she thrilled to the thought of never having to see Father Daley again.

"Sure," she said. "I'll try it."

The following Sunday, Emilia Mae dressed up in a pale blue caftan with beige stripes and a pair of beige pumps. She and Xena linked arms against the lacerating wind. As they got closer to the church, Xena said hello to the parishioners. It was a small congregation, and everyone knew everyone else. A stranger was the object of curiosity, and there were stares, not all of them friendly. "Keep walking," whispered Xena, never dropping the smile from her lips.

The church was like a child's drawing, with a steeple and double front doors. Inside, it smelled like a moldy attic. The walls were white and spotless, with a stark cross above the pulpit and wooden pews that looked as if they'd been recently stained. Xena led Emilia Mae to the second-row pew. There was a hum of conversation behind them, which switched off the moment Reverend Klepper strode to the pulpit in a long white robe. He was a big man, uneasy in his body and clumsy in his movements. He was pale and had thick brown wavy hair with glints of gray. He had a large nose that seemed to have been broken and a malleable mouth that could stretch into a hymn and fold to a whisper. His bulging brown eyes took you in. No one knew if they were naturally that way or if he had some big-eye disease, but when he preached, the entire congregation paid attention, because everyone thought he was staring straight at them.

Emilia Mae was certain his invocation was aimed at her: "Welcome. Today I am happy to see some familiar faces and new friends. In the eyes of Jesus, we are all one. So, let us come together in this house of worship in friendship and in harmony." He led the congregation in the hymns "Holy, Holy, Holy" and "How Great Thou Art." Their voices blended exuberantly and lifted Emilia Mae to a place where she floated above herself. They prayed and read from the scripture in unison. When it was time for his sermon, Reverend Klepper walked among the congregants, nodding at people as he spoke.

Father Daley never left his pulpit, never made his sermons personal. Reverend Klepper's white robe swayed as he walked. In this sermon he spoke about a difficult time in his life. "Only when I learned to find within myself the love and affection that had been taken from me did I lose my bitterness and gain my strength. Only then did I learn to forgive." His sermon, about isolation and forgiveness, echoed many of Emilia Mae's own thoughts—though she was unsure about the forgiveness part.

Before she knew it, he was saying the benediction. People were freely crying out "Hallelujah" and "Amen," and the service was over. Xena and she waited in line to say hello to Reverend Klepper. When it came their turn, Xena gently shoved her toward him. "This is the child I told you about. Emilia Mae. Emilia Mae Wingo."

Reverend Klepper took her hand in his. "Emilia Mae Wingo," he said, "we're so pleased to have you here today. I hope you enjoyed the service."

"I sure did," she said.

"Good, then perhaps that means you'll join us again."

"I'd like that."

"And we'd be honored to have you."

Three weeks later, on a Saturday night, John from Albany showed up at the Inn, slipped into Emilia Mae's room, and without words took what he'd come for. In the morning light, as he dressed in his traveling clothes, he saw how she struggled to pull her caftan over her distended stomach. Such a dark expression came over his face she thought he might hit her. "Gee, you look...different," he said.

"Nope, it's still me, I'm fine."

He must have noticed the putty lines under her eyes and how the act of pulling on her caftan put her out of breath. "Well, you certainly don't seem all that fine."

She looked at John, at his smug face and expensive clothes. He was a successful businessman, but so what? He was also a cheater and a liar. She wasn't movie-star gorgeous, but she was okay-looking, and everyone always told her how smart she was. Emilia Mae knew from her own life that you couldn't force someone to love you, but she knew she deserved better. She'd just finished reading *A Tree Grows in Brooklyn* and thought about Francie Nolan, the main character, who always stood up for what was true and right. Like Dorothy in *The Wonderful Wizard of Oz*, Francie had become a friend, one she felt she could rely on in a moment like this. She took a deep breath and said what she thought Francie might say: "Just because you come waltzing in here in your fancy suits and shoes doesn't give you the right to judge me. I'm as fine as anyone you know, probably even finer. I'd *never* marry a man who cheated on me or used my suitcase, which, by the way, reeks of lavender soap. I suppose you take me for some simple girl in the baking business who would never figure that out. Well, I'm more than that."

She heard the sound of raked rocks in her voice, and it made her feel powerful. John gave her a weak smile that showed the tunnel between his two front teeth. It was the kind of smile that told her she would never see him again.

"I suppose this means you're giving me the boot."

"I suppose I am."

She watched as he walked out of her room. The last she heard of him was the tick-tocking of his shoes against the wooden floor. "Holy moly," she thought, "I sounded just like my mother."

Despite her bravado, she was sad. She'd miss the wanting and the waiting. She'd looked forward to seeing a night game at Yankee Stadium and had gotten used to the smell of lavender soap. Knowing that she was going to church this morning and would hear one of Reverend Klepper's plague-free sermons gave her small comfort. But first she needed to see her mother.

Geraldine was alone in the baking room, preparing the dough for the next morning's bread. She didn't see Emilia Mae enter and was startled when she heard "Mother." She turned to her daughter with a smile. "Well, look what the cat's dragged in. To what do I owe this honor?"

The lightness in her mother's voice made Emilia Mae think this conversation would be easier than she had anticipated. "Well, I thought we should talk a little about church."

"Do you mean about how you haven't shown up for the past couple of weeks? You know, I've missed you."

"You have? I wasn't sure you would notice."

"You think I wouldn't notice that my daughter was missing?"

Emilia Mae couldn't remember when or if her mother had ever used the word *daughter* in her presence, and it stunned her to think that her mother might actually miss her.

"Well, it's nothing personal, but I think I've found another church, where I feel more comfortable."

"Oh . . . I didn't know you felt uncomfortable in this one," said Geraldine defensively. "Is there another Roman Catholic church in town?"

"Um, it's not Roman Catholic. It's Baptist. The First Baptist Church."

Geraldine wiped her hands on her apron and pulled a cigarette from her pocket. "You're a Catholic, or have you forgotten that?" The concern went out of her voice.

"Their doors are open to everyone."

"You know I'm as tolerant as the next person," said Geraldine. (Did she notice the look of surprise on Emilia Mae's face?) "But joining a Baptist church? Really, that's stepping one foot over the line. You're a smart girl. You must know that it's a mortal sin for a Catholic to neglect Mass."

Emilia Mae nodded. "It's a little late for mortal sins. Besides, church is church. God's as likely to hear me there as he is at your place."

Her mother picked loose a piece of tobacco from between her

teeth. "Let me ask you something, Emilia Mae. You come here looking like someone's dirty laundry and tell me that you are defying everything your father and I believe in. Are you deliberately trying to hurt us, or do you come by it naturally?"

"Really, Mother, it's got nothing to do with you. The cook at the inn invited me to go to church with her. We've become friends, so I went, and met the reverend and liked him. I feel comfortable there. I've never felt comfortable at St. Bernadette's."

Geraldine stared at her daughter long enough for Emilia Mae to see pain in her eyes. It had never occurred to her that she had the power to hurt her mother. She suddenly felt sorry for her and tried to think of something to say that would soften the moment. But the moment didn't last long.

"I'm sorry it's come to this." Her mother's words came out hard. "But I think it's best if we don't see each other for a while."

And just like that, everything was the way it had always been.

Chapter 6

If Lily Doucet could have seen what a beautiful boy Dillard Fox became, she might not have taken off so fast. He had his father's ocean blue eyes, a perfectly square chin, and a mouth swollen with sensuality. His blond hair against his pale skin gave off the effect of a summer sun. People were always telling Beau that Dillard should pose for magazine advertisements, but Beau was determined to give his motherless child as normal a life as possible, and for a long time that's what he had. When Beau traveled, his sister, Denise, would come and stay with Dillard, sometimes for weeks at a time.

Dillard missed having a mother, more than he missed his actual mother. He barely remembered her. The song "Lavender Blue" played in his head when he thought about her, and the smell of peppermint Chiclets sent him back to vague memories of soft hands running through his hair. Mother love was buried deep within him, and what remained was tenderness and the ability to draw love from other people. He was popular with grown-ups and kids. It was as if whatever he had shone upon them, and in his aura, they were beautiful, too. When he was sixteen, he was elected president of his class, and at seventeen he was chosen to play the lead role in his class play. Girls and their mothers flirted with him. He flirted back, but it was always an uneasy transaction. Women were unreliable.

He had a talent for music, and at his high school graduation, his music teacher presented him with a flute. "You'll always have the music in you," he wrote in a cursive hand. "Now you can have it with you as well."

That's how it was for a while: Dillard won prizes; people gave him gifts. At Black Mountain College in Asheville, he excelled at the flute. There was talk of an audition with the Boston Symphony Orchestra, but it never materialized. Instead, Dillard stuck around for four years after graduation as a teaching assistant in the wood-winds department. He returned home at twenty-six not sure how or where he'd make money as a musician. For a while, he took odd jobs working in a restaurant, playing the flute at charity events and public concerts, but he knew if he ever was to amount to anything, he'd have to leave Skyville.

His aunt Denise argued with her brother. "The boy has no future. He should study something practical, like electronics or plumbing. He's never met a toilet he can't fix."

"The boy has music," said Beau.

"The music is pretty, I grant you that," she said. "But music is just air blown into different shapes. There is no money in that."

"There is if you're willing to be creative," said Beau.

Dillard had run out of ways of being creative. In an effort to jumpstart his life, he went to his local draft board. The Korean War had been over for a few years and he was hoping to get shipped off to Europe, or maybe a more exotic location in the Far East.

The doctor who examined Dillard took his time palpating this and probing that. He checked his ears and throat and held the ophthalmoscope to his eyes. He had him stand on his tiptoes to see if a visible arch formed. When none did, he stamped his application with a 4-F and clapped his hands together. "Nope, you're not army material. We'll keep you right here in Skyville, where you belong." Without the army as his next move, Dillard was at a loss.

Because his father traveled so much of the time, Dillard thought of Beau more as a friend than a father. Beau confided to Dillard about his business and love worries, and Dillard had no problem telling his father how eager he was to get out of town.

Beau said he'd heard about these places in the Catskill Mountains of New York that hired young musicians to entertain their guests. "Handsome young men are catnip for these places. I'll bet you could get a job in a heartbeat." Beau gave Dillard fifty dollars, which would cover his three-day bus trip to Liberty, New York, and then some.

By then, Beau was well into his seventies and in ill health. He'd stopped peddling his antique instruments and laid them aside in their leather cases. Days before Dillard was to catch the Greyhound to New York, Beau sat him down for a man-to-man. "I want you to know this. You're a good son. I wasn't around nearly enough for your growing up, yet despite my absence you turned out okay. I also want you to know that your mother's leaving had nothing to do with you. You may have been the only person she ever loved. She was a woman who acted solely on whims. In my heart, I knew she'd never stick around long enough to see you grow up. But she, like you, had the gift of music. You have her spark and some of your old man's charm, if that's what they call it. You have real talent. Don't give up on it. Make something of yourself. I don't have much to leave you except my instruments and a few dollars in the bank. You stay in touch and make your old man proud."

On the night before he was to leave, Dillard fished around for his duffel bag in his father's bedroom closet. In the back of the closet, he came upon a moth-eaten primrose shawl and an old handbag. Both smelled of peppermint Chiclets and brought him back to his earliest memory: His mother packing her suitcase, his father shouting things as he paced back and forth, and his four-year-old self getting out of bed, wrapping his arms around his mother's legs, and singing with all his might: "Lavender blue, dilly dilly... Mommy, don't go." His mother telling his father, "I never did love you."

He left the shawl and the handbag behind.

Chapter 7

The one piece of advice that Beau Fox had passed on to his son was to never tell anyone everything at once. Beau parceled out his own history the way people rationed bits of bread during the Depression. It wasn't until Dillard was ten that he heard the true story about his mother. He was fourteen before he learned that his father never really lived in Orlando before he came to Skyville. In fact, he'd been a bootlegger in Miami during Prohibition and was on the run from the law when he took off in his car and zig-zagged up the state, taking refuge in Orlando, which was nothing more than mangrove swamps and citrus groves. That's where he'd acquired the antique musical instruments in leather cases in exchange for four bottles of rum. He'd always listened to music and knew a great deal about it, but it was the supple and rich-smelling leather cases that drew Beau to the instruments in the first place. He'd thought, *Now that's a way to make a living*, so he had some cards made up and painted a sign on his car that said BEAU FOX'S GENUINE LEATHER AND MUSIC. He said the name was confusing enough to make people stop him and ask what was the leather and where was the music? It was when he got lonely at night in the cheap boardinghouses he stayed in on the road that he took a shine to the fiddle and taught himself how to play.

This was what Dillard knew of his father. He'd always figured if he'd stuck around Skyville long enough, he'd have learned even more. But the lesson stayed with him: No one needed to know everything at once.

When people asked him why he'd taken up playing the flute, he'd tell them that he was drawn to the sound of its unearthly whispers. The truth of it was more prosaic than that.

His Selmer flute had been a graduation gift from his eighth-grade music teacher, Mr. Alden. At the time, Mr. Alden seemed so much a grown-up, but in reality, he was probably only ten years older than Dillard. A hulk of a man, slightly unkempt, with an auburn beard and shoulders wide as a bench, Mr. Alden attracted Dillard's stares all through class as he imagined what it would be like to run his fingers down Mr. Alden's back. Dillard was certain everyone else had the same urge. How could they not? It was only later that he realized maybe they didn't.

Three weeks before the annual winter recital, Mr. Alden asked Dillard to see him at the end of the day. When Dillard went to Mr. Alden's classroom, the teacher told him, "Take a seat, any-where." Dillard sat at the desk closest to him; Mr. Alden pulled over the desk next to his until they were close enough for Dillard to smell the mothball musk of his sweater and see the hairs inside his ears. Mr. Alden mentioned the upcoming recital. "I have some-thing special in mind for you. I want you to play a flute solo, Erik Satie's 'Gymnopédie Number One.'"

Dillard started. "I'm not good enough to play that!"

Mr. Alden shook his head. "You certainly are, and I'll help you. We'll meet every day after school, and you'll learn that piece inside out."

Dillard objected. "I've only been playing the flute for a year. Satie's for a more advanced player than me."

"You underestimate yourself, Mr. Fox. Trust me, you'll be a star."

Their heads were so close now that Dillard suddenly had the impulse to kiss Mr. Alden. "I don't know about that," he said.

"I do." Mr. Alden laughed, as if he knew what was going through Dillard's mind. "Don't let's tell anyone. Let this be our little secret until we get to watch them go hog wild at the recital."

"Alright then. Satie," said Dillard, his voice a bit jagged.

"Alright then, Satie," said Mr. Alden, shaking Dillard's hand.

For the next three weeks, Dillard came to Mr. Alden's classroom at the end of every day as Mr. Alden helped him understand the complicated lyrical melody of "Gymnopédie No. 1."

After that, Mr. Alden would occasionally invite Dillard to his house so they could listen to his record collection. His sparsely furnished clapboard house had heavy beige curtains on all the windows that turned everything inside the color of potatoes. He would pour them Coca-Cola and bring out snacks as they sat around listening to Schubert, Glenn Miller, Billie Holiday, Ella Fitzgerald. Mr. Alden told Dillard about each artist and what influenced their music. He'd make Dillard distinguish between major and minor keys and listen for the bridges and chord changes. Sometimes they would improvise together on Mr. Alden's piano. Dillard always thought of the potato-colored living room as the place where he became a musician, and of Mr. Alden as his first real crush.

Not that it meant anything, Dillard knew that. Students always had crushes on their teachers, especially those who took a special interest in them. Didn't they?

Chapter 8

Try as she might, Emilia Mae hadn't been able to hide her secret.

By the beginning of February, even the blousiest of smocks billowed in front of her as if she were hiding a kettledrum beneath it. She bicycled to the bakery every couple of days and would try to sneak in and retrieve the pies and cakes when her mother wasn't there. The Neptune Inn became home; Xena and the Reverend Klepper, her surrogate family. She could feel the thing move in her. Her face had gone puffy, and her rear was so big, she had to sit sideways on most chairs. At night, she tossed and turned, unable to settle into a comfortable position. She was constipated. She farted all the time, had to go to the bathroom every twenty minutes, and had searing pains running down the backs of her legs. Her body had gone crazy; nothing about it was hers anymore. As far as she was concerned, the only thing she didn't have was pus-filled boils up and down her legs. Not yet, anyway.

She was pregnant, no doubt about it. Even worse, counting back from the last time she and John from Albany had been together, this baby would be due in May or June. Motherhood was frightening to Emilia Mae. She'd learned little about how to love a child from her own mother. She worried that she would do to her own child what her mother had done to her: leave a void where love ought to be. No child deserves that, she thought. Emilia Mae figured she didn't have time to waste. An abortion was what she needed, and she needed it quickly.

She remembered how Father Daley would go all frothy when he talked about abortion. "A grave evil," he called it. "A sin against God." Well, tough for Father Daley; she was no longer in his hands.

Nobody she knew had ever had an abortion. She didn't know how they were done or where they were done. Certainly not in New Rochelle, which didn't even have its own record store. She couldn't run the risk of asking anyone in this gossipy town. She'd have to find someone to take her into Manhattan. She thought about talking to Xena but realized how painful that would be for her, given her own lost baby. The only person she felt safe enough to ask was Reverend Klepper. She couldn't tell him about John, but maybe she could make him believe that she had the devil in her, just as her mother had believed. It would have worked with Father Daley; maybe it would work with him.

The following Sunday, she told Xena she'd meet her at the inn, then waited in the back pew of the church until Reverend Klepper had spoken with all his parishioners before she came up to him and shook his hand.

"Can I talk to you about something?"

"Sure," he said with a broad smile.

"It's a personal thing."

"Whatever you say inside this church stays with me."

Suddenly the urge to vomit spiraled through her. The double dose of Pepto-Bismol she'd taken that morning clearly wasn't working. She willed herself not to make a mess of the Reverend. "I think I'm going to be sick."

He took her by the elbow, led her to one of the pews, and brought her water. They sat silently, the only sound coming from the sudden rain shower that pattered against the window. Finally, the nausea subsided.

"Did you ever have the feeling something inside of you isn't right?" she asked.

"Often," he laughed. "Every time we go to my mother-in-law's and she cooks her scalloped sweet potato casserole, I eat way too much. For days after I feel like there's a boulder in my stomach and the darn thing won't move."

"Not like that," said Emilia Mae. "I mean something different than food, something that really doesn't belong in there. My body doesn't feel like it's mine anymore."

Reverend Klepper rubbed his neck and looked down at her stomach. "Have you been with a man? I mean, have you had relations with a man?"

She reddened at the thought of him knowing what had gone on between her and John and decided to play the innocent.

"Just a little."

"You do understand what happens when a girl and a boy have relations?" He glanced at her belly.

"Sort of." She stared out the window.

Reverend Klepper continued, trying to find common ground. "When two people love each other very much, they come together in the way the Lord intended them to, and they create a child. You know that, right? Do you love this man with whom you've had relations?"

"Oh no, I don't even know his last name. I'm not sure that's what this is. It could be something else, you know."

"No, Emilia Mae. Pregnant women can feel the baby moving around months before it comes out."

"Maybe there's something inside me, not a baby, but the devil's work, something that ought not to be there. We need to come up with a way to get it out."

"Listen, Emilia Mae. I don't know what you're thinking, but I'm certain what you have inside you is the most precious kind of love there is. Trust me, the first time you hold that newborn child in your arms, you will know a love like no other."

"This isn't about love," she insisted. "It's about something bad that's not meant to be. I really hope you can help me get rid of it."

Reverend Klepper's face turned somber. "Even if I had the power to help you get rid of this child—and I don't—I wouldn't. By getting rid of it, you mean having an abortion. That would not only be a sacrilege, but you'd be putting yourself in serious danger. Do you understand that you could die from an abortion?"

"If I am pregnant, I can't have this baby. I'm too young, plus I have no idea how to raise a child."

Reverend Klepper shook his head. "Here's how I can help you. I can help you see your way spiritually through this time. I can help by suggesting that you tell your parents to take you to see Dr. Rogan as soon as possible. That's what I'm qualified to do."

Emilia Mae shook her head. "I don't need Dr. Rogan. I need..." Reverend Klepper interrupted her and raised his voice to sermon level. "Emilia Mae, you need to see Dr. Rogan. You need to talk to your parents. You're going to have a baby. That baby needs attention, and so do you."

"I don't want attention." She tried to keep her voice calm. "I just don't want to have this baby."

"I understand that. Do me one favor, talk to your parents. After that, we'll talk again."

Emilia Mae allowed herself the thought of her mother as a grandmother. What if she liked this child? What if she was kind to it the way she was kind to the kids at the bakery? Emilia Mae had to smile at the thought of her mother calling this child "sweetheart." If her mother loved this child, maybe she'd love her for giving birth to it. The thought hung in the air for a few moments before reality butted in. Her mother would be shamed by having a daughter pregnant out of wedlock, maybe never speak to her again. Then another thought interceded. What if this wasn't about her mother at all? What if this was a way for Emilia Mae to have a little family of her own? A child who loved her, whom she would love back. The thought came and went, sometimes as a fantasy to indulge, other times as a concept too frightening to contemplate.

That night, Aloysius told his wife, Cora, about Emilia Mae. "She's pregnant and wants an abortion. I'm not sure why, but she latched on to me to help her. I know this is an uncharitable thing to say, but I wish she hadn't."

"The young and unfortunate always latch on to you, Ally," said Cora. "You're a compassionate man, and you have God's ear. Why wouldn't they pick you?"

"This one's different. She's stubborn and inflexible. Nothing I say reaches her. All she wants is for me to find her an abortionist. What am I supposed to do with that?"

Cora rolled her startling green eyes skyward in an exaggerated manner.

"Very funny, Cora. God's not a referral service."

"Then seriously, what are you going to do?"

"I don't know. I really don't know."

Every Sunday for the next few weeks, Emilia Mae and Reverend Klepper had the same conversation. She'd plead with him to help her find an abortionist in the city, because that was the only path she could see clearly, and he'd tell her she had to tell her parents and see Dr. Rogan.

After a particularly infuriating session, Klepper walked into his house, threw off his coat, and flopped down on the couch. "That girl has really gotten under my skin," he said to his wife. "If God is testing me, he's sent me one worthy opponent."

Cora pulled off his size thirteen shoes—each as large as a planter—and brought him a cup of tea with a shot of rum. "Ally, you got into this business knowing it would be more than bake sales and christenings. Isn't that your job, to tend to the lost sheep and all that kind of stuff?"

He had to laugh at her unsentimental view of his job. As she was fond of telling him, being a minister's wife was never what she'd had in mind: "The Lord led you here. I simply tagged along." Still she did her best, showing up for as many funerals, baptisms, and services as she could tolerate, but never without reminding him that there was still time, he could always go into her family's flower business.

"This one's different. She's hardly a lost sheep. She doesn't want any tending from me. She just wants me to help her get rid of this child."

"So, find her one of those homes for unwed mothers."

"God, no, I could never do that. Those places are filthy and crowded. Besides, she's so far along now, no one would have her."

"What about talking to her parents?"

"I can't do that without her permission, and she doesn't seem to take them into account any more than she does me."

The following Sunday Reverend Klepper saw how the fabric of Emilia Mae's dress stretched tight across her stomach and asked again if she had spoken to her parents.

"I saw my father at the bakery last week," she said. "He made some comment about how old Sam Bostwick was feeding me well. But I could tell by the way he watched me waddle that he knew it wasn't the food. When I asked him what he meant by that, he said that he and my mother saw what was happening and did I understand that this was a small town and that they couldn't afford to have people gossiping? I told him I did, but he shouldn't worry, you were going to help me get free of it."

Reverend Klepper stepped forward. "I hope your father doesn't think I'm going to help you get an abortion."

"I didn't say how you'd help, just that you would." Emilia Mae spoke in a flat tone until she got to this part. Then she raised her voice: "It's time now, don't you think? This thing is kicking and pushing me, and if we don't do something soon it will be too late. What are you waiting for?"

Reverend Klepper sighed, his shoulders fell. He prayed for patience. It came fitfully. He took her hand. It felt warm and fleshy. "I'm going to tell you some very grown-up things so listen carefully. My wife,

Cora, and I have been married for twenty-two years. We've wanted a child for all that time, but God has never blessed us with one. What you have is a miracle, one that Cora and I still pray for every day. Wanting an abortion is only your way of saying that you're terrified. That's understandable. When your time comes, it will be bloody and painful and very scary, I'm sure, but on the other side of it you'll have a child, your own child. Then you can decide whether or not you want to keep the child or give it up for adoption. Do you understand?"

She stared at him as if she were puzzling something out. "Do you think it's possible that maybe you and Cora would like this baby? You know, to adopt it?" Emilia Mae's eyes had sunk into her cheeks in the past month. It took Reverend Klepper a moment to realize she was crying.

"Don't say things like that unless you've given it lots of thought. Adoption is a decision you can't un-decide. As for me and Cora, it's a kind thought." He placed his hand gently on her stomach. "But I think we'll wait until the Lord blesses us with one of our own." His smile was faint. "Right now, this child's life depends on you. You matter more than anything in the world to it. Please take care of yourself."

"I'm glad I matter to somebody," she said loudly.

Reverend Klepper lowered his head and rubbed his brow with his thumb and forefinger.

"I'm sorry," Emilia Mae whispered.

"No need to apologize. We all raise our voices in times of excitement."

"Not about yelling," she said. "I'm sorry about you and your wife."

★ ★ ★

On the morning of June 9, Emilia Mae woke up in a pool of sweat. An unexpected heat wave bore down on New Rochelle with such ferocity that the main roads gave like mud underfoot. Nauseated and dizzy, Emilia Mae felt as if her insides were wringing themselves out. She turned on her side and waited to die. When the pain subsided, she called out for Xena, but Xena didn't come. She gathered her soaked bedclothes around her and walked in slippered feet to Reverend Klepper's house, only minutes away from the inn. Cora was awakened by the sound of what she thought to be a cat in heat. Or was it an injured dog? She got out of bed and went to the window. In the first light of morning she saw the young girl lying on the ground, curled up as if she'd been shot.

"Aloysius," she cried. "It's Emilia Mae."

Emilia Mae must have passed out, because she had no memory of what came next. When she woke up, she was in the New Rochelle hospital. She swam in and out of the ether; the bitter taste of it stuck in her throat. Figures moved about like shapes on the other side of a rain-splattered window. Someone was asking, "Emilia Mae, can you hear me?"

Reverend Klepper.

She closed her eyes and tried to re-enter the tranquility of darkness, but it was too late. Pieces of reality were starting to float together.

"It's over," he said.

She tried to ask what happened, but had trouble moving her lips.

"It was touch and go there for a while. The baby had its cord wrapped around its neck. You had a cesarean. Thank God for Dr. Rogan."

Emilia Mae tried to sit up, but the parts of her body required to do so felt as if they were ripping. She lay back down and saw that Xena was sitting at the foot of her bed with a bundle in her arms. Just then, Cora Klepper walked into the room with Earle in tow. "Look who's here," said Cora. "It's Grandpa!"

Earle blinked back tears as he looked at his daughter and the baby. "Your mother sends her love," he lied. "She's holding down the fort at the bakery, but she'll come soon."

"You have a little girl," said Xena, placing the baby on Emilia Mae's chest. "God bless her."

Reverend Klepper showed Emilia Mae how to hold the baby's head just so. Cora's eyes widened as she watched her husband. "How do you know so much about how to hold a baby?" she asked.

"I have done a few baptisms in my life," he answered, still fussing with the baby.

All these people gathered around her brought Emilia Mae back to her fantasies about the Oz brothers. She wished she still believed in them; they would have loved this.

For the next two days, Emilia Mae lay in her hospital bed getting to know her baby. She had a tiny red face and looked unlike any creature Emilia Mae had ever seen. She was swaddled in a blue and pink blanket and had a pink cap on her head. She was as light as a freshly baked loaf of bread and smelled like one, too. Emilia Mae would stroke her face. Her nose was so small that Emilia Mae wondered how would she be able to breathe out of it. Her lips were red, and her cheeks were as soft as flower petals. Emilia Mae would loosen the swaddle to play with the baby's fingers and toes. She'd put her finger in the baby's hand and the baby would squeeze it. Once the baby even looked her straight in the eyes. Emilia Mae thought, *She must already recognize me.* When she drew the baby to her breast, the baby would put her mouth around Emilia Mae's nipple and suck. Her body was warm, and Emilia Mae thought she could feel the baby's heartbeat. Or was it her own? She could do this. She would be a good mother, unlike her own. She promised herself that this child would never feel unwanted.

On the third day, Xena was visiting Emilia Mae when Cora and Reverend Klepper showed up. "We have a surprise guest," Cora announced, then left the room for a moment.

"Ta-dum!" she announced as she led Geraldine through the door. Geraldine looked nearly as shocked as Emilia Mae. She was still wearing her bakery apron and hadn't had time to wash the flour from her hands. "Yup, here I am. Not that I had much choice. Cora showed up and said she wouldn't leave until I came with her. I would have come anyway, I just needed to find the right time."

"Well, this was the right time then, isn't that so, Ally?" said Cora.

Aloysius shook his head. "That's my Cora."

Geraldine leaned over the baby. "She's a pretty one, has my family nose."

Cora laughed. "Oh, she does not have your family nose, she hardly has any nose."

"Well, she will have my family nose when she grows one."

Emilia Mae couldn't believe Cora talking back to her mother that way, but her mother just laughed and made a swatting motion toward Cora.

Cora stroked the baby's cheek. "She really is a beauty, isn't she? What will you name her?"

"I've been thinking about that. I'd call her Aloysius, but her life is going to be hard enough without that. So, Alice, I'm going to call her Alice."

Cora looked at Aloysius. "Well, God bless little Alice," he said, with tears in his eyes.

"Amen," said Cora, as she stroked Aloysius's arm.

"Amen," said Xena.

"Amen," said Emilia Mae.

Later, Geraldine would tell Earle that she felt as if she'd walked into a revival meeting. "Aloysius was crying and the rest of them were practically hallelujahing all over the place. I won't have any grandchild of mine raised by holy rollers, I'll tell you that right now."

Maybe it was true or maybe it wasn't, but that was the reason Geraldine gave for telling Sam Bostwick that Emilia Mae would not be returning to the inn, because she and the baby were moving back into the house with her and Earle.

Chapter 9

Reverend Klepper had always been the subject of speculation among parishioners at the First Baptist Church. Although he was friendly with many of them and often shared meals in their homes, no one ever had the nerve to solicit information from him, and clearly he was not comfortable putting any forth. What they knew was what they saw. A large man. A strong man. A kind man. Cora's husband. A childless man. At one point or another, most of the congregation had burdened him with their secrets; it was hard to imagine that he had room in his heart for any of his own. Of course, it's wrong to underestimate what the heart can hold. Reverend Klepper had a past filled with burrs and secrets as painful as those of his parishioners.

His parents ran a small farm in Kingston, New York. Because he was the oldest and largest of two brothers and a sister, most of the hard labor had fallen to him. He'd split wood; cut, raked, and baled hay; gathered and hauled away manure; in addition to milking the cows, cleaning the chicken coops, and feeding the livestock. This life, built around sustaining the lives of his family and the creatures they raised, had brought him immense satisfaction and peace. His relationship with God evolved naturally. He saw Him in the young animals he helped to birth and heard Him in the songs of birds and the cries of summer crickets. The reliable strength of his own body was, he felt, a gift from God.

His father's people were Baptists from Valdosta, Georgia, and religion was a fixture in the Klepper household. They all had the inflection of the church in their speech. Every Sunday, they'd gone to the small Baptist church in town. During the week, his mother would bring food and sometimes clothing to the less fortunate parishioners. Although his parents hoped that their brawny son would continue to run the farm when they were gone, Aloysius always knew that he would be part of a ministry and tend to the living, as he'd been raised to do. The pastor at their church had studied at the Southern Baptist Theological Seminary in Louisville, Kentucky, and promised Aloysius that whenever he was ready, he would try to help him get a scholarship there.

At seventeen, with a full scholarship, thirty dollars in his pocket, and a secondhand suitcase loosely filled with one pair of slacks, one pair of shoes, three shirts, and various underwear and toiletries, Aloysius had set off on a bus to a strange city eight hundred miles away, having never spent a night apart from his family.

His living quarters at Southern Baptist were modest: a cot, a desk, and a chair. Raised in the outdoors, Aloysius found the drab cinderblock room confining. Whenever he could, he took long walks, which inevitably led him to the Parklands of Floyds Fork, where he would watch the birds, pet the dogs, feed the ducks, and long for the life he'd had back home. Sometimes, he lingered so long that he'd forget the time and have to jump on a bus in order not to miss his next class. On one of those bus trips, he noticed a woman carrying an armful of groceries. She was tall, nearly six feet, with a long, pale neck that flushed when he offered her his seat. For a moment, they stood eye to eye. "Thank you," she said. "It's so nice to see a man my size."

It was a provocative thing to say, for sure, but Aloysius understood what she meant. In those days, a woman that tall was a rarity, and she probably towered over most men. When the seat next to her became available, Aloysius took it.

"You from around here?" she asked.

Aloysius explained about Kingston and why he was in Louisville.

"Are you one of those holy rollers then?"

Aloysius laughed. "No, ma'am, just a farm boy hoping to get an education and help people out."

"I guess I'm sort of hoping to do the same thing," she said. "I want to be a nurse. Right now, I work as a secretary in a law firm, but when I save enough money, I plan to go to nursing school in a big city up north."

She held her groceries on her lap and talked with her hands; lovely hands, slender and graceful. Her name was Marguerite. She was Canadian, with a beautiful French accent, and eyes the color of a blue jay. It had been months since Aloysius had talked to anyone, particularly a female, with the ease that he found while talking to Marguerite. When she stood up to get off at her stop, he stood with her. "Mind if I walk you home?" he asked.

She laughed and said, "It won't be a long walk; I live across the street."

That afternoon, Aloysius missed his class on the Old Testament.

The two fell in love, quickly and completely, and gave no thought to how hastily they'd jumped into a relationship. When Marguerite became pregnant, six months after their meeting, Aloysius took an evening job as a busboy at the Oakroom Restaurant in the Seelbach Hotel. They rented a two-room cottage near the seminary and spent the next seven months fixing it up and preparing for the baby. Marriage would come later. They joked about the very tall and strong child they would have and decided that if it was a boy, they'd call him Lionel, and a girl, Linden, after the tall and graceful linden tree that stood in front of the Kleppers' farmhouse.

Aloysius splurged on a yellow cashmere baby blanket with the letter *L* monogrammed onto it. The two of them would hoist that blanket over their shoulders and carry it around the house pretending it was their newborn. When her time came, Marguerite gave birth to a beautiful girl, who would have her mother's blue jay eyes and long neck. The nurse who delivered her said she'd never seen a newborn with such big hands and feet. The first time Aloysius held her he was afraid she would wriggle out of his arms. The nurse showed him how to rest the baby's head and neck in one hand and her back and rear in the other. The baby grabbed Aloysius's finger, and for the next half hour, neither of them moved. She was a big girl with a firm grip, and the name Linden seemed just right.

Linden was an easy child with an even disposition who only cried when hungry or wet. At night, Aloysius would sing lullabies to her: Brahms, "Frère Jacques," "Hush Little Baby." Although he had only an octave range, his resonant voice must have soothed her, because she'd go to sleep without a fuss. Aloysius recalled her infanthood as the happiest time in his life. Often, in his sermons, he would use the phrase "someone touched fire," meaning how someone burned with joy. With Marguerite and Linden, he had touched fire. He and Marguerite made plans to move back to Kingston when he finished at Southern Baptist. It wasn't the big city that Marguerite had fantasized about, but his parents would take care of the baby while Marguerite went to nursing school, and he'd find a job with a small congregation.

Late the following winter, when Linden was nearly eight months old, she developed a sore throat and swollen glands. At first, they thought it was a cold, but when her breathing became jagged, Aloysius scooped her up and ran her to the nearby hospital, where she was diagnosed with diphtheria. For the next eleven days, Aloysius and Marguerite sat by her bedside. Aloysius reassured Marguerite that he had a special relationship with God and that his God would not let their child get worse. Yet despite the antitoxins the doctors gave her, Linden's breaths became shallow and wheezy. Her face turned a bluish gray, which Aloysius knew was really not a color but notice from the body that it was beginning to shut down. He and Marguerite were holding Linden's hands and singing a lullaby when they saw her breathing stop and her face go slack. They kept singing and squeezing her hands as if by treating her as alive, they could keep her so. They sat like that for what could have been ten minutes or two hours, until a nurse came into the room and gently told them it was time.

They got home well past midnight. In the darkness, Aloysius lay on their bed and held Linden's yellow blanket over his face, trying to inhale her. He begged God to give him the diphtheria and take him, too, even though he knew the unreasonableness of his request. He prayed that, by some miracle, Linden would be restored to them. When that didn't happen, he asked for the strength to care for himself and for Marguerite. Over time, it became clear how that wasn't going to happen, either.

In her despair Marguerite turned on Aloysius. So much for him and his God. How could she believe in a God who let an eight-month-old baby die? They didn't fight, because Aloysius had no fight in him. He became angry with God, convinced that He had abandoned him. His faith and devotion dried up until he was left only with grief. He retreated into himself. Sometimes, he found it hard even to look at Marguerite. That face, those eyes, so reminiscent of Linden's, could make his heart jump with the momentary belief that she had reappeared. Then reality would hit with pain as fresh as the day she'd died.

Without his faith, his studies became irrelevant. He stopped going to classes. He quit his job at the restaurant. Four months after Linden's death, he and Marguerite were broke, and broken. When Marguerite said she wanted to move back to her parents' in Toronto, Aloysius didn't protest. She packed up her few belongings, leaving Aloysius alone in the cottage. There was no choice but for him to return to Kingston after nearly two years. He left everything behind except Linden's yellow cashmere blanket, a reminder of what could have been.

Back at the farm, his parents tried to interest him in his old chores, but he remained sullen and immutable. Early one morning, before anyone was awake, Aloysius crept down to the barn, picked up an ax and brought it to the house, where he threw all his weight and rage into trying to fell the linden tree. His father ran out in his bare feet.

"What are you doing?"

Aloysius kept whacking the tree and didn't look up.

"Stop, now!" yelled his father. "Do you really think you can get even by killing that tree?"

"Does anyone ever get even?"

"If you think God will take pity on you because you're having a tantrum, think again. He's heard you. He knows you're in pain. You'll heal, but not like this. Put down the damn ax. Anyway, you've chosen to mess with the wrong tree. This one's a whole lot stronger than you are."

Aloysius dropped the ax. "I'm tired."

His father opened his arms, and Aloysius came to him. After a time, his father said: "You need to go get yourself a job somewhere. Hiding out with us is a mistake. You've already started manhood; there's no turning back. You're always welcome here, but it's time to move forward."

It took a few days for his father's words to sink in. Aloysius knew he was right: By staying on the farm, he was hiding. It had been six months since Linden died, six months since Aloysius had left the world and everything that held meaning for him. He and Marguerite hadn't been in touch, but he'd still try to honor his promise to her and get a job in the city. He'd work until he got his feet on the ground, then maybe go up to Toronto and find her. With no qualifications except a strong body, he'd take any job requiring physical strength.

At the Kingston library, he scoured the New York newspapers until he found what he thought to be the perfect opportunity: the Panonia Plumbing Company, in a place called the Bronx, was looking for a truck driver who didn't mind "long hours and heavy lifting." He was ready for both and applied. It was during the Depression, when jobs, even labor jobs, were scarce. But Aloysius, in the only suit he owned, with his hair slicked back and his assertive voice, cut a fine figure. The owner hired him on the spot, saying, "If you turn out to be as good as you look, this will be one happy marriage." Aloysius moved to the Bronx and rented a room at the YMCA.

In this new place where no one knew who he was, he slowly learned how to put one foot in front of the other and live again. Seeing Marguerite would only open the door to pain. The longer he didn't contact her, the less necessary it seemed.

One afternoon, nearly a year after he moved to the Bronx, he was asked to deliver a porcelain high-back sink to a florist in a place he'd never heard of called New Rochelle, twenty miles outside of New York City. The sink had clawlike legs and felt as if it weighed close to one hundred pounds. He carried it into the florist shop as he might carry a calf, with all four legs tucked behind him. The woman behind the counter laughed when she saw him: "Well, you are a sight. Who's that you've got with you?" Her laughter got his attention, as did her green eyes. She had enough freckles on her face to cover the side of a barn. Before he knew it, the two of them were laughing together, though he hardly knew why. That young woman was Cora, and for the third time in his young life, Aloysius felt as if he'd touched fire.

Eventually, he forgave God. Cora talked him into returning to school, the Union Theological Seminary in Manhattan. Cora wasn't from a religious family, but because her family owned the only florist shop in town, they knew everyone, including the pastor at First Baptist. When Aloysius graduated, he was able to get a job as the assistant to that pastor.

After they married, they took a small apartment not far from the church, and once again, life was as it was meant to be. Although he had told Cora about Marguerite, he would keep Linden to himself until Cora got pregnant. When, after a year, and then two, that didn't happen, he decided that telling her would be like rubbing salt in a wound. He never told her about the recurring fish dream either, the one in which he held a baby who became smaller and smaller until it was the size of a goldfish and slipped out of his hands.

The secret of Linden weighed almost as heavily on him as her death. He promised himself he would tell Cora when the time was right. But the time never seemed to get right.

Chapter 10

As she grew, it quickly became clear that little Alice Wingo was the exact opposite of her mother. She had Grandma Geraldine's swirly black hair and dark skin and Grandpa Earle's pin-straight nose. At five years old, her white teeth flashed like a constellation when she smiled, revealing someone else's gap between her two front teeth. The gap between her teeth was all she knew about her father.

Emilia Mae had a beaky nose and was as round as Alice was slender. Alice had a gaudy grin that people took personally; her mother rarely smiled, which people also took personally. Her mother also wore bright red, pink, or orange lipstick, depending on what she was wearing and, lately, so much pancake makeup that Alice thought her face sometimes looked wooden, but in 1953 New Rochelle, it was important that makeup matched your outfit.

Alice lived with Grandma Geraldine and Grandpa Earle in a white stucco house about a mile from the bakery. The house had an orange tiled roof that you could barely see because of the two-hundred-year-old white oak that loomed over it. Inside, it was always nighttime, even in the morning. There were three bedrooms, a kitchen, a small dining room, and a living room with a brick fireplace. Her mother worked at the bakery every day. Though she and Grandma didn't speak all that much, her mother and Grandpa got along just fine; everyone got along with Grandpa just fine.

At night, Grandpa would tuck Alice into bed and sing to her songs he'd picked up on the radio, like "Don't Let the Stars Get in Your Eyes" and "Vaya con Dios." His voice was thin and almost girlish, but he could carry a tune perfectly. One night after supper, he played his new album for Alice, *Ella Sings Gershwin*. Alice particularly liked "Someone to Watch over Me" and had him play it three times. The next evening, after he tucked her into bed, Grandpa pulled a sheet of paper from the book he was carrying. He'd written out the lyrics and told Alice: "Put them under your pillow before you go to sleep, and they'll seep into your memory."

Three nights later, after Alice had listened to the song many more times, she told Earle: "It worked. I've learned the words by heart. Want to hear?" She was wearing a flannel pink and white nightgown with eyelet lace trim around the yoke. She sat up in bed and sang. Her voice was as sweet and pure as her open face. Earle cupped his hand over his mouth. In the realm of events in his life that made him believe there was a higher being, this angel voice coming from his granddaughter secured a place in his prayers for her and it.

When they sang together, his reedy voice blended with her sweet one in a way that seemed preordained. "We sound like the Andrews Sisters," he said. He told her that she had a beautiful singing voice and that one day, she could become a professional musician.

Years later, when Alice listened to old Andrews Sisters records, she could hear their voices in the sisters' harmonies. It reminded her how it was Grandpa who made her see beyond the bakery. It was also Grandpa whom she called out to when she had nightmares, and Grandpa whom she ran to first at the end of the day. He made her feel safe. She wished he were her father, but he was the next best thing.

When Alice was six, Emilia Mae went to work full-time in the bakery and brought her there on weekends. Alice's earliest memories of the bakery were that it smelled like chocolate and butter and was always warm inside. There was always a spool of red-and-white–striped string on the counter, and Grandpa taught Alice how to loop it around the box twice on each side before tying it in a bow.

Sticky buns were Alice's favorite. After that, she liked the crullers and red velvet cake best. The black-and-white–tiled floor was slippery. One of her favorite games was to slide across the floor with Grandpa Earle. He thought it was funny and would reach out and grab her hand, but Grandma Geraldine would scold him: "This is not a playground, Earle. You should know better than that." Grandpa Earle would make a sad face, like it mattered that Grandma had yelled at him, but as soon as she'd leave the room, he'd put his finger over his lips and grab Alice's hand, and off they'd go.

The game stopped when Alice was eight. Grandpa Earle said his legs were sick. Sometimes they hurt so badly he had to lean on Grandma when he walked. His hands were always cold, and sometimes the tips of his fingers turned blue. Emilia Mae would rub them until they got warm and Grandpa always said Emilia Mae had "the touch." By then, Alice's job was to sit on a stool behind the counter. When a customer ordered fudge cookies or buttermilk biscuits, Grandma would put them in front of Alice and let her wrap them in wax paper before she stuck them into a white cake box.

One day, while she was packing up muffins for a skinny man with brown and white shoes, the man leaned in close. "You're a mighty cute little girl," he said, something mean in his voice. "I've seen your mother and you don't look nothing like her. It makes me wonder, who's your father?"

Before Alice could say what she'd been taught to say, "My father's gone," Grandma Geraldine spoke up. "For whatever business it is of yours, and it is no business of yours, this one's got no father. That's just the way it is." She stared at the man in a way that made him step back and put his hands in the air as if he were being held up.

Grandma Geraldine looked out for Alice that way. Alice knew Grandma loved her by how she'd stroke her cheek when she walked by and spoke to her in a tone that was different from the way she spoke to Emilia Mae. Oh, she could be nice to the customers when she wanted to, but Alice could hear the forced sweetness in her voice when she'd say things like, "Bless you, honey. Won't you be my guinea pig and try these chocolate drops I just baked," and "Please, come again, dear." Deep down, Grandma was a good person. She was always lecturing Alice on the virtues of kindness and generosity even though, when it came to her daughter and husband, it seemed to Alice that those virtues sometimes slipped Grandma's mind.

Grandpa Earle chatted naturally with customers. He flattered them and remembered their children's names. He could talk about everything: politics, the new polio vaccine, *The $64,000 Question*. When kids came in, he gave them free sugar cookies. Like Grandpa,

Alice remembered babies' names and was up to date with what was going on in *Lassie*.

Customers always told Emilia Mae what a polite daughter she had, and Emilia Mae always answered, "She sure doesn't get it from me."

Reverend Klepper once explained to Alice: "Your mother doesn't have a natural bakery personality. That's why the Lord sent you. You could light up death row. You need to help her out." She promised that she would, even though the troubling image of death row stayed with her for a long while.

By the time Alice was nine, Earle had so much pain in his bones that it was all he could do to wipe down the counter and take in money at the cash register. Alice picked up as many of his chores as she could. She scoured the bread trays, scrubbed the oven, and washed out the tubs used for the rising dough. No matter, Grandma always complained how all the work fell to her. As Earle lost weight, Geraldine would tease him in front of customers and say, "Earle's doing a piss-poor job of advertising for Shore Cakes these days." Her laugh was thin, and Grandpa played along with it, but Alice could tell neither of them thought it was funny. Soon, Grandpa got so sick he stopped coming to the shop.

Her mother worked full time, and Alice would come directly to the bakery from school and stay until they closed at six. Grandma spent most of her time in the baking room, leaving Alice and her mother to take care of the customers.

On the last day of fourth grade, Alice and her friend Sheryl sang "Jamaica Farewell" at the school talent show.

Two days later, on June 13, 1957, Grandpa Earle died.

At nine, Alice felt as if she'd lost the only father she'd ever known.

Geraldine mourned his pale blue eyes, his sweet voice. The man who'd loved the lavender robe she used to wear, the one with the embroidered calla lilies on it. The Earle who'd always hungered for her before Emilia Mae was born.

Emilia Mae wept for the kind man who had understood her loneliness but hadn't had the strength to drag her out of it.

Now it was only the three of them.

With Grandpa Earle gone, Alice began experiencing phantom limb pain, not for a body part but for her father. She watched every man who came into the bakery, particularly the ones around her mother's age.

The first time a man with a gap between his yellowish front teeth came into the store, Alice studied his pockmarked face and turtle eyes. Her own skin was smooth and her brown eyes wide, but the gap was nearly identical to hers. She watched the man as he bent down to study the cakes behind the glass. He had a bald spot in the middle of his gray-blond hair. His hair was coarse; hers was fine. Still, the gap. She wrapped up the two brownies he bought and tried to engage him in conversation. "Are you new to town?"

"Nope."

"I haven't seen you around here."

"Don't really have a sweet tooth," he answered as he zipped his brown windbreaker and left the store. Alice saw that he turned left, toward the center of town.

She wondered if he was heading to his car. Maybe his kids were waiting for him, maybe his wife. *I'll just follow him a bit*, she told herself. *Not too far.* She told Grandma she was running out to get some Life Savers and would be right back.

Alice followed him down Main into Woolworth's. He walked through the kitchen supply department, stopping to glance at pans and potholders, then to menswear, where he looked around quickly before stuffing four pairs of socks into his pocket.

Not my father, decided Alice. My father wouldn't be a shoplifter. She headed back to Shore Cakes.

A few months later, when Alice and her mother were alone in the bakery, a short chubby man with baby-pink cheeks and windblown auburn hair came in. He reeked of Canoe and wore an ID bracelet the size of a handcuff. Alice knew the type: a cocky rich guy from Wykagyl. Her mother and grandmother hated them. Every time one of them left the store, her mother would stick her nose in the air and say, "Hoity toity," in a fake English accent. He was definitely one of those.

"Hello, doll face. You look as if you could point me to the perfect red velvet cake." The man practically stepped on Alice's toes.

She moved back. "Every red velvet cake here is perfect."

"Atta girl. I'll take your most perfect one, then." He smiled, and when he did, the gap between his teeth nearly sucked her in like a wind tunnel.

She wrapped up the cake, and when the man left, she told her mother she'd be gone only a minute, she wanted to get a Coke. Alice followed the man as far as his Impala convertible, a half block away. As he drove off, he must have glimpsed her in the rearview mirror because he waved and shouted, "Thanks again, doll face."

Following gap-toothed men became a habit. Alice followed them to a pool hall and a podiatrist's office, and once she even followed a man to his home. She had no intention of talking to them; mainly she wanted to glimpse their lives and see if she could find a place for herself in them. Each time, she'd come up with a reason that the particular man she'd followed couldn't possibly be her father.

The search would go on.

Chapter 11

In Skyville, the summer breeze smelled of jasmine and the moon shone like a crown over the mountains.

The water in Lake Lure was so clear, you could see twenty feet down to the bottom, where people had dropped shoes or sent flying a bottle of cola.

It was a waste not to be in love in Skyville summers, if only in love with love.

In the summer of 1959, Dillard Fox was in love with more than love.

He'd been working in the Catskills resort for two years. He finally quit in late May and came home to the little Skyville cabin his father had left him and where he hoped to settle down and recapture whatever was left of his soul. One Saturday night in June, he decided to go to a summer concert at the bandstand by the lake. He was walking barefoot when he stepped onto a broken Coke bottle. The bottle ripped open the bottom of his foot. As he hopped around searching for a place to sit, he left a trail of blood behind him. When he finally made it to a nearby picnic bench, a well-meaning man pulled a handkerchief from his pocket and wrapped it around Dillard's foot. An older man stepped in and yanked the handkerchief off: "Don't do that, it'll infect it. I'm a doctor. I'll take care of it."

By then, a small crowd, including a woman pushing a baby carriage, had gathered around the table. The doctor pointed to her and shouted, "Do you have any clean diapers in there?" She rummaged around and turned up a neatly folded fresh cloth diaper.

"I'll take it," said the doctor, who quickly fashioned a tight bandage around Dillard's foot then asked another man to help get him to his car. He drove Dillard to the Skyville General Hospital, where he lay on an examining table as the doctor cleaned the cut, sewed it up with five stitches, and wrapped his foot in a bandage. "You came yay close to nicking your tendon," said the doctor when he finished. He patted Dillard's foot. "You're a lucky fella. But you got yourself a nice wound there; you're gonna need to stay off it until it heals a bit. I'll order up a pair of crutches for you. Come see me on Wednesday. In the meantime, keep that foot clean and dry. My name is Dr. Moore, and you are?"

Dillard said his name softly as the doctor put his arm around his shoulder and helped him off the examining table. He must have seen something in Dillard's eyes—sadness, loneliness, fear—that made him keep his arm around Dillard a moment longer, then pat his shoulder and say, "Don't worry, buddy, you'll be fine."

For the past two years, Dillard had been anything but fine. His work at the resort had been humiliating. He'd been made to feel the clown, performing for all those guests who couldn't care less about the entertainment when they had mountains of food planted in front of them. Management treated him and the other musicians like servants, snapping their fingers to get their attention, calling them names like "tart" or "show boy," and paying for room and board and little more. So, no, Dillard was not fine. Nor had anyone reassured him that he would be in a very long time.

Dr. Moore's words and comforting touch stirred feelings that Dillard had tucked away for all those months. In an uncharacteristic gesture, he threw his arms around the doctor. "Thank you for taking care of me and for your profound kindness."

Dr. Moore hugged him back: "Nothing to thank me for, son, you'll be fine."

"It's been a long time..." said Dillard into Dr. Moore's shoulder.

The doctor put his hand behind Dillard's head and pulled him closer. "I know. Sometimes it feels as if we are the lonesome spot on this planet, as if we are a species unto ourselves. I really do understand. You take care, now."

By Monday, Dillard's wound was infected, so much so that two people who saw him hobbling down the street pointed to his red, swollen foot and said, "You need to take care of that." One nun caught his eye and whispered, "God bless you." His foot felt hot and achy, and at night he could feel it throbbing. Even Dr. Moore was taken aback the following Wednesday when Dillard limped into his office. "You're the saddest sight I've seen all day," he said. "Why'd it take you so long to come here?"

"I didn't want to bother you," said Dillard.

"Well, let's have a look." Dr. Moore unwrapped the bandage and lightly palpated the swollen foot. "That's some infection you've got festering. Right off, I'm gonna put you on penicillin. I want you to soak it at least three times a day in a mixture of two parts water, one part hydrogen peroxide. And don't you be shy about dropping by here if this thing doesn't start healing up. Are you at a job where you can keep off your feet?"

Dillard half smiled. "I'm at no job right now."

"What did you do when you were at a job?"

Dillard explained about his music and the Catskills and how he'd just quit.

"Are you in the market for something?"

"Anything," said Dillard. "I'm in the market for anything that will pay a decent wage."

"Just so happens my receptionist is going off on maternity leave. I could use someone who's personable and reasonably organized." Dr. Moore smiled. "Think you might want to give it a try?"

"Sure, that's awfully kind of you. But I've never been a receptionist before."

"Two things," said the doctor. "One: This isn't brain surgery. It's sitting behind a desk, answering the phone, taking messages, scheduling appointments, and making people feel welcome and less nervous than they probably are. And two: You can call me Nick when it's the two of us. Just throw in the doc part when we're in front of patients."

Dillard smiled. "I think I can do that. When can I start?"

"She leaves in three weeks. Enough time for you to be off the crutches and to memorize your lines: 'Dr. Moore's office. How may I help you?'"

Dillard was surprised at how much he enjoyed his job as a reception-ist. He liked having a place to go to every day. He liked his oak wood desk and the leather chair that had wheels on it, so he could roll back and forth to the filing cabinet without getting up. He liked the window behind his desk that looked out onto a giant Douglas fir, a year-round Christmas tree. Having been so mistreated at the resort, he took care to treat the patients with sympathy and respect. He called the ladies "ma'am" and the men "sir," and kept a large jar of gumdrops on his desk for the kids. He flirted back with the women and their daughters and bantered with the men and their sons. Sometimes, when Nick needed an extra hand lifting a patient or holding down a child, he'd call Dillard into the examining room to help out. For a time, Dillard even considered studying medicine. But that was before Mr. Axelrod, an older man who worked as a custodian in the high school, came in with a gash in his leg from a broken window pane and bled all over Dr. Moore's table. While Dillard was able to hold Mr. Axelrod's hand while Dr. Moore sewed him up, the moment it was over he ran into the bathroom and vomited. That's when he realized he'd best stick to music.

Still, Dr. Moore said Dillard was the best receptionist he'd ever had. He remembered the patients' names and reassured them when they called with their questions or worries. Dillard had been there six weeks when, at the end of the day, Dr. Moore stepped out of his office, took off his white coat, and rolled up his shirtsleeves. "How 'bout you and I leave all this blood and gore behind us, pick up a couple of beers, and go sit down by the lake?"

"Sure," said Dillard, who had no other plans.

Because of a morning thunderstorm, the air at Lake Lure smelled of wet clay. Their feet squished in the mud. Nick took Dillard's arm as he stepped over a log: "It gets slippery around here," he said. "Gotta watch yourself." Dillard was aware of the doctor's strength and how he towered over him with his six-foot-three-inch frame.

They found a dry patch of grass next to the lake. Its metallic surface was regaining its composure after the rains. "This is where I learned to swim," said Nick. "If you can call it that. My older brother pushed me into the deep one day when I was around three. Like a dog, I paddled back to where I could stand." He shook his head. "We humans have more animal instinct in us than we care to admit. I suppose that's why we survive the things we do."

Dillard thought back to when his mother walked out and how he'd felt as if he would die. He remembered after, how he and his father slept in the same bed for a while, curled around each other like cats. He told Nick about that, about his mother insisting on his long hair, how she'd told his father that she'd never loved him, the abuse he'd felt at the resort. Stories spilled out of him, personal things that he'd never talked about to anyone. There was something about Nick's arching presence that made him feel safe.

Two beers in, Nick told Dillard that when he was five, the boy next door named Judah and he were cutting out paper rockets when Judah suddenly turned to him and sliced him in the face with his scissors. "The only memento I have left is this one." Nick licked his upper lip where a *J*-shaped scar bifurcated it. "It bled like a sonofabitch, my lip and my chin," he said. "I was so proud of myself because I didn't cry. I just got up and went home. Shortly after that, Judah and his family moved away, and we never heard from them again."

"Why'd he cut you?" asked Dillard.

Nick shrugged. "Why do grown men climb mountains or hunt deer? Because they can. Judah was two years older, but I was probably twice his size. Maybe that was his way of showing dominance over me? Primal instinct? We humans are a funny species, don't you think? Because I'm a big guy, people assume that I like to fight, I'm good at sports. And you? You with your handsome face and big blue ones? People must make assumptions about you all the time."

Dillard laughed. "I never thought of it that way. I always thought that girls were nice to me because of my good personality and my immense intellect."

"I'm sure that's part of it," said Nick. "You and I, we're members of the same tribe, separated only by time and circumstance." Nick had a way of talking that was circuitous at times, but Dillard found it intriguing. His largeness, his kindness, the way he took care—all of these things were an enormous comfort to Dillard, who'd never felt taken care of.

Nick patted Dillard's hand. "Gee, your hand is cold. Lemme have a look." He studied Dillard's fingers, and rubbed them where they were bluish. "You have Raynaud's syndrome. Ever hear of it? Not enough blood gets to your extremities. Gotta be careful in the cold."

Dillard didn't move his hand, and in the evening dusk, Nick leaned into Dillard and whispered: "I feel like kissing you."

"Me too," said Dillard, surprised to hear those words come out of his mouth.

Nick tasted of beer and the earth and Dillard fell into the kiss as if it were home. When Nick folded his arms around him, he didn't have to say, "I'll take care of you." The tenderness of his touch and the way he held him made that clear.

A man with no memory of a mother's caress or a father's dependable hugs can only fantasize about what they might have been like. But once he feels that touch, he knows without knowing how that this is what he has longed for always.

★ ★ ★

Nicholas Moore was forty-three, fifteen years older than Dillard, and four inches taller. He had thick, wavy black hair and that scar on his upper lip, which made his smile at once lopsided and endearing. Because he was tall and muscular and dressed in the conservative fashion of the day—solid oxford shirts, khaki pants, and cordovan loafers—people took him for ten years younger. His house, on a bluff at the edge of town, was a simple log one with a sloping roof, a big open porch, and a year-round view of the Smoky Mountains. He owned an old turquoise Chevy station wagon, which had just enough room for him, his wife, three children, and one German Shepherd. Until he met Dillard, his only indulgence had been cashmere socks.

The two of them became as inseparable as it was possible for two men in Skyville to be. Sometimes they'd leave work early and take walks together at Lake Lure. They kept bathing suits in the car in case they decided to jump in the water and cool off. They'd swim to the floating dock in the middle of the lake and lie in the sun. They befriended the lifeguard at the lake, who called them Doc and the Kid and never asked any questions. After work, they'd duck out to Dillard's cabin, where Nick would whip up pancakes or mac and cheese. Sometimes, Dillard would play his flute. On the rare occasion when Nick could get away overnight, they'd go twenty miles away to Asheville and stay in one of the big hotels there. Nick wrapped Dillard in a cocoon of safety and love. He wrote Dillard letters, funny quips, or love notes that came by mail at least four times a week.

Once in a while, Dillard went to Nick's house for dinner with his wife, Sharlene, and the kids. Sharlene was an English teacher who spoke formally and in complete sentences. Everything about Sharlene was neat. Her long, straight brown hair was held back on both sides by tortoiseshell barrettes and nicely framed her vase-shaped head. Her small brown eyes were close together, but perfectly congruent with her thin, straight lips, like those on a ventriloquist's dummy. She and Dillard had an easy rapport; she'd recommend books to him, then they'd have long discussions about them. When Sharlene was being thoughtful or rendering an opinion, she'd bite down on the knuckle of the index finger on her right hand before she spoke, a habit he found touching.

Dillard taught the Moore boy, Zeke, how to play the drums and the twin girls, Eve and Ava, how to harmonize. The dog, Lucy, took a fancy to Dillard and would roll over on her back waiting to get her stomach scratched the moment Dillard walked in the door. With the Moores, Dillard had found a family the likes of which he'd never known. Anyone looking through the picture window of the Moore home would see that family, a happy and handsome one, the kind that trouble tends to ignore.

And for a long time, trouble did just that.

In late November, as the weather turned colder, Nick and Dillard were in bed when Nick looked at his watch and realized it was nearly seven. He kissed Dillard on the forehead and sat up. "I hate to do this, but I promised Sharlene I'd pick up the girls from Scouts."

Dillard kissed him back, not on the forehead.

"Every time I leave you, pieces of my heart break apart," said Nick.

"Me too," answered Dillard in a sleepy voice. "But I'll see you in the morning, Dr. Moore."

Moved as he was by Nick's sentimentality, Dillard was also amused by how overwrought his words could be. Dillard was Nick's first male lover. Nick said he'd always liked girls; he didn't know he had it in him. He told Dillard that he and Sharlene had met as teenagers and become best friends. They stayed that way until Nick entered med school, when marrying Sharlene seemed a logical step. "She took care of everything and supported me through those years. Without her, my life wouldn't have worked. She's the reason I became a doctor. She's the one who's basically raised our kids and taken care of the house. I love her, I really do. Just not in that way. I assumed that was the price I had to pay for the life, the kids, the profession, the whole shebang. Then you came along."

In one of the many letters Nick wrote, he said, "When I met you, my hands, my heart, and my head abandoned all judgment. They would not rest until they possessed you. Nothing in my body or soul prepared me for the happiness I would discover with you, my Dill. I can't imagine life without you."

Dillard stayed in bed and watched Nick get dressed. Methodical down to the last detail, he never threw his shirt and pants on the floor, but folded them neatly, placing them on the wicker chair in the corner with his shoes and socks tucked directly underneath. As he slipped his loafer onto his left foot, a look of concern fell over his face. "Dill, have you seen my sock, the gray cashmere one with the white trim?" Nick held up the other sock to show him.

Dillard looked under the covers and on the floor. Nick got on his hands and knees to search under the dresser and behind the door.

"Odd," said Nick when he sat up. "How can a sock get away just like that?"

"It must have a mind of its own," said Dillard. "I'd blame the dog, but I don't have one."

"Funny," said Nick, slipping his loafer onto his naked foot. "Well, if a cashmere sock turns up somewhere, you'll know it's mine."

"Okay, I'll remember that. What'll you tell Sharlene if she notices you're minus a sock?"

"Hmmm, I'll tell her I was in a hurry and forgot to put it on."

Dillard laughed. "Nobody who knows you would believe that. You're far too meticulous to do something like that."

Nick came and sat on the bed next to Dillard. "That meticulous thing is just for show," he said, stroking Dillard's face. "When it comes to matters of the heart, I'm a goofy slob. You know that, don't you?"

Dillard took Nick's hand and held it to his cheek. "You're my goofy slob, that's all I need to know."

Nick kissed Dillard on the mouth and stood up. "Always will be."

Before he left, he put on the new brown tweed flap cap he'd bought and pulled it down to the middle of his brow. Dillard shook his head: "I hate to say this, but you still have that bald spot, whether you wear a hat or not."

Although Nick wasn't a vain man, he took pride in his hair: the thickness of it, the way it curled around his ears, how there were just enough strands of gray in his sideburns to make him look distinguished. It was Dillard who'd noticed how the top had started to thin out a tiny bit. No bigger than a coffee cup stain, he told Nick. Nevertheless, it was enough to make Nick check out the spot in the mirror each morning and put his faith in the cap. Nick made the case to Dillard: "Hair follicles tend to release when the air around them is cool. The heat is what keeps them closed and stabilized, so it's important for me to wear the cap and keep my head warm at all times."

"Is this a scientific theory?" Dillard had asked.

"It's Dr. Moore's scientific theory, is what it is."

"Sounds like bullshit to me," Dillard had said. "But you look pretty sexy in the cap, so who cares?"

Dillard never did find Nick's sock, and Nick never mentioned it again, although he now kept his socks on in bed, claiming his feet got cold on winter afternoons.

Sharlene invited Nick to spend that Christmas with the family. "It won't be anything fancy, just a traditional holiday dinner with us and the kids. Please, you mustn't feel it necessary to bring us presents, we have more than enough."

Of course, Dillard ignored Sharlene's instructions and brought her a leather-covered notebook with her initials; a Mr. Potato Head for Zeke; the soundtrack to *Oklahoma!* for Eve and Ava, twins who were obsessed with the movie; and a bag of Milk-Bone biscuits for Lucy. When Nick opened his present, a pair of gray cashmere socks with white trim, he shot Dillard a quick knowing smile.

They ate turkey and stuffing, green bean casserole, candied yams, and pecan pie. They sang Christmas carols around the piano and opened presents. Sharlene gave Dillard *Lolita* and *Doctor Zhivago*, and Nick gave him a blue stocking cap with the note reminding him to keep his "hair follicles warm." As Dillard left, Sharlene kissed him on the cheek and said, "Thank you for sharing this special day with us. Your presence has simply added to the festivities." He thanked her and said her pecan pie was the best he'd ever had.

If there was anything awkward about that day, Dillard missed it.

Chapter 12

Dr. Moore's office remained closed for the week between Christmas and New Year's. Although Dillard had assumed Nick would finagle a way to get in touch with him, when he didn't, he figured Nick was busy with the family. He was surprised that he didn't receive any letters from him during all that time but excited about the two nights and three days they would have together the following week. Nick had been invited to speak at the Continuing Medical Education Conference in New York City, something about the treatment of rashes in primary care. They would be staying at the Roosevelt Hotel, which Nick said was in the heart of downtown. Dillard had never been to New York City, though he'd passed near it on the way to the Catskills. He'd never even been on a plane. Nick had promised him jazz in Greenwich Village, a walk through Chinatown, a ride on the Staten Island Ferry. He'd bought a New York City guidebook and earmarked the pages of all the sites he thought they should see. Mostly, Dillard looked forward to spending unfettered time with Nick. They'd be able to go everywhere without worrying about being seen. Nick had reserved an extra hotel room using an assumed name so there'd be no awkwardness about their checking in to the same room. He paid for both in advance.

Dillard took the window seat on the plane and started reading the guidebook. He ordered a cup of hot chocolate that was so hot he turned on the overhead air nozzle and stuck the cup right under it to cool it down. He hadn't anticipated the strong flow of air that would manage to splash hot chocolate all over the guidebook, his khaki pants, and his white shirt.

Nick looked startled. For a moment Dillard thought he was angry and started to apologize, but Nick smiled and said, "Well, that settles that. I was debating about whether or not I should take you to Macy's." Dillard wiped the hot chocolate off the book and shoved it in his duffel, which was overhead. When they got to New York, they headed straight to Macy's. Nick bought Dillard new khaki pants, a white oxford shirt, and a heavy brown car coat with a faux fur collar. Dillard wore the coat out of the store, and as they walked up Thirty-Fourth Street, Nick turned Dillard's collar up around his ears. "Now you look like a real New Yorker."

New York City did not disappoint. There was music everywhere, even when no one was playing: the garbage trucks, the sirens, the kids roller-skating, the traffic cops blowing their whistles. Nick was quieter than usual, which Dillard attributed to nerves about his Tuesday speech. Dillard predicted he'd be a hit, that the audience would love him, and he was right. Nick even managed to throw a few jokes about ringworm and eczema into his speech. That night, they went for a steak dinner at Keens Chophouse. They sat in a dark, wood-paneled room that smelled of searing meat and pipe smoke—not a surprise since thousands of clay pipes lined the ceiling. The slabs of steak were enormous, and so were the prices. "What's the occasion?" asked Dillard, after reading through the menu. "This is an awful fancy place."

Nick smiled his lopsided smile. "You. Me. Our last night here. Do we need another reason?"

After dinner, Nick suggested a walk uptown. On Broadway, between Fifty-Second and Fifty-Third Streets, he stopped in front of a blue and yellow striped awning that said BIRDLAND PRESENTS. Underneath was a small box to the left that said THE FIRST LADY OF SONG and in large red capital letters: ELLA FITZGERALD.

Nick bowed and held one arm out toward the entrance: "Care to step inside?" he asked in a mock formal tone.

Dillard clasped both hands over his heart. "Ella Fitzgerald? Is this a joke or something?"

"Nope," said Nick. "I know how much you like her. Lucky for us, she's performing here tonight."

Dillard was accustomed to not showing affection to Nick in public, but on this night, with the prospect of seeing his musical hero, he threw his arms around Nick: "Ella! I can't wait for you to hear her."

Nick took off his flat cap and placed it on Dillard's head. "Tonight belongs to you, Dill. Merry belated Christmas."

The cap was too big on Dillard and hung down to his eyebrows. "I never realized what a big head you had," he said.

Nick laughed. "Bigger since I met you."

They got a table near the front of the room close enough to see the sweat running down Ella's temples. When she sang "The Man I Love," Dillard rubbed Nick's knee under the table. And when she sang "Someone to Watch over Me," Dillard could swear he saw Nick's eyes get misty. She sang every song as if no one else had ever touched it. Nick and Dillard left Birdland well past midnight. Dillard hooked his arm into Nick's and said, "Thank you. This has been the best day of my life with the person I love the most. There's so much more I want to see and do with you."

Nick stared straight ahead and said, "I hope you'll always feel that way."

When they came back to the room there was a bottle of champagne on ice waiting for them. Nick said he'd ordered it before they left. They undressed, put on the two thick terrycloth bathrobes that were hanging in the closet, and watched out the window as a light snow began to fall. "I ordered this, too," said Nick. "There's hardly anything more beautiful than New York in the snow." That night they made love slowly, as if discovering each other for the first time. Dillard rested his head on Nick's hairy chest and fell into a peaceful sleep.

The shades at the Roosevelt Hotel were flimsy enough to allow in the first light of morning, which meant that by 7:20 a.m., the flat winter sun nudged Dillard awake. He looked over at Nick, usually a lighter sleeper than he was, and saw he was still sleeping. Their plane wasn't until noon, so Dillard thought he'd let him doze some more. By nine, Nick hadn't stirred. "Nick," he whispered. "It's time to get up." Nick didn't move. Dillard shook him lightly, but nothing. He put his hand on Nick's stomach to feel his breathing. He was still. He put his hand under Nick's nose. No air. He lifted Nick's arm. The arm was icy and fell back onto the bed when he let go. He felt his legs, his chest. Everything was cold. He shook him by the shoulders and called his name.

"No," he cried. He grabbed Nick's hands and tried to pull him up. "Nick, come on. We've got a plane to catch. I promise I won't spill hot chocolate all over us. I'm an experienced flyer now, thanks to you. Nick. Nick." His body was heavy and fell back onto the bed. The breath went out of Dillard. "Don't go. Please, don't go." He doubled over making the sounds of someone sobbing and retching, but no tears came. Nick. How could this be?

In a haze of terror, he lay next to Nick and watched him, as if staring would bring him back to life. Nick would know what to do. Should he call the hotel? The police? An ambulance? How would he explain who he was, what he was doing there? Theirs was a dangerous love, and Dillard knew it. Men loving men got arrested. Now here he was in the same room, in the same bed, with a man. A dead man. He lay staring at Nick a bit longer. *I've got to get out of here*, he thought. *Sharlene can never know we were here together. No one can ever know.*

It was a plan, of sorts. Whatever it was, it calmed Dillard down enough to tend to the tasks at hand. He straightened the sheets on his side of the bed, so it looked as if Nick was sleeping alone. He packed his bag. He even rinsed the second glass in the bathroom, so no one would see that two people had brushed their teeth there. He scoured the room for any signs of himself. There were none. It amazed him that he could be so practical while heartbroken. He told himself that Nick would have done the same thing. He walked back to the bed, where he leaned over and kissed Nick. He saw that his hair, his thick black hair, trailed little rivulets of curls on the pillow. The thought that Nick's hair was still alive gave Dillard small comfort. It made him think about Nick's hat, and how he'd shoved it on his head the night before. Nick's hat. He'd take that. It sat on the small writing table across from the bed. He picked it up and saw there was an envelope in it addressed to him. Whatever happened, Nick must have known that Dillard would find the hat.

Dillard slipped the hat and note into his suitcase. He'd read the note later when he was far away from the Roosevelt Hotel. Now he would go to the room that Nick had booked in an assumed name, unmake the bed and make it look slept in. He opened the shades, as one might do in the morning, and turned the cup in the bathroom right side up and filled it with a little water so it would look used.

He walked eleven slushy blocks down to Macy's, the only place in New York City where they'd used the public bathroom. He locked himself inside one of the stalls, sat on the toilet, opened his suitcase, and read Nick's letter:

Dearest Dill,

Sharlene knows about us. She doesn't know for sure but infers. She picked up on the way I smiled at you when you gave me those socks for Christmas. She's not a stupid girl. She said she didn't want me to tell her whether it was true or not, about you and me, but if it was, that I had to stop immediately, or she and the kids would leave me. If she had to, she said, she would spill the beans to the hospital. This kind of thing could get my license revoked. I've been in agony, Dill. I didn't say anything about us to her but I'm sure she could tell that something was up. I mean, I stopped eating; I couldn't sleep. I could barely talk. I couldn't bear to think of life without you. And yet my kids. My family. I was at wit's end. I didn't know what to do.

I thought about giving up my practice and moving away with you. Or that you could move to another town and we could see each other every now and again. Sharlene said there's treatment for this sort of thing, but honestly, there isn't. I don't even know if I'm one of those men, I just know I'm in love with you.

What I'm doing is the coward's way out; I know that. But Dill, I can't face life without you, and the alternative is impossible to bear: Did you notice how my eyes filled up tonight when Ella sang that song about someone to watch over me? We were sitting so close I could hear your heart beat. It broke mine. Forgive me. Remember me. And please know that wherever you are and whatever you do, we will always remain connected by our love, as pure and beautiful as anything I've ever known. I did my best, Dill. I really did.

Love,

Nick

P.S. Now you must distance yourself from me. I've left my I.D. in the breast pocket of my suit so that when the cops find me, they'll know to contact Sharlene. There is no way for anyone to know you were with me. Remember, I checked you in under an assumed name and have already paid for both rooms in cash, so there is no record of this. If the police call on you, you last saw me at Christmas, when we celebrated with my family. I've left nothing in your name, nothing that would make them suspect we were anything more than professional colleagues. Before I left, I told Sharlene that you might not come back after the first of the year, that you were eager to pursue your music career.

I'm going to swallow Miltown—a whole lot of them—so there should be no signs of foul play or anything like that. Also, check the back pocket of your new khakis. You'll find one hundred dollars. Enough to get you back home and tide you over until you get a new job.

One more thing, Dill. Please do go back to music. I've heard you play, I watched you watch Ella tonight. It's what you were meant to do.

The letter was so Nick, touching, honest, and practical. Dillard put his hands over his face, the same hands that made love to Nick last night. He could smell Nick on them. That's when he began to cry. Not even twenty-four hours had gone by. *Eleven hours ago, I was in the best day of my life*, he thought. *Now I'm in the worst.*

His thoughts fired quickly and erratically. *Sharlene. The kids. Do they know? Skyville. I can never go back. I'll fly in tonight. Clean out the cabin. Drive the Pontiac back to New York. Get a job. Maybe at Birdland?*

The Skyville night at eleven thirty. Stars punctured the sky. The air smelled fresh and familiar. *Oh God, get out before you change your mind.*

Driving all night. Breakfast at a Howard Johnson's outside of Washington, DC. Thumb through the hot-chocolate-stained copy of the guidebook. Cheap hotel, the Royalton, at West Forty-Fourth Street, $4.50 a night. The guidebook said it was unexpected oasis of calm. Boy, I could use an oasis of calm.

A small drab room. No private bathroom. Who cares? Lay out clothes for tomorrow.

Morning. Beige brick wall out the window. Like being in prison. Nauseous. Close your eyes and count backward from fifty. That's what Nick tells scared patients to do . . . forty-six . . . forty-five . . . forty-four . . . forty-three . . . uh-oh, bowels. Gonna soil bed. Hurry to that bathroom. Phew. Shower. Dress. Walk around until Birdland opens. Times Square. Cops everywhere. Any one of them could be looking for me. Do Sharlene and kids know by now? Times Square too crowded. Those sirens! Coming for me? Nick wanted to see the Empire State Building. Go now, it's only a few blocks away.

Jesus, I've never been on the eighty-sixth floor of anywhere. For $1.50, I could go to the 102nd floor. The top. Nick would definitely do that. The guide says we can see six states from up here. Wish I could see Skyville. Now he's handing out buttons to all of us. Pin it on like everyone else. Back on Thirty-Fourth Street. Head over to Birdland. Quiet. Empty. Walk through to the kitchen. Ray Charles on the radio. Lots of men cooking, washing. No one acknowledges me. A guy with pebbly gray eyes is looking at me.

"Well, get a load of this. You got a name, blue eyes?"

I'm sure not giving him my real name. "William Smith."

"Can't hear you, what's your name?"

"William Smith."

"From?"

Dead guy from Skyville found in his hotel. Another guy from Skyville looking for work. Uh-uh. "Orlando, Florida."

Everyone's staring at me now.

"What brings you here?"

"Work. I'm looking for any kind of work."

"Lemme ask you a question, William Smith, do you always like to be on top? Because if you do, you've come to the right place. We've got some bottom guys who could keep you mighty busy."

They're laughing. *Not a friendly laugh.*

"I'm afraid I don't know what you mean."

"On top." *He's pointing at my chest.* "It says here you like to be on top."

The button from the Empire State Building. Shit. It says, "I've been on top." *I never read it. Turn around and get out of here.*

"Nice meeting you guys, but I don't think I'm up to doing the kind of work you do. Thanks anyway."

Someone's yelling, "Try the grocery store on Eighth Avenue. They could use some good fruit."

Take deep breaths. Cold air feels good. Need quiet. Central Park. A few blocks up.

Light's ebbing, park quiet. Sit on one of these benches. Close your eyes and count backward. Fifty . . . forty-nine . . . forty-eight . . . forty-seven . . . forty-six . . . Why did that guy at Birdland make that crack about fruit? Forty-five . . . forty-four . . . forty-three . . . forty-two . . . Plenty of men are handsome without being fruity. Do I look like a man who likes men? Forty-one . . . Forty . . . I don't want to. Thirty-nine . . . thirty-eight . . . I should talk louder, take big strides. Thirty-seven . . . thirty-six . . . Maybe a mustache. Maybe a beard. Nick was a fluke. Thirty-five . . . thirty-four . . . thrity-three . . . thirty-two . . . I've slept with women. They like me. I'm sure I'll marry one someday. Thirty-one . . . Thirty . . . Twenty-nine . . .

Oops, a cop.

"You okay, son?"

"Yes, sir. I must have dozed off."

Oh God, he's going to cuff me.

"You from out of town?"

"Yes, sir." *Please don't ask me where I'm from.*

"Well, I don't advise you to stick around these parts in the dark. Unfortunately, it's not safe. There's an exit right here on Fifty-Ninth Street, good idea to take it."

"Yes, sir, I'll leave right away."

"You take care, son."

"Yes, sir, you too."

Close call. Won't be so lucky next time. Got to get out of this city.

Chapter 13

It surprised Geraldine how much she missed Earle. Secretly, she had thought she'd be relieved if he died. The braces on his legs. The walker. Later, the bedpan and the smell of urine and Lestoil in his room. Those were depressing. Not to mention Earle himself. That rumble in his throat, the edema that swelled his legs. The way he smiled ingratiatingly at the nurses, as if they might rescue him. He'd become an old man. His silky blond hair was coarse and gray. He was rope thin; his arms spindly. When he walked, slowly, the back flap of his hospital gown opened, and you could see his rear end sagging like an old pocketbook.

Geraldine was certain the doctors and nurses thought she must be his daughter or a favored niece. She'd get done up for the hospital: makeup, tight pants or a flirty skirt, and a revealing sweater. No one wanted a pale hag sitting bedside.

She had never really believed he would die. He'd have lapses here and there, but he'd be back by her side at the bakery. She'd tease him about how he made her do all the work, and he'd make some good-natured joke back. But when it happened, when he slipped away while she was out getting a soda, she thought he was faking, lying as still as stone. She shouted his name and kissed his face but none of these things roused him. When the nurse finally came in, she put her hand on Geraldine's shoulder and said, "I'm so sorry dear."

In the days after, she left her world. It was Emilia Mae who'd get her out of bed in the morning. There were things to do, plans to make. Pick out a suit for Earle's internment. What a stupid word, internment. Sounded like a temporary job, but not this. He'd be in that box forever: The snow would come, the rains would rot the wood, leeches and worms would move in with him. Why bother with a suit? But Emilia Mae said it was important, that Earle prized dignity and there was no reason he should leave without it. So, she picked the blue one, the one that lit up his eyes and played against his fair skin and now gray hair like chimes. Alice insisted on singing "Someone to Watch over Me" at the service. People Geraldine barely knew cried their eyes out listening to the young girl with the beatific voice sing about being a little lamb lost in the woods waiting for someone to watch over her. Only Geraldine was dry-eyed. No one was crying for the Earle she knew. The artifice, the music, the priest's banal words. None of it had anything to do with her Earle, the man who gently pulled her back when she overstepped and quieted her when the noise in her head became too loud. What did they know of that man? She'd taken it for granted he'd always be there. Now that he wasn't, she felt stripped bare. Deserted. Scared as she'd never been. She hugged the black wool shawl around her shoulders. Emilia Mae had pulled out the only black dress she'd had in her closet and told her to wear that. Earle would have laughed at seeing her all in black. That wasn't the Geraldine he knew. But even dead, Earle was the man she knew.

She loved him. Not in the way she had when they stood side by side in the bakery all day. Not at night when he listened to his jazz records in the living room. She loved the part of him that was kind and patient and had taken hold of her. She would never be him; that was impossible. But she would always know that something of him was buried inside of her.

Still, Geraldine thought she'd probably marry again. She'd eye the men who came into the bakery, and yet she could never bring herself to flirt with any of them. Two months after Earle died, she snuck out to grab a bite of pizza, and a young bearded man (they all had beards now) asked if he could share her small table. Normally, Geraldine would strike up a conversation or talk in that breathy way she did around certain men. But she didn't feel up to any of that. Men who weren't Earle didn't interest her. Her life now was taking care of Alice and trying to get along with Emilia Mae. God, all those stupid quibbles and spiteful resentments with Emilia Mae. Emilia Mae's weight, her sullenness. What did it add up to? Nothing. Words. Silly, spiteful words. Without Emilia Mae there'd be no Alice, and without Alice there'd be no laughter. They were her family, all she had. Sure, she still had her house; she still ran the bakery. With one less person helping out, with no one studying the books, she worried the business would falter. Earle was the one who was good with money and numbers. With him gone, all that financial dribble-drabble fell to her. One less friend for Alice, who missed her grandpa something awful. She and Emilia Mae shared Earle stories, quoted silly things he'd say, reminisced about how he'd talk to the customers.

One day, when they were cleaning out Earle's closet, Alice

found a tattered old sign: FREE SWEETS AND BREAD. When she asked Geraldine what that was about, Geraldine shook her head. "During the Depression, we handed out free three-day-old bread and cake. Earle's idea. Someone had chalked an X on the back door, which signaled to those who had nothing that the people on the other side of the door had something. Oh my God, those rolls were as stiff as papier-mâché, and I remember how the pie filling crystallized. But they were still edible, and people waited in line to get them because that's all they had to eat in one day."

Alice looked at the sign. The paper was browned at the edges, and pieces of the words painted in red had chipped off. "We could do that again," she said. "In honor of Grandpa. Grandpa would like that, wouldn't he?"

Geraldine smiled at Alice. "You sure as hell didn't inherit your kind genes from me, but yeah, I think you're right."

Alice took it upon herself to make a new sign. Using the same words and red paint, she'd plant it in front of the store every Tuesday and Friday at five p.m., and sure enough, thirty years after the Depression, a handful of hungry people would be waiting patiently out the door by 5:05.

Chapter 14

His father's old Pontiac was a metallic rust color, which Dillard had always loved because it glistened gold in the sun and reminded him of fall in Skyville. Now, as he drove the car down the Hutchinson River Parkway heading out of New York City, the car looked decayed under the muted winter sky. Or maybe he was projecting onto the car how he felt.

He was going to a town called Baychester in a borough called the Bronx, to a destination that held promise in its name. Freedomland USA. He didn't know much about Freedomland other than it was going to be an American-themed amusement park about the history of the country. What appealed to Dillard, aside from its name, was its reputed size: The *New York Post* said it would be the world's largest amusement park and called it "the Disneyland of the East." It was to open in June, but the *Post* said they were hiring now to help get the park up and running. Freedomland sounded like the perfect place to lose himself.

Dillard parked his car in the empty parking lot and found his way to the reception area, nothing more than a wooden shack with a tar roof. He'd scheduled the appointment for noon, and got there at

11:50, just to wait in line with other applicants, each of whom spent no more than four or five minutes in the shack. When it was his turn, a man who said his name was CV sat in a folding chair with a clipboard on his lap. He had long gray hair and craters of old pockmarks on his face. The only things in the shack, aside from CV, were a chair, a small table with a call bell on it, an electric space heater, a trash can, and a map of Freedomland tacked on the wall.

"Holy cow!" said Dillard, when he noticed that the park was to be in the shape of a map of the United States.

"That's what everyone says." CV glanced up at him, and held out his hand: "Resume?"

Dillard pulled out the handwritten resume he'd cobbled together the night before.

CV barely skimmed it: "You a doctor?"

"No, sir, but I've worked as a receptionist for one."

"Won't need any receptionists around here." He kept skimming. "I see music school. Can you sing?"

"Yes, sir."

"Play the banjo?"

"Yes, sir."

"We need a fella to sing stuff like 'Oh! Susanna' and play the banjo for our paddleboat on the Great Lakes. Ever been to the Great Lakes?"

"No, sir."

"Me neither. Doesn't matter. Think you can handle the banjo and singing?"

"Yes, sir," Dillard lied. He'd never played the banjo.

CV looked up and scrutinized him. "You'll do. There'll be crowds, lots of kids. You like kids?"

"Sure."

"Me, I don't care for them," said CV. "I'm a behind-the-scenes kind of guy. Anyway, we'll work something out." He made a note on Dillard's resume and told him to come back in three months.

"Umm, I wonder, sir, if you've got work for right now?" asked Dillard. "I'm available, if you do."

"You good with your hands?"

Dillard looked at his hands. His fingertips were numb and blue. Must be the Raynaud's. He quickly hid his hands behind his back.

"Yes, sir."

"There's a whole lot of building to do. Between you and me? I don't see how they're going to pull this place together in the next four months. Then again, that's not my concern. But I'll tell you this, they need all the help they can get. I could put you to work this afternoon."

"Yes, sir, I'd like that."

"The pay is one dollar an hour. We have barracks for the workers, nothing fancy, but it's a roof over your head, and you get three meals a day, which we will naturally deduct from your pay."

"That suits me fine, thank you," said Dillard, trying not to sound too grateful.

"I'll have Louis get you settled." CV tapped the call bell.

"Mind waiting outside? Louis will be by in a moment. And can you send the next fella in?"

Dillard wandered around while waiting for Louis. There were sawhorses everywhere and the wooden frames of things that were about to be something else: a stagecoach here, a fake shooting gallery there. The land felt soft and muddy beneath his feet. With no structures to bar the wind, the cold ripped through him. He'd never worked outdoors in this kind of weather. Even with gloves, his hands were already numb. He wondered how he'd manage, then told himself that if he was surviving Nick's death, he could survive anything.

Someone came up behind him and tapped him on the shoulder. "You're a new guy, right?"

Dillard turned around and stuck out his hand. "Dillard. You must be Louis."

"He says it Louis, but it's Louie." He shook Dillard's hand briefly, then pulled his away. "Names aren't so important here. Guys come and go, no questions asked. That's the beauty of it." He led Dillard down a hill toward a wooden structure with a tin roof next to a small running river. The place was as bare bones as something with bones could get. Dillard understood why they called it the barracks.

For the next two months, he and more than twenty men lived in a large, cold room, despite the two electric space heaters. With only a crack between them, the beds were practically touching each other. Each was fitted with a woolen blanket, a small flat pillow, and one sheet. Dillard thought the mattress might have been stuffed with horsehair for how coarse and itchy it was. There were two showers and barely any hot water. Although he became intimate with the farts and foot odors of his roommates, he kept his distance, not wanting to give any of them reason to become curious about him. At night, they put their names on a sign-up sheet, which was posted at six each morning delegating each man to a different task. The only thing that came close to horseplay was when they'd read their new posts and one of them would say, "Goin' to old New

York today," and another would respond, "Gonna build me a great fire in Chicago."

The work was exhausting and the food meager: thin farina in the morning, watery soup at lunch, mysterious meat stews at night. Dillard lost weight but developed ropey muscles in his arms and legs. His face was ruddy from all the outdoor work, and his lips were always chapped.

He recognized that, despite the grind of it, this work was perfect for him. It left him so spent at the end of the day that he barely had time to think about anything before falling into a deep and dreamless sleep. For the next three months, he became a citizen of Freedomland. He never left the premises but never felt claustrophobic as the old Great Plains, Southwest, San Francisco, and New Orleans were being built up around him. He knew it would sound crazy if he said it out loud, but he looked forward to June, when he could play the banjo and sing corny songs on a paddleboat in the Great Lakes.

Then, in late April, the mosquitoes came.

Not just a few: an army, a cluster. At night, they'd keep up a steady drone as they bore down on the most tender pieces of their victims, puncturing their skin and feeding on their blood. In the morning, the men would find welt villages on their inner thighs, behind their knees, down their necks. They were maddeningly itchy, but scratching made things worse, as the welts got hot and red and infected. One night, shortly after the infestation began, CV called a rare meeting of all the employees.

He stood in front of a box that said 6-12 in big numerals. "There's been complaints about the mosquitoes, and we're doing what we can to fix the situation. In the meantime, this here is bug repellant.

Each of you will get a stick of this stuff. Rub it all over you before you go to bed, and in the morning before you go to work. Should keep those critters away. As I said, we're doing everything we can to correct the situation."

For the next two weeks, the men covered their bodies with the waxy 6-12. While it gave off a pleasant floral odor, it did little to ward off the mosquitoes. With his fair skin, Dillard was a favorite target. He ended up sleeping with netting covering his bed. Still, they found him, keeping him awake with their humming and biting. By now, he'd scratched so hard and often that his body was a rash of angry red, boiling over with pus. Although CV kept promising they would look into the situation, nothing was done; things got worse. Turned out the marshy land right off the Hutchinson River, which flowed right by the barracks, was a breeding ground.

With mosquitoes always hovering, Dillard spent restless nights slapping them away. When he did fall asleep, he'd invariably be awakened by the buzzing and itching. Sometimes, he heard the buzzing when there was none. He began to dread the nights, and the tedious days that followed. He told himself he could stick it out until June, but after three consecutive mornings of not being able to get out of bed, he realized that he had reached the end. The mosquitoes had won.

Despair, he concluded, came in different textures. When Nick died, his pain was internal: heart, stomach, head. But he'd kept moving, afraid that if he stopped, he'd stop forever. This despair was different, external, but exhausting to the point where he couldn't move and didn't have the energy to even try. If he stayed like this, they'd throw him out in a matter of days, so he forced himself to pack his few belongings and pick up his final paycheck before that happened. Back in the Pontiac, he headed north on I-95 only because if he went south, he'd find himself back in New York City. He had $52 in his pocket and no clue as to where he was going.

He turned on the radio. Johnny Cash. "I Walk the Line." The song brought him back to Nick, because everything brought him back to Nick. For the time they were together, Nick was his destination, the only one he'd ever had. Other than that, he'd never settled. Music school here, the resort there. His ties had been tenuous, at best. No mother, a half-present father; no strong friendship. What was just his? His father's instruments. Music. Thank God for music. For a blessedly short time Nick was his, totally and completely—yet not totally and completely, because Nick also had Sharlene and the kids. He thought about them often and how they'd made him feel part of a family, something he'd never had and knew in his bones he'd never have again. Because of him, they would never have that again, either. Sharlene must hate him, understandably, hate him so much that he couldn't imagine setting foot in Skyville again for fear of bumping into her.

Skyville. That was another thing he'd had completely and totally, and now that too was gone. The word *solitary* fixed in his mind. He kept repeating it: *Sol-i-tar-y sol-i-tar-y sol-i-tar-y.* That's how it went for the next nine months. Dillard in his car driving, singing, talking to himself, picking up the odd job here or there. The talking out loud had become a habit, an isolated word *(ca-coph-o-ny)* or phrase *(my life is a sym-pho-ny of ca-coph-o-ny)* here and there, a conversation with Nick (*You're not gone, you're just sleeping*). He kept Nick's brown tweed cap in the back seat.

In those months, he was a bottlewasher in Pelham, a house painter in Yonkers, a busboy in White Plains, and a janitor in Mamaroneck.

When he had enough money, he'd stay at a motel; when he didn't, he'd sleep in his car. When he had enough money, he'd eat three meals a day. When he didn't, he'd live on 20 cents a day—mostly franks and potatoes. Weighed down only by his sadness, Dillard got so thin, he couldn't sleep on his side because his bony knees hurt when they knocked together.

For now, the itinerant life suited him. He told himself he needed time alone with Nick. He didn't want anyone to try to comfort him, didn't want to talk to anyone about who he was or where he'd been. Once, in Pelham, Ira the dishwasher invited him out for a beer after their shift. They talked about books—they'd both recently read *Doctor Zhivago*—about young John Kennedy running for president, about Dillard's love of music and Ira's ambitions as a photographer. When they left the bar more than an hour later, Ira squeezed the back of Dillard's neck. He told him he'd enjoyed their time together and asked if they could have a drink soon again. Hours after Dillard said, "Sure thing," he got in his car and drove east from Pelham. He'd heard how plainclothes cops cruised at night trying to entrap queers and wasn't taking any chances.

In mid-morning, he came to a town called New Rochelle. Something about this place pleased him; it wasn't Skyville, but it felt familiar. There was a lake, there was Long Island Sound, trees—not the live oaks he remembered from Skyville, but oaks nonetheless. He drove by a log house that reminded him of Nick's house, and on this February day, with pewter clouds low in the sky, he could envision them as mountains. It seemed a place he could settle into for a while.

With less than $30 in his pocket, he had enough to pay for a warm room while he looked for a job. In the local classifieds, he found a listing for the Neptune Inn, a boardinghouse that cost $3 a night including breakfast and was only a couple of miles out of town.

Dillard drove up to the old inn and was certain that, given its decrepit condition, it had already been shuttered. The large wrap-around porch showed stained wood under its gray peeling paint. What were once detailed posts and ornate cornice brackets were now rotted and rusted. There were a few old slat-wood rockers on the porch that looked as if no one had rocked in them for years. The faded green front door still had a holiday wreath hanging from it even though it was February. *This must have been some place in its glory years*, he thought as he tried the front door. Surprisingly, it opened. The woman at the front desk was named Martha. She wore her bleached hair in a chignon and had an ample amount of lipstick on her teeth. He heard whiskey and cigarettes in her voice when she said, "It's a bit used up, but what remains is still clean and well tended." Dillard smiled gratefully. As he followed Martha up the stairs, he thought that the same might be said about her.

She led him to a room that had also seen better days: There was a dark brown spot on the ceiling where there must have been a leak. The thinning, blue chenille bedspread had a stain in the middle that someone had unsuccessfully tried to bleach out. *Don't even try to figure out what that might have been*, he told himself. The room was small and clean but had a musty odor that made Dillard feel as if he were breathing air from twenty years ago. Still, there was a hot shower down the hall, and he had his own bed with two sheets, a blanket, and a fluffy pillow. No complaints.

Within two days, he found a job on a construction site. Having glorified the building work he'd done at Freedomland, he was hired to work on an office tower being built downtown. The job required him to work on the fourteenth floor. The height was not the problem, but that fact that he had to often work without his gloves in this exposed and windy spot was. The Northeast was going through a cold spell that winter, and the frequent sub-freezing temperatures turned his hands so blue and numb he became incapable of lifting and carrying the heavy steel pipes and framed tubes. Two days later he quit, knowing he'd be fired if he didn't. After that, work was hard to find. He was too old for the pizza delivery job and too inexperienced for the bartender spot at the Beechmont Tavern. Eight days later, his money was running out, and he was back living in his car eating one meal a day. He'd give New Rochelle one more week, and if he didn't find anything by then, he'd keep driving north on I-95 until he did.

After a job interview for a clerk at Woolworths, he noticed a sign two doors down that said FREE SWEETS AND BREAD, 5 PM.

For the past two years, nothing had been free for Dillard. He figured this was some kind of scam, but he also figured he had nothing to lose.

PART 3

The music sustained him. The swoops, the dives, the trills spoke a language that no words could convey.

Chapter 15

In February 1961, a man started showing up at the bakery on free food days. Something about the dark valleys beneath his light blue eyes caught Emilia Mae's attention. He didn't say much but thanked her for whatever he'd taken. After his fifth visit, he said, "Ma'am, I don't feel right accepting your food day after day. I'm a hard worker. I'll work for you for nothing in return for whatever food you might give me."

He was so pale he looked as though he might faint. His skin was taut against his forehead, and his large pulsing veins made it look as if some creature was burrowing through his temples. He had long, wavy blond hair, a strong jaw, perfect white teeth, and full lips, all of which suggested to Emilia Mae that he'd once been handsome. He wore a brown car coat with a faux fur collar, khaki pants, a green and blue plaid button-down shirt, and a brown tweed Irish flat cap. The cap was so big for him that he looked as if he were balancing a plate on his head. The clothes were clean, but they hung on him as if the body beneath them had disappeared.

Emilia Mae studied his hands, sinuous and strong. She imagined they would easily be able to lift the weight of an electric mixer or a twenty-five-pound bag of flour. His voice was soft, and his words came out slow and Southern, as if half melted. Yet, despite his appearance he had the vocabulary of an educated man. He was clearly a stranger, but something about him was familiar. Emilia Mae had the feeling that who he was now was a nightmare away from whoever he'd been. If loneliness gave off an odor, she smelled it; if longing cried out, she heard it. It surprised her how this man tugged at her. She was determined not to let him get away. She told herself that they could use a man around the shop, that free work was free work. No harm could come from hiring someone in need; besides, it would make Geraldine feel righteous, and Emilia Mae knew how her mother loved to feel righteous.

Emilia Mae was right about her mother. She put the man to work the next day.

His name was Dillard Fox. He appeared to be in his early thirties and said he lived nearby. Emilia Mae figured what that really meant was that he lived in an SRO, or something like it. She assumed from the lack of a ring on his fourth finger that he was unmarried.

After a few days, she saw what a hard worker he was. He washed dishes, stacked the racks of trays into the ovens, stocked flour and cornmeal, and swept and scrubbed the floors. He spoke to no one. Emilia Mae searched for something to say to him and finally resorted to the chitchat she despised: "Fine day we're having, aren't we?"

"Yes, ma'am, we sure are."

Oh God, she thought. *He's as bad at this as I am.*

She tried again a few days later. "I hear we're getting a doozy of a snowstorm."

"Yes, ma'am, feels like snow."

As promised, the Wingos paid him a small wage and fed him three meals a day: eggs and bacon for breakfast; toast with peanut butter and jelly at lunch; chicken, pork, mac and cheese, or whatever else they were eating for dinner. He never ate at their home or inside the bakery, preferring to take his food while seated on a stool in the baking room. After a few weeks, it was Alice who finally got him talking. "I've never seen you pick off some cookie or cake crumbs," she said one afternoon. "Don't you like sweets?"

Dillard considered her question as if she'd asked him whether he believed in God. "I do like sweets," he finally said. "Though not all of them. Take pies, for instance. The fruit is too sweet, and the crust leaves a soggy taste in my mouth. Something crisper, like a gingersnap, is more to my liking. Or shortbread. Now that's something to sink your teeth into."

"You'll love our gingersnaps," she said. "And our shortbreads taste like heaven. Hey, what do you think of this?" She reached into one of the white enamel display cases and passed him a fistful of dream bar bits. He shoved one into his mouth and, before swallowing, then another and then another.

"Delicious." For the first time since his arrival, he allowed a smile.

Alice watched him. "You eat like a hungry person."

He stopped chewing. "I'm fine."

"I know," she said, pointing to a row of éclairs. "But there's a whole lot more where those came from."

After that, whenever she could, Alice slipped him pieces of cookies or messed-up pieces of cake. He'd always snap them up and devour them with no more than a bite or two, as if afraid someone would take them away before he finished.

Emilia Mae kept her eye on the two of them. Dillard hummed as he worked. He had a pure tenor voice. When he swept, he made sure to move close to Alice, who would hum along with him. When Dillard took his break, Alice took hers. They'd walk around the block or sit on the old stone retaining wall out back. Sometimes they sang; other times they talked or sat in silence.

"You two have certainly become chummy. What do you find to talk about?" Emilia Mae asked Alice after Dillard had been there a month.

Alice shrugged. "Nothing much. What cakes he likes. Sometimes he asks me if I've heard of this song or that."

"Is he a musician?"

"Maybe. He has a nice voice and plays a few instruments, but I'm not sure which ones."

"I wonder where he goes when he's not here?"

"He lives at the Neptune Inn."

"Where's he from?"

"Someplace called Skyville. I never heard of it. Why're you asking *me* all these questions? Why don't you ask him?"

"He doesn't seem like someone who likes to answer questions. A real loner, that one. He must have a family or a girl in Skyville—wherever that is."

"He says Skyville is the most beautiful place in the world, but he's never mentioned a family or a girlfriend."

Emilia Mae stared at the ceiling as if what she was about to say had just dawned on her. In fact, she'd been hatching this idea for the past few days. "What would you think if we invited him for

Sunday dinner? Nothing fancy, just you, me, Grandma, and the Kleppers. Grandma seems comfortable with him. Might be nice for him to meet some new people."

Alice jerked her head forward. Since Grandpa Earle died, surprises of a happy sort had not visited the Wingo household. In fact, if asked to name the last good thing that had come to her unbidden, Alice would have to say Dillard Fox. "That would be great. Will you ask him today?"

"I'll get Grandma to invite him," said Emilia Mae. "I'll tell her she'd be doing a charitable deed and make her think this whole thing was her idea."

Geraldine kept a handkerchief tucked in her brassiere. Even in winter, the baking room could heat to well over one hundred degrees. She poured sweat and was always mopping up puddles from her neck or arms. Usually, she wore a work shirt over a pair of dungarees and pulled her hair back into a small ponytail. Emilia Mae thought her mother looked younger when she let her hair fall loosely around her shoulders, that it hid the creases in her high forehead and softened the angles of her cheeks. Although she'd start the day with lipstick and blush, by ten in the morning, when the lipstick and blush faded away, her face looked naked except for her hard coffee-bean eyes, which told you all you needed to know about Geraldine's durability.

It was thirty-six degrees on this cloudless winter morning, yet the baking room was already scorching. Geraldine had just popped a batch of sticky buns into the oven and was dabbing her handkerchief behind her ears when Emilia Mae stepped in.

"Mother, I have something to ask you."

"What is it?"

"I thought you might invite that Dillard fellow to Sunday dinner. He doesn't seem to have any friends or family and seems a bit lonely. It would be the charitable thing to do, don't you think?"

Geraldine wiped her neck with her handkerchief. "Lord knows he probably has no other plans for Sunday." She stared at the handkerchief. "Yeah, I suppose I could do that."

"It would be really kind of you."

At first Dillard refused. "No, ma'am, you don't want me as a dinner guest, trust me. But you are kind to ask."

Geraldine persisted. "We'll invite Cora and Aloysius Klepper. He's the reverend at First Baptist, a very nice man. Can't hurt to know a man of the cloth." Her laugh rattled. "His wife, Cora, is a florist, very easy to talk to. Then it'll be me, Alice, and, of course, Emilia Mae. Nothing fancy. I know Alice would be particularly pleased if you came."

Dillard smiled at the mention of Alice. "Well, I'll come on the condition that I can contribute to the meal."

"Fine. We're cooking a turkey. My husband used to carve them, but none of us know what to do with the damn thing, so we end up pulling it apart with our fingers." Geraldine gave him a sidelong glance. "You look like you'd know what to do with a carving knife."

"Yes, ma'am," said Dillard. "I can handle that."

Emilia Mae couldn't remember the last time they'd had a dinner guest. The house, with its dark little rooms, hadn't breathed in strangers since long before her father died. He was the only one who ever brought people home: a friend from the church choir, a buddy, Dr. Rogan. But since Earle was gone, the house was musty and looked worn out. Making it ready for a visitor would require work.

Early Sunday, Emilia Mae polished the old walnut table and pulled out the remaining pieces of her mother's chipped wedding china. Geraldine put on her favorite Mantovani records. Alice snuck in *Ella Sings Gershwin*. There were no flowers to pick on this February morning, so Alice gathered branches from outside the house, stuck them in a vase, and hung old Christmas ornaments from them. Geraldine told her they looked odd, but Alice said she didn't care. "It's my first ever dinner party, and I want there to be decorations."

Geraldine hummed "Tammy" as she and Emilia Mae worked side by side preparing turkey, stuffing, and corn bread. This was what mothers and daughters did together, and they were doing it well. The noon light pierced the drab room, setting aglow a red glass bird ornament, which looked as if it might fly off the branch, while the tin snowball next to it seemed ready to melt. Even she had to smile at the sight of it.

No one admitted how special this day was, yet each Wingo dressed for celebration in her own way. Geraldine let her hair fall loose, put on rouge and lots of 4711 cologne. Emilia Mae painted her nails red and squeezed into a pair of burgundy stilettos that she thought made her legs looks slimmer. Alice tied a yellow ribbon in her hair and kept on the green velvet dress she'd worn to church that morning.

After the table was set, Alice picked up seven stones from the yard. She wrote each guest's name on a stone with India ink and used them as place settings, making sure to seat herself next to Dillard. When the doorbell rang, Alice ran to open it while Emilia

Mae and Geraldine stayed in the kitchen. Listening for conversation, they heard no words, just a low tinny sound coming from the living room. When they peered out, they saw Dillard and Alice sitting side by side on the couch. Dillard was playing the harmonica and Alice was humming along.

"What song is that?" asked Geraldine.

"An Elvis song, 'Can't Help Falling in Love,'" said Emilia Mae.

"Oooh, Elvis!" said Geraldine in a mock shriek. She wiggled her hips and shimmied.

Emilia Mae turned away and tried to change the subject. "Alice hasn't been this happy since Daddy was alive."

Geraldine stopped shimmying. Her voice got tight. "Well, that was a fine idea, inviting this young man to dinner. We know nothing about him other than he's broke, lives in that old rat trap where you used to work, and looks like he hasn't eaten in two years. Now he has Alice wrapped around his little finger. For all I know, he'll disappear as soon as he takes his last bite of pecan pie. And then what? We're stuck with that girl's broken heart." Sweat bubbled from her brow.

Emilia Mae was always taken aback by her mother's feelings for Alice: pure and tender, as they never were for her. How could she be jealous of Alice? She felt the same. And in some way, Alice was Emilia Mae's bridge to her mother's love. Her mother's concern made her smile. "So far he hasn't gone anywhere," she said. "So, you can put the guns and knives away for now."

But once Geraldine got going, there was no stopping her. "Heaven only knows what's on his mind, hanging around with a pretty twelve-year-old girl like that. I say we keep a close watch on him."

"Oh my God!" said Emilia Mae. "Sometimes, your mind goes straight to the gutter. What makes you think he'd do anything to her?"

"Don't use the Lord's name in vain," said Geraldine. "You don't know men the way I do."

"Wrong you are. I know plenty about men."

Geraldine gave her daughter an assessing look. "Unless you've been sneaking around behind my back, I've seen no sign that you've been near a fella in the thirteen years since Mr. Mystery Man." It was an unkind thing to say, she knew that. But every now and then she reverted to her old self.

Emilia Mae shook her head. "I'm not having that conversation. Tell you what, you finish the cooking, and I'll watch over Dillard to make sure he doesn't try to kidnap Alice."

When the bell rang again, Emilia Mae went to the door. "Must be Cora and Aloysius."

Dillard shoved the harmonica in his pocket and folded his hands like an obedient child.

Because of his size and bearing, people tended to stand up when Aloysius Klepper came into a room. He was nearly a foot taller than Emilia Mae. Even in her stilettos, she had to stand on her toes to give him a hug.

"Aloysius. Sorry, I mean Reverend Klepper, Cora, I'd like you to meet our friend Dillard Fox."

"It's alright, Emilia Mae, when we're with friends, he's Aloysius. Isn't that right Ally?"

"Sure, Cora," said Aloysius.

Emilia Mae had always been curious about Cora. She seemed to take her husband's eminence in stride, goading him in a way that bordered on taunting. Cora also had the ability to let Geraldine know when she got out of line in a way that never made Geraldine angry. Sometimes, Cora's words even made her laugh. Next to Aloysius, Emilia Mae thought that Dillard looked desiccated. His long-sleeved faded shirt seemed grubby and out of place. His hat balanced precariously on his head, but his voice was firm when he stuck out his hand and said, "How do you do, Reverend Klepper. Since we're not friends, I feel it is only proper to call you that."

"We are not friends *yet*," he said, folding his large hand around Dillard's.

"And I'm Cora," said Cora, sticking out her hand. "I'm always Cora."

After they sat down to dinner, Dillard took off his hat before they said grace. "May I take that for you?" asked Emilia Mae.

"No, thanks, I'll hold on to it." Dillard placed the hat on his lap.

Geraldine clinked her glass and said, "I want to welcome everyone, particularly our new friend. I'm so glad you could all come to my little dinner party."

Did Geraldine notice the smirk that Emilia Mae and Alice exchanged?

Everyone except Dillard made small talk. "It was Alice's idea to use the Christmas decorations," said Emilia Mae.

Cora turned to Alice. "They're wonderful, so fanciful. And my, you look pretty today, all dolled up in that beautiful dress, our own Alice in Wonderland."

"Is that who you were named for?" asked Dillard.

Alice smiled at her mother.

"I'd have named her Aloysius, but I figured her life would be

138

complicated enough without that, so I decided on Alice," said Emilia Mae.

"Aloysius is hard enough for a boy to carry," said Cora. "Don't you think so, Ally?"

Aloysius lowered his eyes. "My great-grandpa was named Aloysius. He owned a bookbinding business in Valdosta, Georgia, Aloysius & Co. As a boy, I would see his name engraved in gold on the spines of books. I thought he might have been a very famous man, so the name always spoke of distinction to me. I never got teased about it. Then again, I was six-two by the time I was thirteen." He laughed his rusty laugh. "I've always been honored that Emilia Mae chose to name Alice after me. I'm sure Great-Grandpa Aloysius would be, too." He placed both palms on the table to punctuate the conversation's end.

Dillard went into the kitchen to carve the meat. When he came out carrying a neatly arranged platter of turkey, Aloysius looked to him. "We heard you playing the harmonica when we arrived. Have you always been interested in music?"

Dillard contemplated the question. "Music, above all things, is my salvation."

Aloysius asked if he'd been studying music for a long time.

"Yes, sir, I've been playing all my life, and I studied for a few years. I play a few instruments, the harmonica being one of them, piano another, but my instrument of preference is the flute."

"Ah, the breath of God," said Aloysius.

"I'm afraid my reasons are more prosaic," said Dillard. "I was given a Selmer flute at my high school graduation by a special teacher. He said I had promise as a musician and, as musicians tended to travel around a lot, he thought this would be an easy instrument to carry. Now, when I hear music in my head, it comes to me through the flute."

Emilia Mae couldn't stop staring at Dillard. She'd never heard him string together more than three words, much less a whole paragraph. His cadence was slow and deliberate, his mouth so beautiful.

"What are some of your favorite songs?" she asked.

Alice and Dillard exchanged a smile.

"'Walk the Line.' I like 'True Love Ways' by Buddy Holly, 'Walkin' After Midnight.' Nobody does longing like Patsy Cline. I admire the Everly Brothers, and I'd say Ella Fitzgerald is the greatest singer of our time. Alice knows my repertoire."

Alice caught a glimpse of her mother, who couldn't take her eyes off Dillard. Underneath the table, Emilia Mae was jiggling her leg so hard that Alice swore she could feel the draft from her stiletto. Her mother was stuck on this man. She'd never thought about her mother that way.

Dillard fidgeted with the rock that had his name on it.

Cora said that Ella was one of their favorites, too. "I think we have all of her albums, don't we Ally?"

Aloysius smiled. "Cora knows the words to every one of her songs and sings them beautifully. Not me, I can carry about three tunes. The rest sounds like gargling."

Cora hit him on the arm and in a taunting voice said, "Oh, Ally, that's not true, and you know it. Sometimes when I can't sleep, he sings me the sweetest lullabies..."

Aloysius cut her off with a severe look. "I think that's enough about us. Surely there's something else to talk about."

The table went silent. Through lowered eyelids, everyone stared at Aloysius. He tried to deflect the attention by mentioning the new lights on Main Street and how much more pleasant it was to stroll there at night. When that brought no response, he turned again to Dillard.

"So, Mr. Fox, you're a stranger to New Rochelle. I wonder, what brings you here? Do you have relatives in this area?"

Dillard regarded Aloysius with the same grave look he'd given Alice when she'd asked him about sweets. "No, sir." He looked down at his plate. No one spoke, hoping he'd say more. He didn't. He slipped the rock into his pocket and pushed up his sleeves. "Fresh start."

Emilia Mae got up and went into the kitchen. She came back carrying a pecan pie and some ice cream.

Dillard looked at the pie. His stomach flip-flopped, and he felt himself wanting to vomit. He coughed a few times to cover the gagging sounds coming from his throat. This had happened once before in a diner near Pelham. He was seated at the counter next to a pie container. When the waitress opened it to cut a piece, the smell of pecan pie caught in his throat. That time, he was able to get up and move. Now he was stuck. The pie. It was the same pie Sharlene had served Christmas night at Nick's house. That night, that family, his undoing, their tragedy. Now, here he was with another family. A fine family. He needed to get out of here before he caused them any harm.

"I understand what you're saying," said Aloysius. "Sometimes a fresh start is the only answer, don't you agree?"

Alice looked around to see if anyone else felt as puzzled as she did. Were all grown-up dinner parties like this, with people making odd confessions and other people saying things she didn't understand?

Emilia Mae stood over Dillard with the pie and ice cream. "Can I serve you some of this?"

Dillard still stared at his plate and shook his head. "No, thank you."

"You know it's one of our specialties," said Geraldine.

"Thank you, ma'am," said Dillard, "but not right now." His eyes searched the room before he pushed back his chair, placed his hat as firmly on his head as he could, and stood up. "I'm sorry, but I'm feeling ill," he said in a loud voice. "I don't want to ruin a perfectly lovely evening. Forgive me, but I think I'll take my leave now."

Aloysius got up and held out his hand. "Sorry you're feeling poorly, but I'd welcome a chance to continue our conversation. I preach every Sunday at the First Baptist Church a few blocks from here. Meet me after service, and we can walk together. I'll show you the town."

Dillard nodded. "Thank y'all for your hospitality. And Alice"— his voice softened—"thank you for all the treats and conversation. You've shown me a rare kindness."

"See you Monday?" asked Emilia Mae.

"Sure," said Dillard.

They all rose as he left the room, then sat as he shut the door behind him.

"My goodness, wasn't that something?" Geraldine shuddered. "I'm sure it wasn't about the pie. I hope we haven't just fed an escaped convict. I mean the way he talked made me wonder if he's left a trail of bodies behind him."

Cora shook her head. "Now, Geraldine, I think that's uncharitable. He has a kind face, though it would seem he's running or hiding from something. Don't you think, Ally?"

"Something like that. Doesn't look like a criminal to me, more like someone bearing secrets. He's obviously taken a shine to Alice."

Alice sat up. "He's not an escaped convict, is he, Mom?"

Emilia Mae cut the pie and scooped out the ice cream. "No," she said. "He just seems a little lost."

Chapter 16

Dillard came back to work on Monday. As always, he tended to his chores in silence. If he hummed, only Alice heard it, and if he said anything to her, she kept it to herself.

It took Emilia Mae days to work up the nerve, but finally on Thursday she said, "I guess dinner was a bust the other night. How are you feeling?"

Dillard looked at his shoes. "I'm fine. I probably shouldn't have come. Maybe it was too early."

"Early for what?"

Dillard shook his head and looked down. "Nothing," he said.

The winter of 1961 was unrelenting. When it didn't pour, dark clouds shaded New Rochelle. The wildflowers that usually colored in bare earth by mid-April stayed blanketed under mud. It was the kind of cold that dug in despite the scarves and mittens resisting it. One Friday afternoon, when business was slow and most of the day's chores completed, Emilia Mae found herself in the bake room alone with Dillard. Both were rubbing their hands trying to warm up. Emilia Mae saw that the tips of Dillard's fingers were bone white and that the rest of his hands were tinged blue. She remembered how her dad's hands were often like that.

"Raynaud's disease," she said. "My dad had it. I used to rub his hands to warm them up. He said I had the touch; that I heated them right up. Seems to be more common in pale and thin people. Obviously, I don't have it." She held out her pink sturdy hands. "Can I give it a try?"

Dillard looked to each of his hands as if for agreement, then gave them over to her. She took one at a time and massaged it until the blood started to flow again. His hands were like a child's in hers.

"Your dad was right," said Dillard, flexing his fingers. "This is the first time I've felt them all winter." He thought back to his two days on the construction job and shuddered.

"It must be hard to play the flute without feeling them," said Emilia Mae.

Dillard laughed or coughed; it was hard to tell which. "I do enough damage to the flute with my fingers intact. Numb ones would simply add insult to injury. Thank you for this."

"Any time. This is one of my very few talents."

"I doubt that." For the first time, he looked Emilia Mae in the eyes.

Emilia Mae had never been keen on eye locking. She never understood those couples who could stare at each other, cow-eyed, forever. Until now. This man cracked open a door inside of her. It was as if light fell on places in her that had become dark. He aroused thoughts in her that no man ever had. She wondered what it would be like to kiss the back of his neck between his hair-line and shirt collar. She felt protective of his ravaged face and gaunt fury, and wanted to hold him, stroke his head, and put back whatever had been taken from him. She thought back to the days of tending to those lost souls at the Neptune Inn and wanted to tell him that she understood despair. She wanted to talk to him about real things. She understood how neglect could make a person hungry for everything. She fantasized about feeding him, not only crullers and pies from the bakery but meat, spinach, citrusy juices. Not since Alice was born thirteen years earlier had she felt this way about anyone. So yes, she would lock eyes with him and in doing so, hope she could convey some of these thoughts.

By early May, spring finally settled in. Crab apples, daffodils, columbine blazed by the roadside. The water reflected the new greens, and New Rochelle was restored to its pastoral splendor. As if to mirror its landscape, Emilia Mae's world was graced as well. Dillard started asking her small things, like did she think they might add some honey to the cream cheese frosting on the cupcakes (yes), or where was the nearest lake (Glenwood Lake). Their conversation became more comfortable. Small talk, something she could never endure, became her currency.

One afternoon, the two were sitting on the stone wall drinking iced tea. Dillard asked how old the bakery was, and Emilia Mae said she wasn't sure but that her mother's parents started the bakery when they came over from Italy, so it had been around a long while.

"Oh, she's Italian. That explains her dark eyes and skin. She's an attractive woman."

Emilia Mae shook her head. "She was a real knockout when she was young. Then I came along, and apparently sucked the life out of her."

"Your coloring's just the opposite, the light skin and hair."

"From my father. Oh wait..." Without thinking, she grabbed Dillard's wrist. He wore one of those watches that showed the date and time. "What's today? May fourth, 1961. Geez. In four days, he'd be..." She used her fingers to count. "Wow, in four days he'd be fifty-two. Pretty old."

"May I ask how old you are?"

"Getting up there," said Emilia Mae. "I'm thirty-two. How about you?"

"On my next birthday I'll be thirty."

"When is your next birthday?"

Dillard opened his mouth to speak, but Emilia Mae stopped him. "Let me guess." She closed her eyes and waved her hands around her temples the way she'd seen mind readers do it in the movies. "Ummm, I'm seeing May. Late May!"

She opened her eyes in time to catch the startled expression on Dillard's face. "Did I tell you that before?"

"Nope."

"Did I write it down anywhere?"

"Nope."

"Well then, that was amazing. Yes, my birthday is May twenty-eighth. How could you know that?"

"Dunno, I just felt it."

"What do you mean, you felt it?"

She rubbed her eyes with her palms. "Can't explain it. You look like someone born in late spring. Your smile, maybe. Also, Alice's birthday is June ninth. My father died on June thirteenth. Everything important in my life seems to have come around then, so it made sense." Emilia Mae blushed, realizing how much she'd given away.

His eyes roamed her face; she had his attention.

Maybe it was that, or his memory of her warm hands massaging his frigid fingers, but after that, they were more at ease with one another. When she shopped for the bakery, he'd come with her to carry the heavy loads. If the weather was nice, she'd sit with him on the back stairs as he took his dinner. Other times, she'd invite him home with Alice and Geraldine.

Geraldine also liked having Dillard around. As he filled out, he looked less skeletal and more handsome. She let her fantasies override her worry that maybe he was an ex-convict. Yes, he and Emilia Mae had gotten friendly, but Dillard's compliments to Geraldine were more than friendly. He made her feel noticed in ways she most enjoyed being noticed. One day, after she returned from church, he told her, "That dress really emphasizes the curve of your neck, Mrs. Wingo." Another time, when she and he were folding the tarp they kept over the well outside the bakery, he stared at her arms before saying, "Mrs. Wingo, you have the smooth skin of a young girl." It was not out of the question that he was flirting with her. The way he looked at her, how he always held the door for her and poured her coffee in the morning with just the right amount of sugar and milk, was certainly admiring. His flattering words filled up parts of her that had long gone empty. She hadn't had a fling in so long. Jesus, no one had even looked at her indiscreetly in years. These thoughts, which had once been second nature to her, had all but evaporated. She told herself it was as if God himself had delivered this young man to her doorstep. Hell, their union was practically preordained. She was twenty-two years his senior. Who cared? Much older men used to flirt with her all the time; why should it be any different for a woman?

The next time he called her Mrs. Wingo, Geraldine gave him a gentle jab on the shoulder. "Who're you calling Mrs. Wingo? I'm Geraldine, okay?"

"Yes, ma'am," said Dillard.

"I'm not *ma'am* either." She laughed. "It's Geraldine. Just plain Geraldine."

She began wearing her hair piled on top of her head in order to show off the curve of her neck. She wore boatneck blouses made of luscious fabrics that draped around her shoulders just so and made sure to refresh her fire-red lipstick every few hours. To her delight, she even found a bottle of White Shoulders cologne at Ware's Department Store. Every morning, she'd douse herself with enough of it that she smelled like a field of gardenias.

Dillard became such an integral part of the bakery that Geraldine increased his wages. After a few weeks, the green and blue shirt disappeared. He bought himself a pair of white linen trousers and a few crisp white and blue button-down shirts. The brown tweed flat cap remained. Because Earle and Dillard had roughly the same build, Geraldine gave him some of Earle's old clothes, hemming the cuffs that were slightly too long. One day in midsummer, when he showed up at the bakery in white pants and one of Earle's white rayon shirts, Geraldine grabbed him by the arm and trilled, "Oh my God, you look like Clark Gable in *Gone with the Wind*. Emilia Mae, doesn't he look like Clark Gable in *Gone with the Wind*?"

Her mother's voice was coquettish. Emilia Mae had noticed the perfume and lipstick, but not until this moment did it dawn on her that her mother must fancy Dillard.

"Mother," she said. "Clark Gable had a mustache and dark slick

149

hair and was taller than six feet. But sure, other than that Dillard looks exactly like him."

Later, when Dillard left, and Geraldine and Emilia Mae were alone in the shop, Geraldine shook her head and said to her daughter, "You really can't stand to see your mother have a little fun, can you?"

"It's not that. I just don't want to see you make a fool of yourself in front of Alice."

"Alice is not the one I worry about," said Geraldine. "She accepts me for who I am. It's you who have never given me a break."

"And I suppose you'd call pulling me out of school and sending me away from home when I was fifteen your idea of giving *me* a break?"

"I thought it was your choice," said Geraldine, picking the polish off one of her nails.

"I suppose it was, but what choice did I have?"

"We did get Alice out of all that," said Geraldine in a meeker voice. "There is that."

"There is that, thank God," said Emilia Mae.

For the next weeks, Emilia Mae watched her mother dance around Dillard, calling him "honey this" and "honey that," as if the dark-eyed beauty had returned. It surprised Emilia Mae how happy it made her to see this version of her mother.

Dillard always responded to Geraldine's compliments the same way: "Thank you, ma'am, that's very kind."

It drove Geraldine crazy. "No need to call me ma'am. Geraldine will do."

Emilia Mae also saw how Alice was always by Dillard's side and how she'd watch him with her wide brown eyes as they sang or talked together. One afternoon, when she was coming out of the bake room, Emilia Mae saw Alice say something to Dillard, though she didn't quite catch the words. Dillard started laughing. Alice laughed with him. Dillard had tears streaming down his eyes, he was laughing that hard. This is what he looks like when he's really happy, she thought. I wish I could make him that happy.

Alice had become his surrogate. "Dillard prefers pancakes with bananas," she'd tell them. Or "Dillard says that rock and roll has become more important to the culture than jazz." She also taught him how to cup his hands around a ball of bread dough, rub his thumbs against the surface, sink his fingers into it, tug at it to see if it stretched. In turn, he taught her how to ride a two-wheeler and how to play the harmonica.

With Dillard's pale, slender good looks and gentle nature, it was as if a version of Earle Wingo had been returned to each of the Wingo women.

On one of their walks, Dillard asked Emilia Mae about her parents. "The first thing to know is that my mother believes I was born with the devil in me. She's always resented me for stealing away her beauty and sex appeal. She sent me away from home when I was fifteen. I don't think she's ever liked me very much, but Alice has made things easier between us. My father saved me from her when he could."

"His death must have been hard for you."

"It was. He was the only man who was ever kind to me."

Dillard winced. "Well, now there are two of us." He put his arm around her and squeezed her shoulder. There was nothing tentative about his gesture. He kept his arm around her as they continued walking.

"What about your parents?" she asked.

He spoke faster than usual. "As I might have mentioned, I'm from Skyville. It's the most beautiful place in the world, tucked down there in the Smoky Mountains. It's becoming a bit of a tourist trap now, but when I was growing up, it was just the folks who came from there. My father sold antique musical instruments. I still have them. My mother wanted to be a singer. What I remember about her is how I'd sit on her lap and she'd sing this song: 'Lavender blue, dilly dilly...' She called me Dilly because her name was Lily. She liked that our names linked. Funny, your mother thought you were the devil; mine thought I was an angel. I guess they were both wrong. What I most remember about her was her leaving when I was four. She said she couldn't stay with us and become who she wanted to be and that I'd understand when I got older. I never did find out if she became a singer, or where she was. I guess we also have that in common, mothers who didn't want us. Anyway, my father traveled a good deal, and left me with his sister, Aunt Denise. I tried to be a good companion to her and always helped with chores around the house: toilets, lamps, broken faucets. I became quite the young Mr. Fixit. But I think she wanted more than a handy nephew. She'd call me her little man. I learned how to talk to grown-ups and would go with her to visit her friends. They'd ask my opinion about things like what dress they should wear to this or that or how to respond to a friend who'd been rude to them, and I'd always try to have smart answers. They never treated me like a little boy.

"Aunt Denise had these violet circles under her eyes. No matter how long she slept, they seemed to get bigger and darker. She didn't leave me a lot of time for my own life, so while I had friends and was popular at school, I was pretty miserable at home. I knew I had to get out of there."

"Where did you go?"

"I went to this wonderful music school, right outside of town, called Black Mountain College. After I graduated, I worked there for four years as a teaching assistant in the woodwinds department. The teachers and faculty were mostly foreign artists who'd been persecuted and kicked out of Europe. Many of them barely spoke English. It was a very progressive place, all about music and art. Kind of too good to be true. It closed down a few years ago."

"Geez, I wish you'd known my father," said Emilia Mae. "He loved jazz and knew a lot about it. It must have driven him nuts that my mother was such a Mantovani fan."

"Sentiment has its place in music," said Dillard.

"That's kind of you to say," said Emilia Mae. "But have you listened to Mantovani?"

"Not for long periods at a time."

Emilia Mae laughed. "Then what? What did you do after college?"

Dillard shook his head. "That's when things started going bad. What does anyone want with a musician who isn't really an expert in any one thing?" He told her about working odd jobs and suffering through his job in the Catskills. "I did that for two years, then quit and vowed I'd never play music again. I went back to Skyville. Worked as a receptionist at a doctor's office for a bit."

"Did you like being a receptionist?" asked Emilia Mae.

He smiled. "That was a happy time, but when that job ended,

I took work wherever I could get it tending bars, waiting tables, digging ditches. That's what eventually brought me here."

Dillard still had his arm around Emilia Mae. A lifeline. No man had ever touched her that way without the intention of taking something from her. The parts where Dillard's arm touched her back and shoulder tingled. She was afraid to turn her body, lest he take his arm away. She sensed that Dillard could use his own lifeline, and though these gestures did not come naturally to her, she reached out her arm and placed it around him. She felt his ribs and the place where his waist went concave. He smelled like roots and pine, and she wished she could nuzzle into his neck and taste him. Locked into each other as they were, they must have looked like a couple in love.

"You have a girl tucked away somewhere in Skyville, right?"

"Nah," said Dillard. "No time for that."

Aware that they were at an impasse, Emilia Mae changed the subject. "Skyville sounds like quite the place. Do you think you'll ever go back?"

"I hope so. How about you? Anywhere you'd like to go?"

Emilia Mae squinted. Her world was so confined to here, the wish to wander never occurred to her.

"Umm, I'd like to go to a night game at Yankee Stadium. I hear it's something to see. But you, I wonder, how in the world did you end up in New Rochelle and not New York City?"

He dug his fingers into her shoulder. "Oh, that's a story for another time."

Tethered to him as she was, Emilia Mae felt emboldened. With her free hand, she grabbed his cap off his head and said playfully, "Come on. I'll tell you my secrets if you tell me yours."

Dillard went rigid. "No," he said, grabbing the hat and plopping it back on his head.

It scared Emilia Mae, the sudden switch in his tone and body. It reminded her of that night he walked out of the dinner party. Reverend Klepper was right. He did have secrets.

They dropped their arms at the same time.

Chapter 17

In a Skyville fall, the greens were deeper and the reds richer than any painter's palette. The air that time of year was so sweet, you could taste it. During the day, it was still warm enough to sit out on the porch. Only at night could you feel winter's breath.

By fall, two things of note had happened. Dillard and Emilia Mae had kissed several times. The first time was more of a peck, but the second time, Emilia Mae centered her lips on Dillard's and tentatively stuck her tongue in his mouth. Initially, it was as if no one was home but gradually, his tongue found hers.

"It's been a long time," he said.

"Well, we have all the time in the world to practice."

They spent the rest of the fall "practicing." They would be on one of their walks or find themselves alone in the bake room. They'd look at one another, eyebrows raised conspiratorially, and one would say to the other, "Shall we practice?" They'd grab each other, the holding feeling more imperative than the kissing. Because they were roughly the same height, their mouths met naturally. They'd lick each other's teeth and let their tongues slide over one another's gums. They learned each other's bodies. They told some of their secrets: "Geraldine snores like a goat." "My mother said she'd never loved my father." "The Scarecrow, Cowardly Lion, and Tin Man from *The Wizard of Oz* became imaginary friends for a while. I believed they really existed." "Sometimes I talked to the trees in Skyville as if they were my friends." "When I was younger, food was my best friend."

Not that she was skinny now, but Emilia Mae no longer needed the weight as her coat of arms. Dillard looked her up and down. "I can't imagine. You look just right to me."

Dillard told himself that everything about Emilia Mae was just right. She liked him, that was clear. She was easy to talk to, smart, well read. She made "normal" seem easy to him, and wasn't "normal" what he craved? Kissing her, touching her body, it wasn't like it was with Nick but it was all right. A fair exchange for what came with her: Alice, Geraldine, a family, a job, a home. Yes, Emilia Mae was just right.

The second thing that happened that fall was that Dillard became a regular at the First Baptist Church. After church, he and Reverend Klepper would walk together while Cora would drive Xena to lunch at the Wingos' house. As was typical at those lunches, Geraldine cooked a hot meal—a pork roast on this day—and the discussions would range from current events to local gossip. Everyone shouted with the hopes that Xena could hear them. On this Sunday, Geraldine became irate about a book someone had described to her. She said it was about a forty-year-old European poet who seduces a twelve-year-old girl, and that there was a copy of it in the New Rochelle Library.

"This Nab-a-ko-vitch, or whatever his name is, ought to be sent back to Russia," said Geraldine. "Imagine, writing such filth and having it in a library where anyone can pick it up. It's shocking. And you know me, I'm as open-minded as the next person."

Cora had to laugh at Geraldine's outrage. "Have you read it?"

"No, and I never will."

"So how do you know it's all the things you say it is?"

"You do know what it's about, do you not?"

"You just told us. I also know what *Bambi*'s about, and it turns out to be a sweet story."

"*Bambi*?" said Xena. "I loved that film."

"Me too," said Cora.

Reverend Klepper, in his early fifties by now, was struggling to keep up with the more permissive culture of the times. "I haven't read *Lolita*, but I know about its contents. Humans often grapple with emotions or inclinations that are not considered proper or even normal. That this writer dared to put those feelings on paper seems to me a great act of courage. Certainly, we ought not to judge it until we've read it."

"I've read it," said Emilia Mae. "And I'll admit, it's disturbing, even brutal at times, but it is one of the truest love stories I've ever read."

"I've read it, too," announced Dillard, pulling off one of Earle's crewneck sweaters while holding his cap on his lap. "Emilia Mae is right. The main character has unnatural yearnings and acts on them, despite the consequences he knows he'll face. Truth be known, I found it more sad than shocking. The author makes you feel empathy for the main character, which, given the subject, is a pretty hard thing to do."

Geraldine folded her legs beneath her faux leather miniskirt. "Honey, I'm sure you're right about all that. But let me ask you and Emilia Mae, would you want Alice reading that trash?"

Dillard shook his head. "Oh, for Pete's sake, not now. She's way too young to understand that kind of obsession and desire. But I'll tell you this: I'll bet when Alice is ten years older and she does read this book, she'll find it in her heart to feel more sympathy than revulsion for the main character."

"And I'll tell *you* this," said Geraldine. "Even ten years from now, I sure wouldn't give Alice permission to read this book."

"Mother, ten years from now, Alice won't need your permission to do anything," said Emilia Mae.

Mercifully, Cora took the conversation off in a different direction when she speculated that ten years from now, no one would read books anymore. Everyone eagerly piped in with predictions of what ten years from now might hold.

By two thirty, lunch was over. While Dillard helped Geraldine clear the table, Emilia Mae walked Xena and the Kleppers to their car. Emilia Mae didn't give the lunch a second thought until Geraldine cornered her in the baking room the following Wednesday morning. She had a dish towel wrapped around her neck and smudges of liner under her eyes. "Let me ask you a question. Did you not think that Dillard was rude to me the other afternoon?"

"What other afternoon?"

"You know, when we were talking about that horrid Russian writer."

"Oh, you mean about the book you never read?"

"Yes, but that's not the point. I thought Dillard was harsh with me."

"Dillard wasn't harsh, he just felt strongly about what he was saying."

"Even so, I didn't appreciate being spoken to in that tone of voice under my own roof."

Geraldine tried again on the following Sunday, and that lunch went much smoother with everyone chatting about their favorite television shows. Afterward, Emilia Mae walked the Kleppers to their car. While Dillard helped clean up, Geraldine came up behind him, wrapped her arms around his waist and rested her head on his curved back. "Honey, why were you so short with me last week when we talked about that awful little book? You know I only have Alice's best interests at heart."

Dillard stepped back so fast that Geraldine fell backward and knocked over one of the kitchen chairs.

"I'm not your honey."

"No need to take offense, it's just a term of endearment," she said in her breathy voice.

Dillard said nothing.

Geraldine regained her composure. "Let me ask you this. Do you find me attractive?"

"Yes, ma'am. I find you attractive, though probably not in the way you'd like me to."

"Well, that pretty much says everything."

In defeat, Geraldine's body seemed to release itself. Her chin sagged; her mouth went slack. Her eyes squinted to the size of paper cuts.

This was the tableau Emilia Mae confronted when she walked back into the kitchen.

"Did somebody die or something?" she asked.

"People aren't the only things that die," said Geraldine as she walked out of the room.

"What was that all about?" asked Emilia Mae, picking up the chair.

"You know how your mother can get temperamental sometimes?"

She laughed. "Umm, yeah."

"Well, this was one of those times."

"What did she get temperamental about?"

"Nothing I care to talk about," said Dillard. He finished washing the dishes, walked to the dining room table, and picked up his cap from where he'd left it on the chair.

When he came back into the kitchen, Emilia Mae rubbed her hand up and down his arm. Dillard was wearing her father's camel-colored crewneck sweater. "This color really complements your eyes," she said. "It was one of my father's favorites. He bought it at Brooks Brothers in the city shortly before he died. He said it was something young John Kennedy would wear. That was the highest compliment he could pay anyone. My mother, on the other hand, has always thought Kennedy is a snob."

"That's too bad," said Dillard, still distracted.

"What's too bad?" asked Emilia Mae. "Don't you like Kennedy?"

"What? No, it has nothing to do with Kennedy."

"He's Catholic, you know."

"Who, your dad?"

"No, but Kennedy is. Reverend Klepper thinks it's stupid that everyone's so nervous about him being a Catholic. Like he's got a hotline to the pope in his basement or something."

"Kennedy has a hotline to the pope in his basement?"

"Never mind, this is a dumb conversation," said Emilia Mae, not bothering to hide her annoyance.

"You're a prickly one, aren't you?" he asked.

"I'm a prickly one?" Her voice rose. "I'm trying to have a conversation with you, and you get all vague when I ask you what my mother got temperamental about. You always do that, tell me that you don't want to talk about this or that. You make it really hard sometimes."

Dillard picked up the dish towel again and started twisting it. "Maybe I should leave; go back to Skyville," he said. "I don't seem to have the knack for getting along with Wingo women."

"That's a great idea, Dillard." When Emilia Mae got angry, her voice went curvy. "Run away, again. That seems to be something you're good at. You bump into a little trouble, and boom, you're off like Sputnik."

"You know nothing about my little trouble." Dillard spoke in the kind of soft voice people use right before they hit someone. "You don't know where I've been, or why I'm here, so I'd be much obliged if you'd keep your opinions about my troubles to yourself."

He took off the camel sweater, set it on the kitchen table, put on his cap, and walked out the door.

"Don't go," Emilia Mae shouted after him.

He stopped and turned toward her. "Why not? I don't seem to be doing anybody here any good."

"That's not true," said Emilia Mae. "You're everything to Alice. You're everything to me. You're as good here as you are anywhere else."

"Look, I'm sorry. I know I can be difficult, but I don't mean to be."

"Yeah, well, who isn't? I'm not exactly Miss Charm School. The truth is, if anything, you've made it better around here. Your leaving would be the worst thing that's happened to any of us since my dad died."

"I'm sorry," he said. "I need a break."

He headed out the door. Emilia Mae watched him walk down the street. His shoulders were hunched. He was rubbing his hands together. They were probably cold. Again, she thought of that first night at dinner, when he abruptly got up and left the table. She tried finding relief in his leaving but couldn't.

At the same time, Dillard was telling himself that leaving was the only rational thing to do, that once again, he was hurting people. Those people had expectations of him. They thought he was someone he was not. They wanted something from him he didn't think he could give. He couldn't bear to tear apart another family. He walked toward Main Street and passed Frank's Music Store, where he'd planned to buy a harmonica for Alice. He wished he'd said goodbye to her. But maybe that was better left unsaid. He would have had to explain himself, and he wasn't ready to do that with anybody. Emilia Mae was right: He was running away. Where was he running to? Skyville? There was nothing for him in Skyville. If Nick were alive, he'd run to Nick, even if it meant exposing their relationship. He walked to the edge of town, to the train station. Trains left for Grand Central on the hour. He could go to New York City. From there he could catch a train to anywhere in the country. California? Texas? Florida? He'd never been to any of those places. He could go there anew. Change his name. Get a job but keep his distance, not get embroiled in another family again. He walked faster. At the station he saw there was only a seven-minute wait for the next train to New York City. This was a sign; his leaving was meant to be. He'd held out false promises to the Wingos. Just like Sharlene and the children, they thought he was someone he was not. The Wingos didn't deserve him and his deception. He dug his hands into his pockets. A late November chill had started to claim them; he could feel the numbness in the tips of his fingers. On the train, he took a window seat in the unheated car. He was barely able to extract the $4 fare from his pocket. He rubbed his hands together the way Emilia Mae did and watched the trees whiz by, most of them bare by now. He wondered if trees mourned their leaves in the fall. It made him sad to think about those trees, so majestic and proud in their summer foliage, bare and stark against the failing sunlight. That's how he felt. With Nick, he was full and majestic. Now, bare and stark.

As the train moved closer to the city, he could see lights on in the humble houses by the tracks. He imagined kitchens with families sitting around the table. In the darkness, he made out a bicycle lying in the front yard, a swing in another. Normal families. Home. Love unspoken. Love was something he'd never taken for granted. He remembered the night his mother left, how his father had slumped when she shot the words at him: "I never did love you, Beau Fox." Until Nick, he'd never thought love was possible. Now that he knew what it was, he craved it more than anything.

It was dark when the train pulled into Grand Central. He walked up the concrete stairs, following people whose quick steps made him think they had someplace to go. Where was he going? Food. He was hungry. He'd eat and then study the train schedule to see where he'd go next. The hot dog cost $1. That left him with $9. He'd walked out of the house with $14. He remembered what it was like to have no money in his pocket, always begging for odd jobs, skipping meals, sleeping in public places. He'd rather die than go back to that life.

There were few places to sit at Grand Central, but he finally found a bench on the lower concourse. The floor was cracked and the dull lighting makeshift. As night turned into overnight, Dillard sat on that bench and thought about where he should go and what he wanted. He was sick of being the guy who kept running. He felt tired and lost. Alice would never understand why he'd left, just as he'd never understood why his mother had left. Emilia Mae had said, "You're everything to me." He'd never been everything to anyone except Nick. Emilia Mae liked him. Possibly loved him. He thought again about normal, and how with Emilia Mae, normal was in reach. Alice, Geraldine, safety, the whole shebang, this was his chance, maybe his only chance. He could love Emilia Mae in his way. He could give her the kindness and home she craved and build a life with her that worked for both of them. He already loved Alice; that would be no problem. And Geraldine? He would flirt with Geraldine and flatter her. This wasn't as it was with Nick's family. He wasn't stealing anyone away, wasn't causing any rupture. He could do this. Yes, he would go back to New Rochelle and hope that Emilia Mae would forgive him.

He went upstairs to find that the sun had risen, and the station was bustling. There was a six forty-five train to New Rochelle, which gave him twenty minutes to get some coffee, a donut, and buy his return ticket.

With $2.50 in his pocket, he disembarked in New Rochelle and headed to the Wingo house.

He got to the house right after Alice had left for school. Geraldine had already gone to the bakery, and Emilia Mae was heading out the front door just as he was walking in.

"Have you come for your things?" she asked in a dry voice.

"No. Do you have a minute to talk?"

She looked at her watch and said, "I told Mother I'd be at the bakery by nine."

"This will only take a few minutes. Please, can we talk?"

Emilia Mae sat on the top step of the front porch. "Talk fast; I only have about seven minutes."

He sat next to her. When he looked her in the eye, she turned away, but not before he noticed that her eyes were swollen. "I know I acted foolishly yesterday. It was an impulsive thing to do. I thought I was doing everyone a favor. Well, that's not entirely true. You were right, I was running away. I was scared of everything. Of hurting people. Disappointing them. You, mainly. I've thought about it long and hard. I'd like to come back, if you'll let me. I could be happy here. We could be happy here. What do you think about that?"

Emilia Mae turned and stared in Dillard's eyes. "Don't ever do that again," she said.

He nodded.

Sunlight shot through the trees and turned Dillard's blond hair silver. The light underscored the circles under his eyes and the traces of wrinkles around his mouth. Emilia Mae saw what he might look like in thirty years. It gave her comfort to think of growing old with him. She was nobody's idea of a dream girl, but at this moment, with Dillard aglow in the sunlight, a feeling of love washed over her. She could be very happy here with him. Before she could think about the consequences, she grabbed his wrists and in a cracking voice said, "Don't go. Please don't ever go."

Her words haunted Dillard. He knew what it felt like to try to hold on to someone, and how futile it was. *Mommy, don't go.*

For the first fifteen years of his life, he lived next door to a plot of land filled with live oak trees. He loved those oaks, with their embracing arms and long shiny leaves. The trees seemed proud and friendly, and he named them Oliver and Peter and other names he'd found in books. Sometimes, when the trees made that *sshhssshing* sound in the wind, Dillard believed they were friends talking to him, and he would reply to their imagined endearments or questions.

Then a family from up north bought the land and built a house on it. Worried that the oaks would shade their front yard, they began cutting them all down. For weeks, trucks would arrive with saws and ropes and hoisting equipment. Dillard would watch the men denude the trees, one branch at a time. He'd cover his eyes and slam his hands against his ears as the saws hacked through the wood. "Don't go, please don't go," he'd plead. The tree killers would saw the trunk down to a manageable height, then lasso a rope around the top of the tree and yank and saw until the tree was beheaded. Dillard cried for each of them. He cried because they were his friends, but he also cried for how powerless he was.

That's what this felt like.

He knew what was behind Emilia Mae's pleas. He knew what she wanted from him was a promise, one he worried would inevitably lead to disappointment. But this promise to her also came with promises to himself that were difficult to ignore. He would have all the things he never thought possible for him. Yes, he could make it work. He couldn't afford not to make it work.

Marriage meant a ring. Maybe two. It meant placating Geraldine, which would probably cost him more than the rings. He put his arm around Emilia Mae. "I promise, I won't do this again."

Later that day as he sat in his room, he dragged out the cigar box of memorabilia that he kept under his bed and pulled out one of the photographs. "If I did this, I could finally stay still, find my place," he said to the photograph. "Something like this might never come my way again. I know you understand."

On his first day off, Dillard went to the jewelry store on Main Street. The wooden floor planks creaked beneath his feet, and the place smelled of Black Flag bug killer. The salesclerk showed Dillard dozens of rings. All of them cost well over $100. Dillard put his hands in his pocket and said to the clerk, "I wonder if it's possible to find one of these that costs less than a hundred dollars?"

The clerk wore a woven striped jacket with wide lapels and brown slacks that had a slight sheen to them. Dillard was no connoisseur of fashion, but something about the clerk's clothes and the way he kept licking his lips as he talked told him that the man didn't have hundreds to spend on rings himself.

"You know about estate sales, don't you?"

"No, sir, I don't."

"After somebody dies, the family sells off some of their possessions, like jewelry, for example." He licked his lips and pointed to a case of drawers. "We get a lot of that kind of stuff around here. Lemme see what I've got." He opened boxes and searched through small bags. He filled the glass counter with silver knives and forks, watches, bracelets, and a bronze statuette of the three wise monkeys before he came upon an old ring. "So, what do you think of this?"

The clerk held the ring up to the light. It looked to be gold with a blue stone in the middle. There were tiny flecks of other stones around it that might have been diamonds. "Sapphire," said the clerk. "Looks real to me, but we'll see what happens when I clean it up. The rest of the stuff, I dunno." He took out a cloth and polished the ring. When he held it up to the light again, he said, "Yup, the real thing. I can tell you right now, for sixty-eight dollars you've got yourself a nice little engagement ring. Whaddya say?"

Dillard held the ring and imagined it on Emilia Mae's finger. She had big hands; apparently so did the person who had worn this. He stuck it on his pinky.

"Sure is pretty," he said. "But I think it'd be prettier at fifty-eight."

The clerk picked at his red lips. "You're not from around here, are you?"

"No, sir, but I'm looking to marry someone who is."

"May I ask who?"

"Sure," said Dillard. "Emilia Mae Wingo. Her family owns Shore Cakes."

The clerk laughed. "Oh, yes, the bakery girl. I've been eating their strawberry shortcake since I was yay high." He held his hands to the height of a three-year-old. "I'll tell you what, you gimme sixty-two dollars and finally make that old bakery gal a bride."

"Thank you, sir," said Dillard. "I'll give you sixty and you've got yourself a deal. I'll need it by Christmas, which means I'll pay you fifteen dollars a week until then. How about that?"

The clerk had to laugh. "Okay, mister, it's a deal. I'll keep this thing nice and safe until you're ready."

"Thank you, sir," said Dillard. "And one more thing. This is a secret, between you and me, if you'll be so kind as to keep it that way."

"Sure thing," said the clerk.

Chapter 18

Dillard told no one of his intentions but set about courting Emilia Mae in a way that he thought suitable. He took her to the movies. She held his arm during the scary parts of *The Curse of the Werewolf.* He wiped a piece of cheese off her chin when they went for pizza at Giovanni's. They walked through town with their arms around each other. When she cut her long blond hair into a short bouffant, he told her she looked like Brigette Bardot. They practiced kissing every day.

His attentions poured life into Emilia Mae. Alice noticed how her mother smiled at customers now and asked about their children. One day she presented Alice with a pair of patent leather pumps and a sleeveless dress with a ladybug pattern and ruffles at the hem. Her mother never gave her presents except at Christmas and her birthday. When Alice asked what she'd done to deserve a new dress and shoes, Emilia Mae smiled and said, "Does there have to be a reason? I thought you'd look pretty in these."

Alice also noticed how her mother would hang around at the end of the day while she and Dillard were sweeping up and taking out the trash. How she'd smile her glowy new smile at him and he'd smile back, and how sometimes they'd exchange a few words in a whisper low enough for Alice not to hear.

At thirteen, Alice knew what she knew about love from romance comics. But this wasn't like that. It was just that her mother was easier, and Dillard, when he sang, sang louder. One afternoon while Alice was crouched holding the dustpan and Dillard was sweeping the dirt into it, she looked up at him and asked, "Are you in love with my mother?"

Dillard stopped sweeping. "Well, that's a very personal question, don't you think?"

Alice considered for a moment, then answered. "Not really. She's my mother; you're my friend. If you drew a picture of the three of us, I'd probably be in the middle."

Dillard crouched beside Alice. "You're right, you would be in the middle. Am I in love with your mother? Let's just say that we have a very special friendship, like you and I have, only different. Does that make sense?"

"I guess."

When Alice smiled, Dillard imagined he could see through the gap between her front teeth into her soul. It wasn't dank and weedy like most people's; Alice's soul was more like sprinkles on a donut.

"You'll always be in the middle," he said.

Early one morning, Emilia Mae stopped by Cora's shop and bought a half dozen mums, which she placed behind the cash register at the bakery. The flowers echoed Emilia's exuberance. "Someone's awful chipper these days," said Geraldine later that morning.

Emilia Mae continued arranging cookies on a tray.

"Don't think I don't know what's going on between you and Dillard. It's there for all the world to see."

Emilia Mae smiled. "I'm really happy."

Geraldine pressed her lips together in an attempt at a smile. "Look, I know you and I haven't always had an easy time of it, but I am concerned with your welfare. Are you sure you want to take up with a man who is basically a clerk with no money and no future? You're a smart girl and not bad-looking. I think you could do better."

Emilia Mae studied her mother's face. She was still pretty, but disappointment tugged at her eyes and mouth and made her look older than her fifty-plus years.

"I said I was happy," said Emilia Mae. "Maybe for the first time in my life. That's got to count for something."

"Happy? Happy is an illusion." Geraldine lit a cigarette, inhaled and exhaled. "Watch this smoke. It's here and then it's gone. That's what happiness is. An illusion that evaporates just like that. You need more than happiness to sustain a life. Believe me."

Emilia Mae scratched the back of her neck. "Wasn't it only a few weeks ago you were calling Dillard 'honey' and telling him he looked like Clark Gable? Are you really concerned about my welfare, or have you turned on him because he's taken a shine to me?"

Geraldine put her hand on Emilia Mae's shoulder. "I don't expect you to understand, but I honestly worry about you getting hurt. Men like Dillard—they don't stick around."

But Dillard did stick around.

By December, he'd saved the money he needed to go forward with his plan.

The Wingo women had a Christmas tradition of opening presents while still in their robes. On this morning, the three of them gathered in Geraldine's living room, sleep still in their eyes. Geraldine sprawled on the couch sipping coffee while Emilia Mae sat cross-legged by the tree. Only Alice seemed fidgety as she paced in front of the door. At eight thirty, Dillard knocked. He was dressed in a suit and tie and his cap and held a shopping bag filled with wrapped packages.

"Merry Christmas," he said in a chipper voice. "I've come bearing gifts." They stared at him as if he were a stranger. "You know, *presents*," he said with emphasis. "One for each of you."

He walked over to the couch, pulled out a big box, and handed it to Geraldine. "This, for the lady of the house. I hope you like it."

The two of them had exchanged only necessary words since the fall. Now he was handing her a box from Bonwit Teller. She sat up, put her coffee cup on the floor, took the box in her hands, and eagerly tore into the periwinkle wrapping paper. Inside was a white cardigan sweater with a white fur collar—fake fur, no doubt. She held it up. "This is beautiful. It must have cost you a fortune."

"No matter. I thought it suited you perfectly."

Geraldine slipped it over her pajama top. The sweater was cut so as to flatter her neck. When she peeked at herself in the hall mirror, she could see how the white perfectly complemented her dark skin. "Thank you. Really, thank you," she said. "This is very thoughtful of you."

"I wanted you to have something pretty."

Geraldine squeezed his hand. "You really are a dear, aren't you?"

With Geraldine's hand still on his, Dillard turned to Alice. "For the singer in the family, who always sparkles and shines."

He handed Alice a square white box with a pink bow.

Alice grinned when she saw what was inside: a tiara with rhinestones and different-colored jewels. She stuck it on her head.

"There you go," Dillard said. "Queen of . . . well, everything."

The last present he pulled from the bag was as small as an afterthought. It was wrapped in white tissue paper tied with the red and white bakery string.

Geraldine's throat tightened. Alice hugged herself, as she was the one who'd wrapped it. Emilia Mae opened it slowly. She recognized the tiny cedar box as something her parents had brought back from a long-ago trip to the Pocono Mountains. Inside was more tissue and inside the tissue was the sapphire ring. She stood up and wrapped her arms around Dillard. She rested her head on his shoulder, and though no one could understand her through her tears, she said either "I do" or "thank you."

In either case, the deal was done.

Chapter 19

Geraldine was horrified at Emilia Mae's choice of a dress. "Who wears blue to their own wedding?"

"I do," argued Emilia Mae. "It's stupid to go out and buy something white so I can make a spectacle of myself in front of ten people. This fits me right, and I'll dye high heels to match."

The virtues of this robin's-egg-blue sheath were the three long curved darts in front and the vertical back darts, which made her look slim in places she wasn't. The dress came with a polka-dotted scarf long enough to drape over her head and serve as a veil. That, combined with Alice's tiara, and there it was, a complete wedding outfit.

On the day of the wedding, the May light shone through the high, slender windows of the Baptist church. Alice wore her sleeveless ladybug dress with her black patent leather pumps, which made a clopping sound as she walked down the aisle with her mother. They walked slowly enough for Emilia Mae to worry that people would see her shaky knees, but no one seemed to notice as the sublime notes of a Bach flute solo oozed from the phonograph.

Emilia Mae caught sight of Cora holding Xena's arm. Xena looked even tinier than usual. She wore a black dress with white palm fronds on it and a black velvet open pillbox with a veil and bow. She had to be in her nineties by now. Emilia Mae thought, *This is what Xena will wear when they lay her out.* Dillard was at the altar. He wore her father's navy suit with its too-wide lapels and too-short sleeves. He greeted her with a shaky smile. His eyes seemed bigger and bluer, his chin so perfectly square, and that full mouth—God, he was handsome.

Reverend Klepper stood next to him. Fourteen years ago, she and he had stood in this same church week after week, with him trying to convince her that she was having a baby and not some satanic creature. What a pain she must have been. And here was Alice, so unwanted and, if she had had her way, nearly unborn, now the delight of everyone's life. How she had produced a creature full of such joy was still a mystery to Emilia Mae, a beautiful mystery. She squeezed Alice's arm before letting it go and taking Dillard's hand. It was cold. When Emilia Mae looked down, she could see the bluish tips of his fingers. She rubbed them until they were warmer.

Reverend Klepper began. "As we share in this wedding ceremony, it is well that we remember that in the beginning, when God created the heavens and the earth, he concluded, 'It is not good for man to be alone.' So, He created woman to share in man's life—to assist in man's striving—to satisfy man's need. He also created the woman to be loved, honored, and appreciated by man."

Emilia Mae had never thought of it that way.

Dillard took his vows in a slow whisper. When Reverend Klepper asked if anyone . . . or forever hold your peace, Emilia Mae glanced at her mother, uncertain what she would do, but Geraldine's eyes were downcast as if she were reading a magazine or pulling a loose thread from her dress.

Reverend Klepper pronounced them man and wife, and then smiled at Dillard when he said, "You may kiss the bride." Emilia Mae put her hand behind Dillard's neck and kissed him on the mouth. He held her around the waist and kissed her back. It wasn't as showy a kiss as Emilia Mae had hoped, but who cared? She was Mrs. Dillard Fox! She bounced down the aisle to a recording of "Fly Me to the Moon," certain how everyone in that church envied her so.

After the ceremony, cake cutting, and first dance, Emilia Mae went up to Geraldine, who was standing alone in the reception hall. "I hope you can find it in your heart to be happy for us."

Geraldine had watched Dillard and Emilia Mae during the ceremony. Dillard's eyes had spilled onto Emilia Mae with such care and affection that she had to believe it was love. For her part, Emilia Mae stood tall and happy. She had cut her hair pixie style for the wedding, and for the first time, Geraldine noticed Emilia Mae's ears. So tiny, like butter cookies straight from the oven. Earle's voice came back to her in a jolt, the sweetness of it when he prodded her to try and love their colicky little girl. "I'll do my best," she'd promised. Now that colicky little girl was asking her mother to love her again, to love her new husband. Geraldine smiled and heard Earle in her voice when she answered, "I'm happy for you, Emilia Mae, I really am."

Dillard turned out to be the perfect husband. He loved Emilia Mae. She loved him. She couldn't keep her hands off him, couldn't take her eyes off him. It made her laugh to remember how she used to gawk at those couples who stared at each other cow-eyed. Now she was one of them. The sound of his voice, his Southern accent, those eyes, that square chin. Everything about him stirred her. If it were up to her, they'd make love every time he kissed the back of her neck or said her name in a certain way. The miracle of it was, he seemed to love her back. Whenever they could in public, they touched each other—a squeeze of the hand, a rub of the back. Alone, they made love almost every night. She felt like Holly Golightly in *Breakfast at Tiffany's*. They were Joanne Woodward and Paul Newman. Nothing in her life had prepared her for this. Her father's love was kindly but dependent on her mother's mood. Her mother's love could be given or taken on whim; Emilia Mae spent more time yearning for it than actually receiving it. Alice's love, a child's love, was sweet. But Dillard's love? It was pure, and erotic, and required nothing more from her than simply being herself. When she thought about all the men she'd slept with at the Neptune Inn, she remembered the sex as numbing, something she'd bartered in exchange for them making her feel liked. Her mother teased her and Dillard and said they were like teenagers. But teenaged Emilia Mae never experienced the kind of happiness that thirty-two-year-old Emilia Mae was feeling now.

Dillard started giving flute lessons, and both of them made a steady wage at the bakery. They scraped up enough money to buy a stucco house not unlike Geraldine's. The house had two bedrooms, a small porch, one and a half bathrooms, and a basement that smelled like wet towels. Dillard painted over the stained yellow in the bathroom with poppy red. He refinished an old mahogany coffee table for the living room and varnished it a rich antique oak. He cut out pictures of all of Alice's favorite television stars—Dick Van Dyke, Lucille Ball, Marlo Thomas, Fred and Wilma Flintstone—made fake silver and gold frames for them, and then hung them in her bedroom like museum portraits. He painted Alice's room bright pink, the living room lavender, and his and Emilia Mae's room sky blue.

Nobody used the basement except as a place to toss old suitcases and clothes they didn't want until Dillard turned it into a music room. He painted the gray walls white and built a bookshelf out of bricks and planks of wood where he set out his father's musical instruments. Next to the bookshelves was one straight-backed chair, where he sat when he played the flute, and a wooden stool for Alice to sit on when she sang. Across from Dillard's chair, a full-length mirror allowed him to check his posture and make sure his arms were lifted and his feet flat on the floor. He built a special shelf in the closet to hold his cigar box full of photographs and old letters.

At a yard sale, he bought three overstuffed pillows and a bedspread for his and Emilia Mae's bed. A few weeks later, he added two stuffed Daffy Ducks to the mix. Each morning, he'd make the bed and settle the ducks on one of the pillows with their wings around each other. "That's us," he would say. "Two odd ducks."

And each time, she'd answer, "Yup, two odd ducks with a home of their own."

Dillard was the one who kept the house clean. Without complaining, he'd put away the boots that Alice had kicked off on the living room floor; he'd wipe away spilled cereal crumbs from the kitchen and was handy with leaky faucets and overflowing toilets. He told Emilia Mae that vacuuming relaxed him.

Emilia Mae never did like the dark. The dark was where her truths and past seeped out. Dillard offered his chest at night, a bony rack of comfort and musk. He held her head and stroked her hair. She would take his hand and move it to her breast. Sometimes he kept it there; sometimes he'd let it wander down to her hip.

Emilia Mae loved the piney smell of him and the way his hands always felt cool against her skin. In bed, he was thoughtful and careful, knowing when and where to stroke and touch her. He loved her in every way he could, and in loving him back, she lost her way as she had all those years ago with the gap-toothed man from Albany.

Of course, Dillard had some eccentricities, but who didn't? Emilia Mae found it odd the way he ate, quickly and furtively, as if someone might snatch his food away. At times he seemed to disappear. His eyes would go stony and he'd look past her as if she wasn't there. Where did he go? Then there were times when he actually did disappear. He said long walks refreshed his mind, though he didn't say where he went walking. But that was all right; that's just who he was.

God created woman to assist in man's striving and satisfy his needs. That's what Reverend Klepper said at their wedding. Wasn't she doing just that by leaving him to his quirks rather than harping on them? She knew what they had. Dillard loved her. She loved Dillard. That's all that mattered.

Emilia Mae wore her first year of marriage like a fur coat. The rich ladies from Wykagyl used to intimidate her with their flashy jewelry and soft manicured fingers. Not anymore. She was rich, too, now, rich in love. Dillard took interest in what she wore, how she felt. Often, he'd bring her and Alice little presents: barrettes, dime-store jewelry, a favorite record. She'd trim his hair, his thick golden hair, and leave him sweet notes under his pillow.

Marriage made Emilia Mae feel grown-up; it also gave her conversation.

"Dillard and I went biking on the South County Trailway this weekend. The foliage was beautiful."

"Dillard made linguine with clams last night. The best I've ever had."

Weeks before their first anniversary, he started telling her that he had a surprise for her. When May 22 finally arrived, he picked an outfit from Emilia Mae's closet: a short navy skirt, a blue and white striped sweater, and blue pumps. He was dressed in all white with a navy vest and his tweed flat cap.

Before they left the house, Emilia Mae tugged at his vest. "Where are we going?"

"What kind of a surprise would it be if I told you?"

They took the New York Central train to 153rd Street, where throngs of people were heading uptown. A light that could be coming from a flying saucer shone through the darkness. Yankee Stadium. They hiked up a few ramps, then took a dark narrow passageway to the gates. Odors from the restrooms mixed with the smell of hot dogs. Dillard held her hand and pushed forward. They walked through a gate, and the world exploded in color. The grounds were a Technicolor green; the banners hanging from box seats a startling red, white, and blue. The scoreboard was lit up so brightly Emilia Mae had to squint to read it. Even the air smelled richer: fresh grass and late spring. A night game at Yankee Stadium.

"I can't believe you did this," she said.

Dillard kissed her neck. "Happy anniversary. I'm so glad you're happy."

He was too good to be true.

Chapter 20

On a late Saturday afternoon in the fall, after the bakery closed and while Alice and Emilia Mae were out shopping, Dillard went down to the music room and rummaged around, as he often did. He dusted his daddy's antique instruments and arranged his sheet music. He opened the closet and stared at the cigar box he kept on the shelf, trying to decide whether or not to open it. He hadn't opened it since he moved out of the Neptune Inn before the wedding. Opening it would mean going back. He was a married family man now, about as far away from his past as a fallen meteorite. One picture couldn't hurt.

He took down the box and sought out the photograph. He stared at it, touching his finger to a face, outlining the contours of the cheeks. So close, so heartbreakingly far away. He shoved the picture back into the box, put the box on the shelf, and stepped back into his life. His life was an easy flow. He'd found his place. He liked having definition. He liked keeping house, playing music with Alice. Even Geraldine had warmed to him and they were back to silly flirty games. Just last week, she'd said to him, "Are you going to give me more grandchildren soon? I'm not getting any younger, you know."

He said what he was supposed to say: "No one could tell that by looking at you."

"Oh, Dillard," she'd said, slapping him on the shoulder. "You're too much."

In truth, Dillard did want a child. Alice was growing up fast and soon would be off to college. He loved teaching her, loved having someone of his own to mold. On a Sunday late that fall, Dillard suggested to Emilia Mae that they walk by the Sound. It was a sparkling day. The leaves were hanging onto the trees and the water slurped at the shoreline. "Come, let's watch the boats," he said, finding them a spot in the sand. He stretched his legs and lay back. Emilia Mae lay next to him. After a while, he sat up, and looked down at her. "What do you think about us having a child?"

"I already had a child."

"That was a while ago, and you did it by yourself. This would be different; we'd do it together."

She laughed. "Oh, would we? We'd share carrying this thing around for nine months and blowing up as big as a VW? We're getting old. Can you imagine that by the time that child graduated from high school we'd be in our fifties? That's too old."

"Not really, Emilia Mae. People do that nowadays."

"Not these people."

Back and forth they went, until Dillard said, "Imagine how a child would brighten our lives."

"I think our lives are pretty bright as they are. It would be like starting all over again."

"Exactly," said Dillard. "When I met you, I was at the lowest point in my life. You gave me a family and a home. If I were inclined to believe in miracles, I'd say that was a big one. Having a child with you would be another one."

"I'm sorry, but having another kid scares me. I'm the devil child, remember? I can't guarantee that another one coming out of me would be as perfect as Alice. I've never particularly liked my life; now I love it. I want everything to stay exactly as it is."

"That's a sweet thought," said Dillard. "But you know nothing ever does."

Alice at sixteen was a beauty. Her olive skin gave off the soft glow of pearls. She was tall and slender with long wavy black hair that seemed to catch the light just so. Her bangs came down to her eyebrows like a curtain about to fall on her wide, mud-brown eyes. The gap between her buckish front teeth made her smile that much more appealing. Girls liked her because she was buoyant and easy to be with, and boys liked her because she was pretty and not as judgmental as most of the other girls.

One night, after Emilia Mae and Alice went out shopping, they stopped for a Carvel. As they sat in the car, licking their ice creams, Emilia Mae said to Alice, "So how's the boy situation this year?"

Alice smiled and brushed her hand in front of her face. "Fine. I do fine in that department."

"Anybody serious?"

"No, not really. I like to play the field."

"Oh," said Emilia Mae, raising her eyebrows. "Interesting."

"Not that interesting. You know, high school boys. They're such babies."

Emilia Mae laughed at her daughter's maturity. Where did that come from? Certainly not from her. Her Alice would never have been friends with sixteen-year-old Emilia Mae. Alice would never recklessly sleep around and certainly would not become a mother at nineteen. Emilia Mae leaned over and kissed her on the cheek. "I imagine you do just fine with them. Do you have any questions? You know, about sex and stuff?"

Alice shook her head in a way that might have been a shudder. "No, I think I'm okay."

"Alright," said Emilia Mae. "But if you do, you can always ask me. Anything. I mean that."

"Thanks," said Alice. "Good to know."

Alice didn't feel the need to tell her mother about Rick, who'd walk her halfway to the bakery after school. Rick had a sixth sense for finding houses with a FOR SALE sign in front of them. Usually, the houses were unlocked, so he and Alice would go inside and make out in one of the empty rooms. Alice allowed Rick to pet with provisions: He could feel her breasts under her sweater, above her bra, but not underneath it. And no unhooking. The one time he tried to undo it, she pushed his hand away and said, "Uh-uh, you know the rules." Rick immediately withdrew his hands. "I'm sorry," he'd said. "I'm just so crazy about you." She loved him a little more for saying that, and they only broke up because Rick's family moved to Scarsdale.

There was also a Bruno and a Jeff, both hardly worth mentioning because she only let them feel her breasts above her sweater and neither lasted more than a month.

Dillard and Emilia Mae worried about Alice. She was halfway through adolescence and they saw no signs of rebellion. Emilia Mae said that maybe she'd had enough rebellion in her for the both of them, but Dillard disagreed. "It'll come, and when it does, it'll be a doozy."

Alice had begun asking her mother questions about her father. At first, Emilia Mae was reluctant to talk about him. "He was never part of my life. His name was John, and I don't even know his last name. Never did. He meant nothing to me and should mean nothing to you."

But Alice persisted. She asked Reverend Klepper and Cora, but they'd never met him. "She didn't really speak of him," said Reverend Klepper. "Mostly she talked about..."

He had started to say, "Mostly she talked about getting rid of the baby," but realized that would hurt Alice. "Mostly she wanted to make sure the baby—you—were healthy."

Alice knew that Xena had been around then. She'd seen her last at Christmas dinner, and then Xena had said to Alice, "Your mother was a fine, smart young woman. I hope you know that." Alice found Xena's number and called her. "Hi, this is Alice Wingo, Emilia Mae's daughter."

Xena's hearing had deteriorated so that Alice had to repeat herself three times. "I'm trying to find my dad," she shouted. "Do you remember a man my mother was seeing when she worked at the Neptune Inn?"

There was silence, as if Xena was going through her Rolodex of memories. "Well, there were a few of them," she finally said.

Alice paused. That had never occurred to her. "I'm thinking of the one who would be my father. His name was John."

"Ah, that one, I think I do remember. He was a smart-looking young fellow. Looked like money."

"Really? What does money look like?"

"You know, clean. Nice shoes. Clothes. Hair. Had all his teeth. Like that."

Alice wondered if she or her mother looked like money. She thought about her mother's short skirts, pixie haircut, and too-high heels; about her own gapped front teeth and the flour that was perpetually in her hair. Nah, they didn't look like money, though they did have all their teeth.

She went to the Neptune Inn. It still had the wraparound porch with slat-wood rockers, and while it was one of the area's older landmarks, the porch was now green instead of gray, and the old white rockers were painted yellow.

The girl at the desk was only slightly older than Alice. When Alice asked if they still had their registers from 1947, the girl looked at her as if she'd never heard of 1947. "I haven't seen them," she said, snapping her gum.

Alice asked to see the manager, who turned out to be as interested in 1947 as the girl behind the desk. "After old man Bostwick died, we threw all that stuff out." He was chewing gum, too.

"Aren't you interested in the history of this place?" she asked.

The manager wore red suspenders that framed his belly and slopped over his pants. "History, schmistory. This place has enough of that stuff as is. I'm moving us into the sixties. Anyways, what does a cute thing like you want with 1947?"

"My mother worked here then."

When the manager shrugged, his belly rippled.

Alice went back to her mother and badgered her until Emilia Mae finally told Alice what she could: John was in real estate; he dressed like a professional. "As I remember, he was a bit of a snob."

"He looked like money, then?"

Her mother shrugged. "I guess he did. He wore snappy clothes and shoes. He was short and stocky. He lived in Albany but commuted back and forth. Worked in New York a lot, but it was cheaper to stay in New Rochelle. He was in real estate. I remember him saying that the suburbs around here were growing like fungus and he was going to get in on the ground floor. He was a little older than me. You have his same mud-brown eyes. That's all I know. Oh, and of course that cute gap between your teeth, I've told you about that."

Alice went to the New Rochelle library and dug out the Albany Yellow Pages. She looked up real estate companies and found only six listed. When no one was home, she would call each of them. Late one Monday afternoon, when her mother was working and Dillard was God knows where, Alice sat in the wooden scoop-back chair next to the round copper table where the telephone rested. How could she make her voice more grown-up? She thought about how the Wykagyl ladies spoke like actresses in old-fashioned movies and sprinkled their sentences with words like "lovely" and "charming."

She gave it a try: "Hello, my name is Alice Wingo, and I'm inquiring about one of your employees, a John somebody. Please forgive me, his last name has slipped my mind, but he was a lovely, well-groomed gentleman who showed me an absolutely charming house in New Rochelle, and I'd love to get back in touch with him about that house."

Six calls later, and no luck. Two of the companies had no Johns working for them, and the other four had no Johns in the entire New Rochelle area.

A few weeks later, Alice was sweeping up and getting ready to close the bakery when the tiny bell over the door jangled. A man of medium height, stocky with thinning brown hair and dark brown eyes came in. He wore a navy coat over a three-piece navy business suit, and black oxford shoes that shined so brightly they reflected his trousers. He smelled like leather and was probably a few years older than her mother.

Alice shook the flour out of her hair and smiled at him. "Hi, how can I help you?"

He smiled back, and she wondered if he saw what she saw staring back at her: mud-brown eyes and a wide space between the two front teeth. "I'm going to dinner at someone's house, and I said I'd bring dessert. Something expensive. What've you got?"

Alice couldn't take her eyes off him. His tie looked to be pure silk. His suit, coat, and shoes were impeccable. He looked like money. She wanted to ask, was his name John? Was he a real estate man? Did she look familiar to him? But she didn't want to scare him off.

"Strawberry shortcake, it's our specialty. People come from all over just for that."

"Sold! I'll take one."

She picked a cake from the shelf, packed it up in a white box and tied the red and white string around it. She saw how he watched her hands as she wrapped it up and wished she'd remembered to dig the chocolate out from under her nails. He pulled out a shiny wallet—alligator skin. As he sorted through his bills, she noticed that his hands were smooth and tan. His nails might have been buffed. He didn't wear a wedding band.

"Thanks, doll." He took the box and flashed another gap-toothed smile.

Alice waited until he was out the door and halfway down the block before she pulled off her apron, grabbed her purse, locked up the store, and followed him down the street.

At home, Emilia Mae prepared dinner—chicken Parmesan. Alice was usually home by five thirty. So was Dillard. By six neither had shown up. By six thirty Emilia Mae began to panic. She phoned the bakery. No answer. She called Alice's school friends and walked down the street, hoping she'd spot Dillard or Alice. Back home, she took the chicken Parmesan out of the oven. The smell of it made her gag. Waiting was the most helpless feeling.

At six forty-five, Dillard walked through the door as if being over an hour late was the most normal thing in the world.

"Smells good. What're you cooking?"

"Where the hell have you been? And I'm assuming you're not with Alice, who's also decided not to show up tonight."

"Well, that's a nice howdy-doo. I was out for a walk, but Alice? Where in the world is Alice?"

"If I knew, I wouldn't be asking you. This is not like her."

"I'll call the bakery."

"I did that. No answer."

"I'll drive down there. Wait here, I'll call you."

"Yeah, well please don't disappear for another two hours."

He kissed her on the head. "You're overreacting. This'll be fine."

"I'm not overreacting. This is *not* fine."

"You'll see. We'll all be sitting around the table eating your fabulous whatever it is before long."

"Chicken Parmesan. I hope to hell you're right."

Dillard grabbed his cap and coat. "I'll call you the minute I know something."

True to his word, he called her a short time later to say there was no sign of Alice at or around the bakery.

"That does it," she said. "I'm calling the police."

"Don't do that. We can handle this on our own. I'll search every street in town."

"Great, and while you search every street in town, I'm calling the cops."

Dillard knew it was irrational, but he thought back to Nick's death and his worry about being arrested. "Please, it's too early to call the cops."

"I don't care. I'm calling them anyway."

"Not until we've exhausted every possibility. I'll call you every fifteen minutes or so."

"You do that," said Emilia Mae, raising her voice. "But my daughter is missing, and I'm calling the cops."

"Not yet," said Dillard. "She probably went to the movies with a friend and forgot to tell us. Don't do anything rash."

"You know as well as I do, Alice doesn't disappear like that. I'm calling the cops now."

"Please Emilia..."

She slammed down the phone and dialed 0.

Chapter 21

Alice was still missing at eight o'clock, and Dillard was still driving around town. Emilia Mae had called the hospital and every friend of Alice's. Two policemen had come and gone, bearing a full description of Alice plus recent pictures of her. "We'll call you as soon as we have something," the taller one had said.

Emilia Mae found waiting alone unbearable.

She called Reverend Klepper.

"Alice is one of God's children," he said. "I know he is looking after her. For now, you must stay strong. You know how to do this."

She didn't find his words consoling. She didn't know how to do this. Her world felt as if it was tilting. She'd never looked to her mother for solace, but frantic now, she called and asked her to come over.

Geraldine breezed in ten minutes later wearing her faux leopard coat over jeans and a pink turtleneck with lipstick that matched. Emilia Mae had to laugh. "You put on lipstick for this?"

"I did it for you. Coming here looking like an old hag surely wasn't going to make things any better."

Emilia Mae understood that by her mother's logic, this was a kind gesture. She started to cry. "I'm really scared."

"I know," said Geraldine, sitting next to Emilia Mae on the couch. "She'll come back. I'm staying with you until she does. I know you're not the praying type, but I am." Geraldine closed her eyes and bowed her head. Emilia Mae wrapped her arms around her legs and rested her head on her knees. Geraldine moved closer to her. "You mustn't let yourself think the worst."

Emilia Mae laid her head on her mother's shoulder. She couldn't remember when they'd been this physically close. She smelled like gardenias and cigarette smoke.

"Poor child," said Geraldine.

She'd never used those words before. Her daughter had been a troubled child, a difficult child but never a poor one. Now, settled against her, Emilia Mae was more of a child than she'd ever been. Geraldine basked in the feeling of being needed.

The man must have heard her footsteps running down the street. Why else did he turn around so abruptly? He had the cake box tucked under his arm and held his other hand in the air as if he were waiting for someone to place something on it. "Hey there, sweetheart. I guess we both knew this was about something more than strawberry shortcake, didn't we?"

That's when Alice should have lied, said she was running home to dinner, but being this close to the gap-toothed man, she wasn't about to turn away.

"So, hi again," she said.

"Well, hello to you."

A wedge of silence stood between them until the man looked

at his watch. "We could stand here saying hello to each other all night, or we could go somewhere and have a drink. My dinner doesn't start for a few hours."

Alice laughed. "I don't drink. I'm only sixteen."

"Well, I'm a bit older than that. Stick with me, and I promise, you won't have any trouble getting a drink." He pointed to a green MG convertible parked at the corner. "I heard about this place off North Avenue, the High Life. Have you ever ridden in an MG?"

"Nope."

"Well, hop in, you're in for the ride of a lifetime."

It was a five-minute drive. No big deal. She knew the neighborhood. She'd passed the High Life many times, with its orange neon martini glass beneath it. This would be an adventure.

"Sure, why not?"

The car smelled like leather. The man turned on the engine, which sounded like a motorboat revving up. He drove fast. She could feel the road beneath her. Her hair whooshed around her face like the hair on a TV shampoo ad, and she wished someone from school could see her now.

The High Life was dim inside and smelled of old popcorn. The man led Alice past a row of barstools to a plum velvet booth in the back of the room, where they sat side by side. In the hazy light, she could see the dappled skin under his neck. He was balding and wore a thick silver wristwatch that kept banging against the table. He was older than her mother. Much older. He rested his elbow on the table, his chin in his hand, while he swallowed her with his eyes. "So...sweetheart. You do have a name, don't you?"

"Alice. And you are?"

"Marty. Marty Stone. Tell me, Alice with no last name, what do you do besides bake beautiful cakes and make the hearts of grown men beat faster?"

"I go to high school," said Alice, trying to think of reasons why John might have changed his name to Marty.

"Yeah, so high school. That's nice. Any favorite subjects?"

"Music. I like to sing."

"I'll bet you have a sweet voice. Why don't you sing a little something for me?"

"Oh, no, not here."

"Then maybe somewhere more private?" He raised his eyebrows suggestively.

Alice had met men like this at the bakery. They'd make off-color remarks or pat her inappropriately. Dillard or her mom and grandma were always close by, so she could afford to shrug them off. This was different. She was alone with a strange man in a strange place who was studying her a little too closely and talking to her in a way that made her feel as if spiders were crawling up her back. Thank God the waitress showed up. "What'll it be kids?" She winked at Marty.

"Two beers, hon."

Alice knew that she could get up from the booth and run out of the bar whenever she wanted. But something held her there: Was it the fear that Marty might run after her? Was she worried about being rude? Maybe she was a little curious. Maybe she felt cool being in a place like this with a man like that. Maybe that's what held her here.

Marty asked her what her dad did.

"We all work in the bakery," she said.

"Got any sisters or brothers?"

"Nope, just me."

They talked about the bakery, and about New Rochelle. "I'm a Bostonian, been here a few times. Seems like a nice place, but everything outside a big city seems like the country to me."

His Boston accent was thick. Alice didn't remember her mother saying anything about John having an accent.

Marty talked about himself with gusto, as if he was used to entertaining people with his stories. That was another thing her mother hadn't told her about John.

Alice took a sip of the beer. It was bitter and made her want to make a face, but she forced herself not to and took two more sips. Emboldened by the drink, she said, "So, Marty, what do *you* do?"

Marty wiped foam from his lips with his monogrammed handkerchief. "A little of this and that, you know."

Alice took another sip. "Like what?"

"I dabble in the stock market. I play the horses at Suffolk Downs."

"Did you ever dabble in real estate?"

"Nah, real estate's a pussy's game."

Now there wasn't a sliver of reason for Alice to be here.

Marty looked at his watch again, stood up, and took Alice's hand. "Come, let's you and me take a look at the jukebox. Maybe there's something there you'll want to sing along to." He took two quarters from his pants pocket and punched a bunch of buttons. Andy Williams's weeper, "Moon River," started playing.

"Dance with me," he said, pulling her close enough that she could feel her breasts crush against his chest.

"C'mon, let's hear you sing," he said, sliding his hand to the top of her behind.

"I don't know all the words," she lied.

She got through "Moon River" but said her throat hurt when Sinatra's "Bewitched" came on.

"I really need to get home," she said. "My parents are expecting me."

Marty glanced down at his watch. "Aw, come on. It's not even eight thirty yet."

"No really," she said, trying to wriggle out of his arms. "I've got to get home."

"You're like a ray of sunshine," he said, pulling her closer. Struggling her way out of his clutch wouldn't work. She'd have to sweet-talk herself out of it.

"What a nice thing to say. I'm sorry to be rude, but I really do have to get home. My parents expected me home hours ago; they're gonna kill me for being late. You wouldn't want that to happen now, would you?"

Marty loosened his grip. "Anyone lays a hand on you, you let ol' Marty know about it."

"I appreciate that," said Alice, not knowing if he was kidding or not.

"So, at least tell me your last name. If you don't, it's easy enough to find out. I'll just come back to the bakery."

"Wingo," she said, slipping out of his arms. "Thank you for the drink and the ride in the MG." She managed a tepid smile, then grabbed her jacket and walked quickly out of the bar.

"Alice Wingo," he shouted, as she headed toward the door. "We'll meet again."

Out in the street, Alice's heart was beating so fast she had to lean against a car to catch her breath. When she started walking, she turned to see if Marty had followed her. He hadn't. She remembered that in her haste to leave, she'd left her purse in the bar. No way she was going back in there. Except now, she had no coins to call home and had no way to get there. Her throat tightened but she stopped herself from crying with the thought that tears were a waste of time; she had to figure out how to get away from the High Life and Marty Stone. She started running in the direction of home, hoping that someone she knew would see her. People were out. It was a Friday night. Surely someone would recognize her.

After about fifteen minutes, her pace slowed to a walk. She sensed a light shining behind her. A car seemed to be following her, its headlights bearing down on her. Marty Stone? She started to run again and didn't turn around. The headlights came closer, illuminating the yellow witch hazel buds on the side of the road. She jumped at the sound of a honk then jumped again at the second honk. It was only when she heard a familiar voice call her name that she turned around.

Dillard. Thank God. He pulled the Pontiac to the side of the road and got out. "Alice, where have you been? Are you okay?"

She hugged him. "I'm fine," she said, and began to cry. She could smell his freshly ironed shirt, the clover scent of Dial soap. He smelled safe, like home. Dillard kissed her forehead. "You're okay, sweetie." They stood that way on the side of the road until another car whizzed by and made them realize they were in harm's way. Dillard took her by the arm, opened the car door, and helped her in. "Do I smell beer on your breath?" he asked.

Alice didn't want to tell him why she was following this man or how she said nothing when he pulled her so close to dance and put his hand on her rear end. She told herself she let him do these things because she was frightened not to and didn't allow herself the thought that she might have also been flattered.

"There was this party after school. And, um, I got a ride with some kids to the party, which is around here. There was a lot of drinking, and then one kid got into a fight with another kid, and I just wanted to get out of there. By the time I was about a block away, I realized I'd left my purse at the party, but didn't want to go back there so I started walking home. That's when you found me. And I didn't call because I thought you all would be mad at me for not telling you in advance. I only had a sip or two of the beer to taste it. I didn't like it, by the way."

Alice watched Dillard's jaw tighten as she told her story. When she finished, he said, "Okay, let's get you home, and we'll deal with all that later." She could tell he didn't believe her.

"So, you've never done anything that seemed a good idea at the time, then turned out to be stupid?" she asked.

"Sure, I have. Who hasn't? I'm as far from perfect as the moon is from the sun. Honestly, sweetie, you scared the crap out of me." His mouth twisted in a funny way.

"I'm sorry," she said. "I love you."

"I love you, too. Please don't pull something like this again."

"I won't. But can you promise me something?"

"Anything."

"Don't tell my mother about the beer."

Dillard laughed. "Okay, I won't, though I think she's heard worse."

He stopped the car when he saw a phone booth. "I'm calling your mom. Let me get this straight: party, fight, you ran out, forgot your purse, no beer. Right?"

"Right," said Alice, ashamed of how easy it had been to lie.

He looked upset when he came back to the car. "Your mother called the police. They'll be there when we get home. They want to ask you a few questions. Are you ready for that?"

Alice shrugged.

"I'm not suggesting that you lied to me, but it matters that you tell them the truth."

"Okay. Including the beer?"

"Yup, everything."

Alice couldn't imagine how she would tell the cops about Marty Stone and the High Life and the dancing. No, she'd stick to the party story.

Emilia Mae must have heard the car pull up when they got home. She ran out in her bare feet and embraced Alice. In the glare of the car's front headlights, Alice could see that her mother had been crying. Geraldine ran out of the house, her faux leopard coat flapping behind her. "Thank God you're okay," she said, hugging Alice, who was hugging Emilia Mae. Then she leaned in and whispered, "The cops are here. They want to interview you."

Dillard shot Alice a look. "Remember what I said."

The tall cop took his notebook out and asked Alice a lot of questions. She told him about the party and the fight and how she'd left early and forgotten her purse there.

The short one asked, "Were they serving alcohol?"

"Some, yeah," said Alice. "But I just had a Coke before I left." She glanced at Dillard, who was staring at the floor.

"Is there anything else you want to tell us?"

"No, sir. I didn't stay long enough to see a whole lot."

The tall cop closed his notebook. "Okay, that's it. I guess I don't have to tell you this, young lady, but going off without telling your folks where you are can lead to a lot of wasted time and unnecessary worry."

"I know, sir."

The tall cop wrote something down, then tore a page from his notebook and handed it to her. "If you think of anything else we ought to know, give us a call."

Alice said she would and tucked the paper into her coat pocket.

The shorter one turned to Dillard. "May I assume you're the girl's father?"

Dillard folded his hands behind his head. "No, I'm no blood kin. I'm married to the girl's mother."

The cop opened his notebook. "Good. May I have your name and birthdate please?"

Dillard hesitated. "It's not really important. I'm not from around here."

"Doesn't matter," said the cop, pen poised. "I just need to know the names of the adults who share the girl's home."

"Okay, so my name is Dillard Fox." He spelled it out and told the cop his birthdate. But he kept his eyes focused on the floor as if waiting for something to happen.

Two days later, Dillard came into the music room, where Alice was practicing. "I just got a phone call from the High Life," he said. "They have your purse."

Alice looked up at him and started to speak.

Dillard raised his hand to stop her. "Doesn't matter," he said. "We all have secrets. Yours are safe with me."

Chapter 22

By 1965, New Rochelle had become a town full of diverse people who only mingled when they had to. There was the North End, with its mansions and grand Tudors: whites only. Black families lived on Lincoln Avenue and Horton Avenue in everything from ramshackle old Cape Cods to apartments and grand colonials. Jews and Catholics filled the center of town's small wood-framed houses, three-story Victorians, or newer sprawling ranch houses. All of New Rochelle coalesced on Main Street, where the jewelry stores, pizzerias, and bars trailed one another on the sloping street. None were higher than two stories or much wider than an Airstream.

But the very center of town, where all of New Rochelle truly came together, was at the Touch Up Salon at 515 Main Street, specifically, at the station of one André Bellini, who was known around town as the Hair Wizard.

Everyone knew that André Bellini was not his real name and that he was neither French nor Italian. His real name was Alberto Lozano and he was probably from someplace South that had given him his toasty coloring and curly midnight-black hair. Small and trim, with black sagging eyes and an accent that no one could identify, he dressed immaculately, with a pocket square in his suit jacket that always matched his shirt. If a customer seemed nervous, he'd stroke her arm and reassure her. "Don't worry, André will make you and your hair extremely happy." He claimed that anyone who sat in his chair became an open book to him. It wasn't just that women confided in him or that he saw them at their most vulnerable; he maintained that their body language, the way they comported themselves, and how honest each was about her hair situation told him all he needed to know about a person. He saw the teenage girls before prom, the middle-aged women pre-cruise, and the older women shamed by their bald spots. In his hands, a flip became the lip of a wave. He turned curly hair into silky pageboys, and thinning hair into rich foam. He knew how much Spray Net to use, and how to tease the hair enough to give it body yet not make it look as airy as a spider web. Some of the richer men in town would see André late at night for color jobs or elaborate comb-overs.

No one ever asked his age or whether he dyed his own hair because, frankly, no one wanted to know. New Rochelle was a gritty town with few myths. The statue of Jacob Leisler that hailed people in the middle of town was one of them. (Did anyone really know who Jacob Leisler was?) The Hair Wizard was another, and everyone was happy to keep it that way.

All they knew about André was that he lived alone in the South End of town and never seemed to have a partner. But all that changed just around the time that Alice went missing for an evening.

★ ★ ★

Elaine Treaster was one of New Rochelle's socialites and a regular at Shore Cakes. She was always buying scones or croissants by the dozen for the many parties she gave, to which Geraldine was never invited. Nonetheless, the two developed a friendship, of sorts, based on gossip and rumor. Geraldine told Elaine which stores were going out of business and who might be embezzling from whom. In return, Elaine told Geraldine who was getting divorced and who might be pregnant. One afternoon, after Elaine told Geraldine about the history teacher at New Rochelle High who was rumored to be sleeping with the school nurse, and Geraldine told Elaine about the man—"some city slicker from God knows where"— who'd exposed himself to a bunch of young girls at the local RKO theater, Elaine leaned over the counter and said to Geraldine in a conspiratorial manner: "Listen, I'm having a little do at my home Saturday night, a fundraiser for the Art Association." She leaned in farther. "I'm a painter, you know. Anyway, it's going to be nothing fancy, but I thought you might like to come."

Geraldine was nonplussed. She had dreams of being a social butterfly in this town, but for whatever reason, she never took wing. "Why yes, I'd be thrilled to come."

"Excellent," said Elaine. "And if you don't mind, could you bring two or three of your splendid strawberry shortcakes? They'll be such a hit."

For a moment, Geraldine had felt elevated out of her world. In this small town, she led a small life in a small house. Her younger self thought it would be bigger than this. Grander even. Oh God, was she just the middle-aged lady who ran the town bakery?

The Treasters lived in one of the expensive Queen Annes that overlooked Long Island Sound. Geraldine could never understand how chinless Elaine, who looked like a gopher with her short brown hair, large overbite, and small probing eyes, had snared Leon Treaster, whom everyone knew was rolling in money that he'd inherited from his parents, owners of Treaster's Ballroom Dance Halls. Geraldine pushed that thought aside and concentrated on her immediate needs. What would she wear? No shopping at Alexander's for this party. Of course, she'd have to get her hair done. The Touch Up was only three blocks from the bakery. She'd gotten friendly with the receptionist, Kitty (not her real name, but what everyone called her because of the cat-motif sweaters she favored), who'd come in on her breaks to buy black-and-white cookies. Sometimes, Geraldine and Kitty had gone out back and smoked together. She called Kitty and asked for a Saturday afternoon appointment. "I've been invited to some fancy shindig and I really need to get dolled up."

"Don't worry," said Kitty. "I'll set you up with the Hair Wizard. Come by at three thirty." Which is how Geraldine Wingo fell under the spell of André Bellini.

From the moment Geraldine sat in his chair, André felt an unease about her. "You are not a satisfied woman, are you?" he said, massaging her scalp. His words were not harsh or judgmental. Geraldine relaxed her head into his hands. "I wouldn't go that far," she said. "But it's true, I don't get out enough, and that doesn't make me happy."

"A woman like you must always be satisfied." He'd taken stock of her black Capri pants, polka-dotted blouse, and fierce red lipstick. "What I see here is a beautiful woman in the weeds. It's time you come out of the weeds, no?"

Geraldine got teary. "Exactly. That's exactly where I am in my life. Stuck in the weeds, and I don't know how to get out. I work at Shore Cakes all day and go to church every Sunday. That's about it. How could you possibly know this about me?"

"I've seen you at the bakery. You make a fine babka, by the way. How you move, in such hurried motions, and the sweat that pours out of you. Your heart is overworked, but not by the right things. We must change you."

"*We* are going to change *me*?" she asked.

"Yes," said André. "But first we wash."

André rubbed shampoo into her scalp, building peaks of foam. He massaged her temples, behind her ears, and places on her head she never knew as pleasure spots. The shampoo smelled of apples, and the water temperature was just right, which put Geraldine in a dreamy state. After the shampoo, André combed out her hair, which fell below her shoulders. "Too much," he said. "It weighs you down." He ran his fingers through her hair and fluffed it up around her ears.

"Insouciance," he said with some drama. "This cries out for joie de vivre. Do you trust André to give you back your life, to get you out of the weeds?"

Geraldine had to laugh. He sounded more like Father Daley than a hairdresser. "What the hell?" She shrugged. "Do whatever you want."

André started cutting. Geraldine watched him in the mirror.

"May I make another suggestion?" he asked.

"Go ahead."

"Close your eyes. Think about other things. Maybe even sleep. I'll tell you when I'm ready. Trust me."

"Okay," said Geraldine, who felt sweat trickle down between her breasts.

She must have dozed because when André said, "You can open your eyes now," she had no idea that time had passed. He stood behind her with his hands on her shoulders. "I'm ready if you are."

Geraldine stared in the mirror. It took her a few moments to realize that the person looking back at her—the one with the bouncy flip and jaunty bangs—was her.

"Jesus Christ, I look like Laura Petrie."

"Exactly," said André. "This is a good thing, no?"

Bubbly Laura Petrie was Rob Petrie's wife on TV's *The Dick Van Dyke Show*, which, coincidentally, took place in New Rochelle. Laura, played by Mary Tyler Moore, was a beloved character in town. She was insouciant. She had joie de vivre. Geraldine studied her Laura Petrie bangs and André's slender hands on her shoulders. She looked ten years younger. He really was some kind of a genius. The realization that she loved this man made her woozy.

She reached up, took his hand in hers and squeezed it. "André Bellini, you are *the* hair wizard, *my* hair wizard."

André must have felt what Geraldine felt because he squeezed her hand back and said, "You may call me Alberto."

New Rochelle was not any more gossipy than most towns. No one had enough time for that kind of thing. Many had jobs in nearby Manhattan and caught early trains, or they worked at home, raising children and keeping house. But somehow, the union of Geraldine Wingo and Alberto Lozano or André Bellini or whatever his name was got tongues wagging.

They made a curious pair: the tall Italian beauty and the diminutive hairdresser. Her brown eyes shone down on his black ones. When they held hands, hers completely wrapped around his, and when they kissed, some folks claimed they saw him standing on tiptoes. Nonetheless, everyone could tell they were in love. The way they'd whisper things to one another and laugh. In a short amount of time, they'd built their own world, populating it with their own funny characters. He called her his Queen of Hearts because, he said, she looked like the lady in the cards. He was her Hair Wizard. He smoothed her edges; she rounded off his pretensions. She made fun of him, not in a mean way, just enough to make him more accessible and less formal. In turn, when she would get angry, he'd hold her and say, "You don't have to go headfirst into the storm."

As an unexpected consequence of their union, the two of them became that year's flavor du jour of the social set. When Elaine Treaster invited them to her July Fourth bash, she did not ask Geraldine to also bring strawberry shortcake.

Chapter 23

Every Sunday night, Dillard made his special dish: linguine with white clam sauce. Canned clams, olive oil, a splash of white wine, chopped parsley, and lots of garlic. The perfect dinner. It was cheap and briny, but nonetheless the perfume of the garlic floated through the house and lingered long after they'd finished. Sunday nights were when Emilia Mae felt safest. She, Alice, Dillard, and sometimes Geraldine and Alberto, nestled in a cloud of garlic: a happy home.

But inevitably, Sundays would melt into Mondays. On one of those Mondays, Emilia Mae woke up in a dark mood. All that had felt in harmony the night before had disintegrated even before her alarm rang. Alice was seventeen and would be going to college next year. About Dillard, Emilia Mae had uneasy feelings without knowing why. And then there was that unnerving incident at the bakery last Saturday, which brought her face to face with her own truths.

It was windy and rainy that day. The radio kept warning of a nor'easter, but no snow had materialized. Yet the day was dreary enough to keep customers away, so the store was empty when

Emilia Mae came in from the bake room carrying a tray of warm chocolate chip cookies. She'd bent over to slide them into a display case when she heard the door open and felt a spray of water trickle down her back. A man in a yellow slicker, white cable knit sweater, and jeans was shaking out his umbrella all over her.

"I'm so sorry, I didn't see you there, and now I've gotten you soaked."

Emilia Mae shoved the cookies in the case and stood up. "That's okay." She laughed. "I thought I was being baptized." The man laughed as well and asked if she had a towel nearby. Emilia Mae had been carrying the tray with two dish towels, so she handed him one. She thought he'd use it to wipe off his wet pant legs, but instead, he dabbed her back a few times then took a long sniff. "Mmm, chocolate, I could live in that smell forever."

There was thunder in his voice, like Richard Burton in *Cleopatra*. Emilia Mae looked him up and down. He was shorter than she was, stocky with a brown crewcut, stick-out ears, and seaweed-colored eyes. He wasn't handsome except when he smiled a brazen smile that overtook his face. He dabbed her shoulders a few times then said with that smile, "There now, I've absolved you of all your sins."

"I doubt it," she said.

She could feel the imprint of his hand on her shoulder. She wanted to reach out and take his hands in hers. Her face was hot. He'd smiled at her in a way that suggested his thoughts might have been similar. She turned on her most professional bakery voice. "So, how can I help you?"

"I'd like four pieces of cheese Danish."

She checked his left hand for a wedding ring. When she saw

none, she reached down and gave him a free chocolate chip cookie, which he popped into his mouth in one bite.

"Thank you," he said, the sweetness clogging his throat. "You're an angel."

"Just so you know, I bake fresh chocolate chip cookies every Saturday around ten. Free samples for favorite customers." She winked at him.

He smiled a different kind of smile. "Noted," he boomed. "I'll see you soon again."

"I hope so," Emilia Mae whispered.

As he left the shop, Emilia Mae stood behind the window staring out at nothing but lost in thoughts having everything to do with trouble. Why had she acted that way? Wasn't she happily married? She might as well have hiked up her skirt and said, "Here, have a go." *Holy moly*, she thought. *I really am my mother's daughter.*

She tried shooing away her Monday morning blues by watching Dillard sleep. The tension bled out of him, his mouth softened as if he was about to blow a bubble, and his long lashes winged his eyes. She could imagine him as a boy, a sweet boy whose mother should have kissed his beautiful face every morning. She leaned over and did just that. As mothers went, Geraldine was no prize, but at least Emilia Mae had always known where she was. Dillard's father had probably been nice enough, but he was never around either, and Aunt Denise sounded like a sourpuss, not at all the type to kiss a sleeping boy. All that love he never got. Emilia Mae always swore she'd make up to him.

Their marriage was a happy one, wasn't it? Everyone who saw them assumed it was. After three years, he was still buying her gifts, making sure the house was tidy and pretty. He still took her hand in public and would kiss her head or cheek for no particular reason. He loved her. She was stupid to even think of jeopardizing all that.

He was a dream father to Alice, not to mention the music. Alice had become an accomplished singer, thanks to their daily practice sessions. Dillard sometimes took her to recitals at Carnegie Hall or Lincoln Center, and never stopped encouraging her. She always landed the key parts in school plays and was taking private jazz singing lessons once a week. Tom Deutsch, Alice's music teacher, said she was a natural and urged her to apply to his alma mater, the New England Conservatory of Music. It was Dillard who helped her fill out her applications and took her to Boston for her interview. Emilia Mae finally had what she'd always wanted, so why was she stirring up trouble, if only in her mind?

It was Dillard. She had questions that begged answers and answers she'd shove away whenever they came too close. Where did he go when he disappeared for hours at a time? When women customers flirted with him, why did he never flirt back? Dumb things annoyed her, like how he crammed food into his mouth when he thought no one was looking. Why was he vague about the missing pieces of his life? Why did he go blank in the middle of a conversation? Just last Saturday, there'd been a terrible thunderstorm. It felt cozy in the house. She'd asked Dillard to lie on the couch with her and watch the rain out the window. He lay down for about three minutes, then jumped up, claiming he'd left his hat on the outside porch and didn't want it to get wet. That ugly tweed flat cap. He wore it everywhere and never explained why. But every marriage had its quirks, right? She remembered her vows about assisting him in his striving, satisfying his needs and all that.

Yeah, sure, but what about her needs? What about having someone who made her feel the way the cheese Danish man had made her feel that morning? Dillard was an adequate lover. He knew all the right spots and tended to them efficiently. She didn't lose her way as she had in the early days of their marriage. They only made love at night, and not before Dillard signaled that they would by making a box of Kleenex ready on his nightstand. Yes, he was able to get hard, even if it was short-lived. He never, overcome by desire, grabbed her from behind or initiated unplanned sex. He preferred to shower alone.

She told herself that all marriages cooled down sexually after a few years, and the important part was that he loved her. But every now and then (like now), the part of her that wanted someone to make her lose herself woke up. Was it wrong of her to wish for more of that?

These were the places she'd trained her mind not to travel, the subjects she'd bundled up and sealed, along with thoughts about other men. These were the times she willed herself back into the sweet garlicky nests of those Sunday nights and resolved that was where she would stay.

Chapter 24

Alice Wingo is an intuitive singer who commandeers a song the way Ella Fitzgerald does a Cole Porter melody. She is that rare talent who manages to give herself to an audience without compromise, and lose herself in the music without sacrifice.

—Tom Deutsch, music teacher

I am the reverend of a small Baptist church in New Rochelle, New York. I have known Alice Wingo since birth and have watched her grow into the beautiful person she is today. Alice has the heart of an angel and the voice of one, too. In my line of work, music is a window into the soul. God has blessed Alice Wingo's voice and soul with beauty and purity. I believe it is His intent for her to share that gift with the world.

—Reverend Aloysius Klepper

What school, in its right mind, would turn down a student with a recommendation from God and Ella Fitzgerald? Not the New England Conservatory. Alice would start there in September. But first she had to live through the spring and summer of 1966.

On a Wednesday evening in May, she went downstairs to the music room to practice some songs. Dillard kept his pitch pipe on the shelf in the closet, and as she reached for it, she noticed the cigar box where he kept his personal stuff. Pieces of letters were sticking out, as if someone had recently rummaged through it and taken no time to put it back neatly.

When Alice pulled it out, envelopes addressed to Dillard dropped to the floor. A photograph fell next to her foot. The envelopes had no return address, but somehow Alice knew they were private and she ought not look inside them. But the picture that lay by her toes was a different story. She wasn't that much of a saint.

She shoved the envelopes back into the box and placed it on the shelf. Then she knelt down and picked up the photograph. It was a black-and-white photograph of some strange man standing next to Dillard. The man was older and bigger and had an arm around Dillard's shoulder. He was laughing, as if he'd just been told a wonderful joke, and Dillard was looking up at him, smiling. They were both dressed in T-shirts and shorts. Behind them was a lake, a floating dock, and people in bathing suits. The man appeared to be nice looking, though Alice couldn't really tell. But she did notice his cap. It was tweed and the same flat cap style as Dillard always wore.

The date printed on the side of the photograph was August 1959, a little more than a year before Dillard showed up at the bakery. Alice studied the man's face to see if he resembled Dillard.

His father? Couldn't be; Dillard's father died years before that. An uncle? An old family friend? Something about the way the two men looked at each other made her think probably not. Her heart raced. Who was this man? Why hadn't Dillard ever mentioned him? Dillard was everything to her; hadn't they told each other all there was to tell about their lives? Well, she never did tell him about the men she'd followed and what really happened that night at the High Life. Maybe there were things he hadn't told her. She felt scared, as if something irrevocable had just happened.

She sat in Dillard's chair with the photograph propped up on her lap. Last night they'd worked out a jazz version of "A Taste of Honey." The music was still swimming in her head: her voice, the filigree sounds of his flute. They were fine. He was fine. She was making too much of it. She put the picture away and tried to push it out of her mind.

On Friday night, she and Dillard practiced "A Taste of Honey"; on Saturday they worked side by side at the bakery. Dillard was the same as always. If anyone was different, it was Geraldine. Since Alberto, Alice thought her grandma had gone through a personality change. She was cheerful, even to Emilia Mae. Dillard and she had settled into their own embarrassing kind of banter, telling the other how beautiful or handsome they looked, with lots of "if only I were youngers" thrown in. Grandma had taken to chucking Alice under the chin and asking, "How's my favorite grandchild today?" Alice always came back with the same answer: "I'm your *only* grandchild." Grandma would laugh as if it were the funniest joke ever.

She and Alberto were always kissing and rubbing each other's backs. When he said something that was clearly meant to be dirty,

Geraldine would punch him on the arm and smile a fake smile that showed her gums. Like so many things, Alice found that embarrassing.

On Sundays, as they always did, she, Emilia Mae, and Dillard walked to church. After the service, Dillard would take his usual walk with Reverend Klepper, and Alice and Emilia Mae would go to Geraldine's and help with lunch. Since Alberto, Sunday lunch with the Kleppers was no longer simply a roast and potatoes. It seemed that when Alberto moved in with Geraldine last fall, Julia Child came with him. Now they had canapés like *celery-rave rémoulade* or *amuse-guele au Roquefort* and things called *bifteck sauté au beurre* and *coq au vin*. None of them, including Geraldine and Alberto, spoke French, so no one ever knew what they were eating, except Alberto, who had followed Julia Child's recipes to a T. He would lay elaborate food platters before them, try to pronounce their names in French, and then pile heaping portions on everyone's plate. Geraldine would explain that Alberto was a gourmet cook. "That's just one of his many talents," she'd say, waggling her eyebrows.

On this particular Sunday, Alberto and Julia had gone to town: *Foie de veau sauté, asperges,* and *riz à l'Indienne*. Despite the pretty sound of it, and the sprigs of parsley adorning it, there was no escaping that the glistening piece of brown meat on everyone's plate was liver. Alice cut the liver into tiny pieces and hid them under the *riz à L'indienne*, which despite its fancy name, she knew to be steamed rice. Reverend Klepper gamely shoved pieces of it in his mouth, followed by gulps of whatever fancy wine Alberto was serving. Dillard made some offhand comment about how he wished there was a big dog under the table, while Emilia Mae poured lots of salt and pepper on the meat and ate it all.

When Alberto came to serve Cora, she put her hands over her plate and said, "Sorry, my friend, no can do. But I'm happy to have some *ritz* and *asper-gees*, however you say it."

Geraldine looked horrified. "Cora! Alberto is a genius cook. He worked all morning on this. You might give it a try."

Alberto walked over to Geraldine and put his hand on her shoulder. "You are sweet, but not everyone has a palate for this sort of thing."

"I have a palate for hamburgers," said Dillard.

Everyone except Geraldine laughed.

"Mmm, hamburgers," said Emilia Mae. "With American cheese and french fries on the side."

For a moment, the entire table fell into a silent reverie. When they came back to the business of liver, Cora pointed out to Geraldine that she had no meat on her plate.

Geraldine swirled her head around to look at Alberto. Her hair, now in a Shirley MacLaine pixie, sprang behind her. She stroked Alberto's hand. "Alberto says that eating too much meat is the reason my pores are clogged. So, I'll abstain. From the meat, any-way." She flashed another of those smiles. When Alberto served *tarte Normande aux pommes*, Geraldine plopped a second helping onto her plate. Cora winked at Alice, and Alice studied Dillard. He was having a good time.

"Does Alberto worry about you getting fat from all that cake?" Cora asked.

Reverend Klepper's eyes got larger than usual as he stared at his wife.

Geraldine answered, her mouth full of apples and *crème fraiche*: "Alberto doesn't give a crap about my weight."

Alberto, still standing behind Geraldine, kissed her on the cheek. "You have a marvelous way with words."

In between all that, the image of Dillard and that man would catch Alice up short, as if someone had thrown a pebble at her window. She got it in her head to mention the photograph to Reverend Klepper and Cora, certain they would tell her it was no big deal. When lunch was finally over and the Kleppers readied to leave, she said, "Mind if I walk you home?"

"We'd be honored," said Cora, lacing her arm through Alice's.

Alice loved Cora. Even with age written on her freckled face, she was still a beauty. Her graying hair was closely cropped, giving emphasis to her wide green eyes. When she laughed, which she did often, Dillard said they blazed like a cat's eyes in the dark.

Emilia Mae always said that Cora was the only grown-up she knew who never talked down to children, and Alice thought she was right. She remembered how Cora had explained to her why people snickered at the lyrics to "Louie Louie," and how, when she was doubled over with cramps at a church picnic, Cora had given her a couple of Midol. The pills were too big for Alice to swallow, so Cora broke them into pieces, slipped a few drops of red wine into Alice's Coke, and said, "Here, these should go down easy now."

It was a beautiful May afternoon with a slight breeze coming off the Sound. The three of them small-talked about the church and some of the parishioners. Reverend Klepper allowed that he was preparing next week's sermon on Vietnam and was unsure how far to take it.

"You take it as far as you can, Ally," said Cora. "It all comes down to morality. This war is all about saving face and money. Morality doesn't even enter into it. So, what's the question?"

Reverend Klepper laughed. "It's not as simple as that, Cora. Some of the parishioners have boys over there. I can't simply swat away their purpose with high-mindedness."

Cora stopped walking. "You're not judging those boys. It's the men who are sending them over there who need to be held accountable."

"True, we have compassion for those who serve, but we have no compassion for those who do not serve yet send these young men off to war," said Klepper in his stentorian sermon voice. He nodded. "Yup, that works."

Alice took this conversation as her cue. "Speaking of compassion, can I ask you two a question?"

"Sure," they both said.

"So, I found this picture the other day. It fell out of a box that Dillard keeps in our music room. I know it's probably no big deal but... It's a picture of a man. Older than Dillard. He's got his arm around Dillard and he's laughing. Dillard is looking up at him and smiling. The weird thing is, you know that cap that Dillard always wears? Well the man's wearing the same one. In fact, it could be the exact same one."

"Do you have any idea who the man is?" asked Reverend Klepper.

"Not at all."

"A relative, perhaps?" asked Cora.

"No one he's ever mentioned."

"Ask him about it," said Cora.

"You know, Dillard and I have told each other everything about ourselves. I'm sure it's no big deal. I should probably just forget it."

"You'll find as you get older, Alice, that people are not always completely revealing about themselves," said Reverend Klepper, glancing at Cora. "Even people who are very close. I have no doubt that Dillard loves you and would be unhappy to know you were troubled about this. Cora's right, ask him who the man is."

"Really? Just like that?"

"Yes," he said. "If you don't, then you become burdened by a secret, and you don't want that. Trust me."

Chapter 25

Nearly a week after Alice found the photograph, Dillard and she were alone seated opposite from one another in the music room. They'd just finished practicing "A Taste of Honey," and Dillard told her she'd never sounded better. "You're going to outshine every alto at the conservatory."

Alice looked at him and studied the room he'd created. She loved the crisp whiteness of the walls and how his father's antique instruments glowed against them. She loved how her stool faced Dillard's chair and how they watched each other while he played the flute and she sang. She'd never shared this kind of intimacy with anyone except her grandpa. She'd miss all this when she went to Boston.

"You know, I'm kind of scared about going away," she said. "I mean, I know it's an honor to go to the conservatory, but I've never been away from home. I'll miss you."

"I'll miss you too, sweetie, but Boston's not so far. We'll see each other more than you think. You might even get sick of me, with all your new college friends."

"I'll never get sick of you. Are you sick of your old friends?"

"What old friends?"

"You know, friends you had before you came here."

"No, not really. I see them sometimes. But you go to new places; you make new friends." He smiled. "I'm not unhappy to see them, but I've never had friends like the friends I have here."

"That reminds me," she said. "The other day I was looking for our pitch pipe, and some stuff fell out of the cigar box you keep in the closet. I put everything back, but there was this one photograph I couldn't help noticing because it fell right next to me. It was of you and a man, older than you. He was laughing, and you were smiling at him. He was wearing a hat just like yours. Or maybe it's the same one, I don't know, but anyway..."

Dillard's smile vanished, and his voice went stiff. "What were you doing snooping through my stuff?"

"I wasn't snooping. The picture fell by my feet."

Dillard stood up and turned away from her. "Jesus, I thought of all people I could trust you."

"You can," she said, her voice climbing.

"God, Alice, you do not go poking into other people's business. I swear, I don't understand."

"I'm sorry, I really am. I was just..."

"Don't. There's nothing more to say." He stormed out of the room without his cap, and then came back a moment later to retrieve it. "I forgot this. Unless you want to keep it as a piece of evidence," he said, before leaving again.

The heat of Dillard's anger scared Alice. She remembered that first dinner when he walked out in the same abrupt manner. Grandma made some crack about him being an escaped convict and leaving a trail of bodies behind him. Everyone thought she was joking then. Now Alice wasn't so sure. She stayed glued to her chair. Tears stung her eyes. She was terrified that Dillard would never speak to her again.

That Sunday, Reverend Klepper delivered his sermon about Vietnam. He paced back and forth with his hands crossed over his heart before he began. In his early sixties, he was slightly stooped, probably from all those years of towering over people and bending to their size. His thick hair was white, and he'd slimmed down so that his large nose and alpine cheekbones rose more prominently from his pale face. Although his voice occasionally broke when he led the hymns, it had not lost its power to move. He still had that odd way of staring that made every parishioner think he was staring at all of them at the same time.

"The piece of God we all carry within us is goodness and purity," he began. "I believe that's how we all begin. But as we age, and life carves its scars onto us, a blackness can creep in that snakes around our hearts, causing us to yield to immoral thoughts and craven temptations. Where there are riches to be had, there is greed. Where there is truth to hide, there are lies. Where there is need for moral rectitude, there is cynicism. In shame or disillusion, we turn away from God just when we need Him the most. Right now, our country is engaged in a war that some say is corrupt, and others swear is necessary. While I am not a military expert, I do know that we are sending our sons, some of whom are members of this parish, to fight a war they didn't choose. Some are in Vietnam out of obligation, others because they believe they are fighting for the freedom of this country. And then there are those who have no idea why they are there. We have compassion for all these courageous young men, but we have little compassion for those who do not serve yet send these young men off to war with little explanation." Cora turned to Alice and winked at her. "Their impulses are not pure; their motives are not genuine. They are turning innocent young boys into embittered adults."

Reverend Klepper went on to talk about these battered souls. "What happens when the darkness lingers, obliterating all hope? Then what are we to do? I've thought long and hard about this. I've spoken unkind words and had vile thoughts, and Lord knows I have tried to pray them away. And when those prayers go unanswered, I pray for restraint. For the will and courage not to act on my impulses or express my bad thoughts. I pray for God to shine a light on my motivation and for understanding what the impact of my bad behavior might be. Sometimes, it's the long way around, but in doing so, I turn my darkness into more appropriate actions and purer thoughts. Let us pray that the men who are running this war take a moment for reflection, a moment when they ask themselves, 'Are my motives pure?' 'Are the consequences of my deeds worthy of the wanton cruelty or the anguish they cause others?' And then let us pray for our young men who are in harm's way, for the end of unwarranted killing and the taking of something that is not rightfully ours."

Alice kept her head down but her eyes on Dillard, who had not acknowledged her since Thursday. She searched his face for traces of a reaction to Reverend Klepper's words but saw none. She wondered what blackness was snaking around his heart that caused him to be so cruel to her. She asked herself what kind of God would tolerate unwarranted killing and cruelty. In all her years of going to church, it was the first time Alice allowed the thought that church didn't have all the answers. There were things in life that couldn't be resolved simply by hymns and prayers.

When the service was over, Alice told her mother and Dillard that she had to talk with Reverend Klepper about choir, and could she take Dillard's place in their usual Sunday walk? "Sure," said Emilia Mae. "We'll meet you at home." Dillard nodded and didn't meet Alice's eyes.

Reverend Klepper and Cora finished greeting the last parishioner when Alice came forward. "You've got me today instead of Dillard. Do you have a moment?"

"For you," he said, "I have all the time in the world. Come, let's the three of us walk together."

Alice wasted no time in getting to the point. She detailed the confrontation with Dillard and how he'd gotten so frighteningly angry.

"You know, Alice, maybe there are some things Dillard needs to keep to himself," said Reverend Klepper.

"Secrets."

"Call them what you will, but probably everyone has something that they keep private because it would hurt other people or maybe it's too personal to share. You can never really know."

Reverend Klepper hugged his wife around the waist and looked up at the sky.

Dillard tried to keep his distance from Alice the following week, just as a heat wave blanketed town. The coolest place in the house was the music room, where both of them took refuge. It made no sense for Alice to sing one song while Dillard played another, so they were forced to communicate through their music. Alice had learned the lyrics to the Beach Boys' "God Only Knows," and Dillard was trying it out on the flute. Before they played together, they'd have to discuss the key and tempo and what style they'd play it in. For the next week, the Beach Boys were the extent of their conversation.

On Friday night, after they finished dinner, Dillard and Alice cleared the table while Emilia Mae washed the dishes. When she finished, Emilia Mae looked at her watch and said, "I hope you don't mind if I disappear for a few hours. I told Nina Tyler I'd babysit while she and Charlie went to a movie." At the mention of Nina Tyler, Dillard raised his eyebrows and said, "No problem. I was thinking of taking one of my head-clearing walks tonight." Both looked at Alice, and Emilia Mae said, "Guess that leaves you to hold down the fort for a while."

Normally, Alice would have asked Dillard if she could go with him, but the way things had been, she worried he'd say no in a way that would hurt her feelings all over again. Besides, she had other plans.

"You guys go ahead. I was going to watch *The Wild Wild West* anyway."

Alice sat in front of the television as first Emilia Mae and then Dillard left. As soon as he walked out, she went to the window and noted the direction he was heading. When he reached the end of the block, she slipped out the door and followed him, sticking close to the curb in case he turned around. He was heading downtown. At Main Street he turned the corner to Lockwood Avenue, right near New Rochelle Hospital. Alice watched from the far side of the street as he passed three storefronts before walking into what looked like a bar with a modest sign outside that said THE SWAN. The windows had blinds drawn across them, so Alice was unable to see inside. She stood outside for a while, not sure of what to do. Someone opened the door long enough for her to peer in. The place was dim and the music loud. She didn't get too close, knowing that if Dillard caught her now, he'd never forgive her. Everything about this was scary, yet she couldn't help herself—she had to find out what was going on.

She stood outside for a while longer before heading home.

Twice more she followed him at night, and each time he ended up at the Swan. The second time, she noticed that young men walked in and out, but no women did. Alice told herself how that made sense. In 1966, women wouldn't go to bars by themselves. As far as she knew, Dillard didn't drink—or at least she'd never noticed him acting drunk or smelling weird. This must be the place where he met those old friends he'd talked about.

Still, she wasn't satisfied. At home, she looked up the Swan in the Yellow Pages, but there was no ad. She searched through the local paper for mention of it, but nothing. Who did she know to ask? Friends at school were too young to go to bars. Aloysius and Cora? Not likely. Her mother? Bad idea. Grandma? Yes, maybe Grandma. She and Alberto were out on the town all the time; maybe this was one of the places they'd visited.

On Saturday afternoon, Alice and Geraldine were alone in the bakery. Geraldine had just scoured a tray that had been filled with butter cookies. She was studying her hands and said to Alice, "Mind if I step out of here a bit early? I need a quick manicure. Alberto and I have a party tonight, and I can't go looking like this." She shoved her hands in front of Alice.

"Yeah, sure, I'll clean up, but can I ask you a question before you go? Have you ever heard of a place downtown called the Swan?"

Geraldine squeezed her eyes shut. "Nope, can't say I have. Why?"

"Oh, nothing. Some kids were talking about it the other day."

"Is it a cocktail lounge?"

"I don't know, more like a bar, I guess."

"Your friends are a little young for bars."

"I know. I was just curious about what it was."

"I'll ask Alberto. I think he's been to every cocktail lounge in town."

When Geraldine saw Alice after church the next day, her voice was hard when she asked, "Exactly which friends of yours are going to the Swan?"

"I don't know," said Alice. "A bunch of kids from school."

"Are they homosexuals?" asked Geraldine.

"Huh?" Funny word, *homosexuals*, thought Alice. She'd never said it out loud, nor had anyone ever said it in front of her. At school, boys called each other fags, queers, or fairies, but she'd always taken it as a joke. *Homosexual*. That was a serious word, like *cancer* or *penis*. No one said those words out loud, either. "I don't think so," she said.

"I asked Alberto, and he knew about the Swan. That's a homosexual hangout, mostly boys from the community college. I can't believe high school kids would have anything to do with a place like that."

Dillard wouldn't have anything to do with a place like that either, thought Alice. Her stomach clenched.

"Oh, that makes sense," said Alice. "The boys who were talking about it, they were, you know, a little . . . well . . . like they might like a place like that."

"I'm sure these boys are not friends of yours," said Geraldine.

"Not really," said Alice.

"So, it has nothing to do with you. Forget about it."

"Um, how does Alberto know about the Swan?"

"Alberto knows about everything." Geraldine put her hand on her waist, stuck out one hip, and laughed a little too loudly.

Chapter 26

Two days before Alice was to leave for the New England Conservatory, Emilia Mae threw a party for her. Alberto whipped up a bunch of canapés that nobody could pronounce. Geraldine, dressed in a red leather miniskirt, decorated the house with crepe paper and a big sign saying CONGRATULATIONS ALICE. She tried her hand at making a papier-mâché musical note, which ended up looking more like a hatchet but was front and center on the mantel above the fireplace nonetheless. Cora brought a rose and calla lily bouquet, which she placed next to the musical note, hoping to distract people from it. Tom Deutsch, her voice teacher, wrote a jazz piece for Alice called "Shiver Stars," which he played on his trumpet. Reverend Klepper sat on the overstuffed couch in the living room, bobbing his head up and down to the music, while Xena, almost completely deaf, sat next to him, occasionally clapping her hands when one of Tom's notes reached her.

Over the summer, Dillard and Alice had played music together, and although their conversations were mostly about music, Alice was grateful that they were talking at all. Right before the party, they both stood in the kitchen helping Alberto pour cheese fondue into two pots.

"That stuff smells like melting tires," said Geraldine.

"It's the Gruyère," said Alberto. "When I add the kirsch, you'll sing a different tune."

"Yeah, well, right now I'm singing 'Ring of Fire.'"

The two of them went on: She complaining about the smell; he rhapsodizing about the ingredients. Alice and Dillard exchanged glances as if to say, "Here they go again." Dillard whispered, "Meet me in the music room. I have something for you."

As soon as she finished pouring the fondue and lighting the Sterno, Alice ran downstairs. Moments later, Dillard followed.

"Have a seat and close your eyes," he said.

She closed her eyes.

"Here." He shoved something into her hands. It was heavy and square, obviously a bunch of records.

"Okay, you can open them."

Alice started to rip open the package, but Dillard told her to read the note first.

For Alice, who's got Fascinatin' Rhythm and so much more. Of Thee I Sing. Have fun at the Conservatory, but Oh Lady, Be Good.

Love, Dillard

Of course, it was the five-record set *Ella Fitzgerald Sings the George and Ira Gershwin Song Book*.

She unwrapped the records and rested her head on his shoulder. "I thought you—"

"Forget it," he interrupted. "My anger had more to do with me than you."

"Why were you so angry?" she asked.

"Memories, I guess. I don't like it when they sneak up on me like that."

"I know what you mean. Every time I hear 'Someone to Watch over Me,' I think of my grandpa. It's the first song I ever learned with him."

He shook his head. "Sappy song, that one."

Dillard was weird sometimes. There were thin lines between songs he found mushy and songs he liked. Yet she was relieved that he still cared enough to make her a card and give her such a lovely present. They were friends again, thank heavens, but since that whole business with the photograph and the Swan, she felt as if she was guarding secrets, ones he didn't even know she owned. She remembered back to when she'd gone with that awful fellow to the High Life bar and lied about having left her purse at a party. Though she never told Dillard the truth, when he found out she'd left her purse at the bar, he didn't ask her to explain. "Doesn't matter," he'd said. "We all have secrets. Yours are safe with me." Now his were safe with her.

A week after Emilia Mae and Dillard drove Alice to Boston, Reverend Klepper called Emilia Mae. "I have some sad news. It won't surprise you, but it will pain you. Xena died in her sleep last night. I'm told by one of the women who lived with her that she died peacefully."

When Emilia Mae didn't respond, Reverend Klepper continued. "You know how fond she was of you."

"Xena was my first real friend."

"Indeed, she had the gift of friendship."

Emilia Mae didn't reply. She was suddenly visited by her younger self, the scared pregnant girl whose family had rejected her. God, she had come so far from that. She wondered what that girl would think if she could see her now: a wife; a mother; a daughter, having made more or less peace with her own mother. She had a family, people who loved her, people who decorated her home with crepe paper and flowers and made stupid canapés in her kitchen. She had a husband who made her linguine and clams every week and bought her presents even when it wasn't her birthday.

"Emilia Mae, are you still there?"

"I'm sorry." She'd been crying and tried to make her voice sound normal. "She was very important to me."

"To so many," said Reverend Klepper. "Ninety-six years old and never lost her faith. All in all, she had a good life."

Emilia Mae was quiet.

"Emilia Mae, are you okay?"

"I'm fine."

"I know this must be hard for you. But remember, she loved you, and that will always be a blessing. The viewing is on Thursday, and I'm conducting the funeral on Friday. Call me if you want to talk."

Emilia Mae wondered about the custom of having an open casket at the church the day before the funeral. Why look at the dead? Why not remember them as alive? She considered not going to Xena's viewing. Then she thought, *If the tables were turned and I died first, Xena would definitely come to my viewing. But I didn't die, and she'll never know if I don't come.* She argued back and forth with herself until she finally decided that not going would be disrespectful, which was the last thing she wanted to be.

She took Thursday morning off from work and put on the only black sheath she owned. She wore no makeup and walked over to the Baptist church. In all the years she'd known Xena, she'd met some of her church friends, but she had no idea there were so many. She waited in line and watched as people bent over the casket and whispered things to her. Some even kissed her. Emilia Mae was definitely not going to do that. Even touching her was out of the question. Who talks to the dead? Especially the deaf dead? Not her. Nope, she'd move along as quickly as she could.

When her turn came, she approached the casket slowly. Xena was laid out exactly as Emilia Mae had pictured her. She wore the same black dress with the palm fronds on it that she had worn to Emilia's wedding. She even wore the same black velvet pillbox hat she'd worn that day. Her hands lay across her stomach and her face was as sweet and relaxed as it had been at Alice's party. But that scarf? Around her neck was a Gucci scarf with swirling purple, pink and yellow flowers. Clearly, she was proud of that scarf and its obvious hefty price tag.

The scarf touched something in Emilia Mae. For all the years she'd known Xena, she never saw the side of her that valued designer scarves. Such a humble woman with such expensive taste. It made her want to hug Xena. More than that, it made her want to laugh. *You pulled one over on all of us*, she thought. Without thinking, she bent down, kissed Xena's cheek, and whispered, "I love the scarf."

She walked back to the bakery thinking about her friend.

Though she didn't see her often, Xena had been a cornerstone in her life. Xena was family, and when it came down to it, family was all she had. It gave her comfort to think about growing old with Dillard; his steadfastness and kindness would always right her when she felt unmoored. During the funeral, Emilia Mae leaned in close to him. Dillard was a kind man. Although he didn't know Xena well, he'd volunteered to come with her. This was right. This was where she belonged.

After the funeral, she said she'd do some grocery shopping; he said he'd take a walk and meet her at home. She bought lamb chops, string beans, baking potatoes, and a bottle of Bordeaux. It was his favorite dinner and one of the few things she made well. Tonight, they'd celebrate their future.

At home, she changed into a pair of bell bottoms and an off-the-shoulder shirt that she thought particularly sexy. A little mascara, and some Orange Kiss lipstick. Not too much—Dillard hated too much makeup. She turned on one of Alice's Bob Dylan records and sang along to "Like a Rolling Stone" as she prepared dinner.

It was nearly seven when Dillard walked in. The table was set with the Georg Jensen candlestick holders they'd gotten as a wedding present five years earlier.

"Smells good in here," he said.

"I hope it tastes as good as it smells."

"What's the occasion?"

"Do we need an occasion?"

"Guess not," he said, glancing at her. "Why're you so dressed up?"

"Do I need a reason to cook my husband's favorite dinner and dress up for him?"

"No. You look pretty."

Dillard hung his hat in the hall closet and took his seat at the table.

She put on the same Bob Dylan record she'd listened to earlier and poured them wine. "Alice is crazy about this singer. What do you think of him?"

"I think he's whiney and pretentious."

"I don't. I think some of his lyrics are pure poetry."

"Each to his own, I guess." He stared into space.

Damn, he could be so aloof. How could anybody *not* be moved by Bob Dylan? She stared at him and thought he looked different tonight. His jaw was set; his lips were thin and taut. She tried to bring the conversation back.

"We got a letter from Alice today. She loves her new roommate."

"That's nice, and I'll bet her new roommate loves her. Who doesn't?"

"Sometimes you have a way of taking a conversation and slamming it into a wall," she said with irritation. "This is one of those times."

"I'm sorry," he said as if he really wasn't.

She'd hoped for an intimate night, maybe even sex. But who was she kidding? Dillard was Dillard. A solid block of a man unto himself. For all these years Alice had made Dillard possible. Dillard, by himself, made Emilia Mae lonely.

They finished the bottle of Bordeaux in silence.

Chapter 27

Though she'd put on a good face in her letters home, Alice hadn't been at all sure she'd wanted to leave home for the conservatory. New place. New people. New everything.

She choked the first time she inhaled a joint, but then her roommate, Carolyn, told her to not swallow but to keep the smoke in her cheeks until she got used to the taste. She didn't do much better when she tried to get drunk. Listerine spurted through her nose after she took a swig from the bottle. Carolyn laughed. "Don't gulp it, silly. Let it dribble down your throat." When the Listerine didn't get them high, Carolyn decided to go for something stronger. Her brother suggested Tab and Four Roses, and that did the trick. At night, the girls would each pour themselves a glass, buy a package of peanut butter crackers from the vending machine down the hall, eat the crackers, drink, sit on Carolyn's bed (she had the bottom bunk), and listen to Simon and Garfunkel sing "The Sounds of Silence."

No one listened. No one cared. Silence like a cancer grew.

The song was deep. Very deep. And that first semester at the New

England Conservatory of Music, so were Alice and her roommate, Carolyn Whitman. Or so they imagined.

Carolyn Whitman wasn't the kind of girl people would call pretty. Tall and slim, she wore her straight dark hair pulled back in a ponytail and hardly wore any makeup. She had a long, straight nose, an elongated head, and brown eyes that looked to Alice like refinished mahogany. She seemed not to care about what she wore and was always "throwing on" this or that, but in her black turtlenecks and Frye cowboy boots, Alice thought she looked like a character out of a movie with subtitles. Although Carolyn eschewed the bright colors of the day, she soaked herself in patchouli every morning. The only jewelry she wore was a pair of large hoop pierced earrings and a stainless steel men's Rolex watch.

Late at night, Alice and Carolyn lay in their beds and exchanged stories. Carolyn came from a wealthy Catholic family in Maine, whose only purpose they seemed to serve in her life was as a dumping ground for her contempt. "Mother still wears those virginal round-collar blouses from the fifties," she said during one of their sessions. "She's dreadfully prudish. You wouldn't believe how concerned she is about my virginity. Before I came here, she kept telling me that 'men don't like to drive used cars.' I finally said, 'Mother, I don't even have a car.' She blushed like a prom girl and said, 'I'm not actually talking about cars, if you catch my drift.' I caught her drift, and I'll guarantee you that by the time I go home for Thanksgiving, I'll have driven this friggin' car so far and fast, it'll be ready for a tune-up. If you catch my drift."

In return, Alice offered up stories about Geraldine and Alberto.

"They're always touching each other and saying things that have double meanings. Honestly, they're like teenagers that way."

"Do you think they do it a lot?" asked Carolyn.

Alice had never thought about that, but threw out a casual "Oh yeah, I think they do it like friggin' bunnies."

"Cool," said Carolyn. "How about your mom and your cute stepdad? You think they do it like bunnies, too?"

Alice thought about the Swan and what that might mean about Dillard. Determined to preserve his secret, she snapped back: "Oh yeah, I'm sure they do it all the time."

Carolyn was at the conservatory to study the cello. Her teachers had always told her what a gifted musician she was. "Everyone assumes I'll be a professional cellist when I grow up," she told Alice. "But I hate to think life is preordained. Suppose it turns out that I'm equally gifted as an engineer or a psychiatrist? I don't think at this age we should have to commit to who we'll be when we're fifty. Mother married Father when she was twenty-one and he was twenty-five. Twenty-three years later, she's still mixing him two Manhattans every night and preparing his dinner. That's my idea of hell. I don't know how she bears it. I think her dependency on him has infantilized her. She wears those horrible granny nightgowns with little rose patterns. Pretty sexy, huh? Honestly, I don't think they've had sex since they conceived my younger brother. Me? I'm not going to marry until I'm at least thirty, or even older. I'd like to see the world, grab some life before I get tied down. How about you?"

The two of them were sitting on Carolyn's bed. Alice was wearing one of those Lanz granny gowns (hers had a moon and stars pattern) that Carolyn had just disparaged. "Um, I don't know.

I haven't really thought about marriage. I know I'd like to be a music teacher. I haven't been anywhere. I mean anywhere except New York City with Dillard. So yeah, I guess I'd like to see some of the world, too."

Carolyn took hold of Alice's hand. "I'm not one of those psychics, but I've heard you sing, and I'm guessing that voice of yours could take you anywhere you want to go. You could be a professional if you wanted."

"You really think so?" Alice squealed.

"I wouldn't say it if I didn't mean it."

"Gee, thanks." Alice threw her arms around Carolyn's neck and went to kiss her on the cheek, but Carolyn turned her head and placed her lips directly on Alice's. They sat for a few moments, lips to lips, until Carolyn slipped her tongue into Alice's mouth. Her tongue was salty and thin. Carolyn wrapped Alice in her arms and was rubbing her back. It felt good, too good to stop. Alice could feel Carolyn's breasts against hers and taste the patchouli on her neck. She was aroused by Carolyn's attention, but confounded by the thought that if she let this happen, what would that make her? She'd never thought of herself as a lesbian. She'd always liked boys and assumed she would marry one someday. So many things in her life seemed skewed right now, she couldn't allow this to be one of them. Gently, she wriggled out of Carolyn's arms. "I'm sorry, I'm not ready for this," she said in a croaky voice. "You know I love you, but maybe not this way."

Carolyn unembraced her. "That's cool," she said. "I love you, too. Let me know if you change your mind."

★ ★ ★

Three months with Carolyn had an impact on Alice. Back in New Rochelle, she decided that her mother wore too much makeup and looked gauche. Worse, she had a false gaiety about her like a sad person trying to pass for a happy one. Her mother had definitely not grabbed life. Alice also saw that something was eating at Dillard. His face was as haggard as when he first showed up at Shore Cakes.

At least Grandma and Alberto were unchanged. He still did her hair every couple of weeks, something that Alice found infantilizing, while she had embraced the miniskirt. Her legs weren't bad for a woman her age (Carolyn said the legs were the last to go).

She found their house in New Rochelle to be déclassé.

These were the things Alice couldn't wait to tell Carolyn.

She would not tell Carolyn about what happened when she tried to sing with Dillard on her second day home.

"I have a new favorite song," she'd told him. "'Paint It Black,' by the Rolling Stones."

"That's bullshit," he'd said. "They're all about preening and yelling. You're better than that."

She'd wanted to tell him that she wasn't better than that, that the new stuff excited her, took her voice to different places, but she'd been afraid of making him more upset than he already seemed to be, so she'd agreed to sing some of his favorites. The songs seemed stale. Dillard seemed old. She'd wished she were back in Boston.

Thanksgiving was at Geraldine's house this year, with the usual crowd: the Kleppers, Dillard and Emilia Mae, and, of course, Alberto. Alice set the table and arranged it so that she was sitting next to Cora. Every year, they'd had the same traditional meal. But this year, Alberto (along with Julia Child) decided to put a French spin on the menu. Instead of turkey, he made a roasted leg of lamb with different herbs and garlic, pork and herb stuffing, green beans, an eggplant casserole, and Brussels sprouts. He had also baked an apple tart for dessert, but thank God for the Kleppers, who'd brought with them a good old American pumpkin pie.

Gigot de pre-sale roti. Farce de porc. Haricots verts. Ratatouille. Choux de Bruxelles. Tarte aux pommes. Pumpkin pie.

Alice tried to memorize all the French names of the food they'd eaten so she could tell Carolyn. When it came time to clear the table, Alice jumped up and gave Cora an imploring look. "Everybody sit. Cora and I will take care of it."

They stacked the plates and gathered the silverware. Once they were both in the kitchen, and the dishes were in the sink, Alice closed the door. "Finally," she said. "I've got you alone. Can I ask you a question?"

"Of course, ask away."

"You see my mother and Dillard at least once a week, right?"

"Yup, I do."

"Have you noticed anything different about them?"

"Different in what way?"

"I don't know, just different."

Alice didn't mention what she knew about the Swan.

Cora turned away from the sink and leaned against it. "As well as you know people, you never really know what goes on in a marriage. Dillard and your mom are two strong people. They're so different, yet they've made it work. Marriages aren't always smooth sailing. They're work, all the time. It's not like there's ever a long spell when you can coast. So maybe they're going through a rough patch right now. That's entirely possible. Especially with you gone."

"Have you and Reverend Klepper ever gone through one of those?"

Cora laughed. "I live with a man who thinks he's one of God's messengers. Dare I say it, sometimes he can be a bit too saintly. And guarded! Wow! That man has secrets buried so deep I don't know if I'll ever get the whole story. Me? I have a big mouth and am far less circumspect, as you've probably noticed. So, have we ever gone through rough patches? What do you think?"

Alice laughed. "Yeah, it's probably just one of those."

Cora tilted her head and studied Alice, who'd tucked her long hair behind one ear and was wearing a pair of gold hoop earrings and reeked of patchouli. "Look at you, a real college girl, although that perfume—they can probably smell you as far away as Manhattan. Anyway, how are you liking school?"

"The work part is hard, but really interesting. I'm doing a lot of singing, all kinds of it. I'm thinking that maybe I would even try to do it as a career. You know, like after I graduate. Does that sound completely crazy to you?"

"Why would that sound crazy? You have a gorgeous voice. It's the sixties, you can be whatever you want to be."

Alice hugged Cora. "Thanks for that. Can we keep that part about the singing between you and me right now? I'll probably change my mind a thousand times before I graduate."

"Sure, but stick with it for now. You have real talent." Cora stepped back. "Oh God, now they can probably smell *me* in Manhattan."

"It's patchouli," laughed Alice. "The perfume—well, it's an oil, really. My roommate, Carolyn, gave it to me. She says I could be a professional singer if I wanted. I'm going to try and join the chorus.

I've also been asked to sing with some guys in a rock and roll band they're starting up. Carolyn says I should experience every kind of music before I decide which road I want to follow."

"Carolyn sounds like a very wise girl," said Cora. "But what do you think?"

"I think Carolyn is right."

Chapter 28

On the mornings when Dillard awoke before Emilia Mae, he'd go downstairs, pick up the newspaper, settle into one of the chairs on the porch, and read the paper. One morning, he came upon a story about a new cooperative housing project in the Bronx on the site of what used to be Freedomland. The article noted that Freedomland had been built on a former municipal landfill that had never been properly drained, which led to its shuttering a few years earlier. The mosquitoes that had forced Dillard out of Freedomland had been a problem through much of the season and had finally forced everyone else out. He remembered how, in an itchy frenzy, he'd fled that place like a fugitive, telling no one, just throwing all his belongings into his car and taking off.

Looking around at the oak dining room table, the Georg Jensen candlesticks, and the mantelpiece cluttered with family pictures, Dillard thought how out of character that seemed to him now. Anyone who walked into this place would figure that an old married couple had lived here forever. In a sense, they had. Dillard was thirty-seven. He'd been with Emilia Mae for seven years. Alice was twenty and a junior at college. He'd had a hand in successfully raising her, even if she was now singing with what he took to be some puerile rock and roll band. He'd lived this life long enough to believe it would always be this way. But when he thought back to his past before Emilia Mae, staying was the aberration. Fleeing was what he'd always done. He'd left Skyville when the army wouldn't take him. He'd left the resort in the Catskills when it became too humiliating. He'd left Skyville after Nick. He'd left himself after Nick.

Nick.

Every thought of Nick still stung Dillard anew. He put the paper down and closed his eyes. He could almost feel Nick's mouth on him, smell his Aqua Velva. He needed a Nick pick-me-up, so he tiptoed down to the basement, where he opened the closet and pulled out the cigar box filled with Nick's photos and letters. In all these years, he'd never read those letters. The pictures were one thing, but reading Nick's odd sentence structures and the almost childlike way he expressed his love would be like hearing his voice. That would be unbearable.

He thought about Skyville. He hadn't been there in nearly ten years, and he missed the smell of it, the light, the mountains, the water. He thought, as he often had, about Sharlene. What had become of her? Had she remarried? Did she still live in the same log house? What were the kids doing? He wondered what Nick wrote in his final note to her. Unfinished business there. He'd often thought to call her or write her a letter and tell her how sorry he was. She'd loved the Nick he'd loved—still did love—and that part of him yearned to see her again. Nick had made it clear in his note that there was no evidence that he'd joined Nick in New York City. The case of Nick Moore had been closed for many years, so he wasn't worried about any legal complications. Maybe Sharlene wouldn't mind being in touch with him. Maybe her attitude toward homosexuals had changed. Maybe she saw him as he saw her: as a piece of Nick.

The idea took hold. He stared at the picture of him and Nick by the lake. They both looked so bright and eager, the way lovers do when everything is new. He could drive down there for a few days. Just to see that lake again would be a miracle. He started to talk aloud to Nick's image. "I'll write Sharlene, if she's still in Skyville, to find out if she wants to see me," and then nodded at the photograph, as if Nick and he had made a pact.

Dillard wrote a brief note to Sharlene's old address telling her about his marriage, his home, Alice. He asked about her and the kids. He said he was planning a quick trip to Skyville and would love to see her. If she thought it was a good idea would she send some dates that might work for her?

The swiftness of her reply startled Dillard. "I'm still where you last saw me, in the old log house. The kids are coming along nicely, thank you, Eve and Ava are almost ready for college and Zeke is in his second year at Auburn. Sadly, we lost Lucy the dog three years ago. Yikes! It's been a long time. As I'm still teaching, a weekend visit would work better than during the week. I look forward to hearing from you." Her handwriting was as unadorned as her face and long straight hair. He could imagine her biting down on the knuckle of her index finger as she wrote her letter, something she did when she was concentrating. In every way, she was a contrast to Nick, but as he'd said of her many times, she was the one who kept their life on track.

Dillard wrote back that he would like to come either the first or second weekend after New Year's. Sharlene quickly answered: "The second weekend would be fine."

That Carolyn Whitman was coming home with Alice for Christmas vacation caused a stir in the Wingo/Fox households after Alice sent out a list of instructions to the family.

"Please don't make anything with a French name or try to speak French in front of her. She is fluent in the language. She doesn't eat white foods. All meats have to be well done. No liver, bananas, or cantaloupe, please. Even the sight of any of those things will make her gag. Peanut butter is a favorite, but no white bread. She likes wine. Chablis, to be specific. Of course, the Kleppers are always welcome, but it would be good if he didn't mention God or any of that stuff as Carolyn's an atheist. She's allergic to dust. Her sheets must be 100% cotton. Cigarette smoke makes her asthma act up. Can we use cloth napkins at dinner? Also, candlesticks would be nice. Just be yourselves. Carolyn will absolutely adore you."

"Christ, you'd think the Queen of England was coming to visit," Geraldine said to Emilia Mae after reading the letter. "I'm sure as hell gonna smoke when I want to. And am I going to tell Alberto he can't make his crème brûlée because some fancy girl doesn't like how he pronounces it? Not on my life. I already hate this girl."

"Mother, she's Alice's friend. We have to be nice to her."

"Oh, I'll be nice," said Geraldine. "I just won't like her."

"This is going to be a nightmare," said Emilia Mae. "Dillard hates her, too. Says she's taking Alice from us, turning her into some sort of snotty college girl. Apparently, she's the one who convinced Alice to join that rock band. Dillard says that's a complete waste of her time."

"Don't worry. It'll be fine. Alberto and I will be our usual charming selves, and Dillard's mostly always a gentleman. If worse comes to worse, we can fob her off on the Kleppers."

Carolyn's visit was fine enough. She was polite, asked lots of questions, and made excellent conversation. After all his apprehension, Dillard actually liked her. She got tears in her eyes when she talked about *The Confessions of Nat Turner*, and knew the words to the newest Jacques Brel songs. The problem was Alice, his sweet, compassionate Alice. He hated how she tossed her hair when she talked, and she reeked of that awful patchouli. "I can't believe that Nixon is going to be our friggin' president," she said the first night at dinner. Coming out of Carolyn's mouth, that sentence wouldn't have raised an eyebrow. But from Alice, it sounded pretentious and unnatural. Worse, her taste in music had taken a turn so far from his, he had nothing to say when she talked about her favorite groups: Cream, Steppenwolf, Sly and the Family Stone.

On the second night at dinner, Carolyn mentioned what a beautiful voice Alice had and turned to Dillard. "Alice tells me you play the flute and she sings along. That's so sweet. What kinds of songs do you sing?"

Dillard brightened. "You know, old standards. After dinner, we can go downstairs and play some for all of you." He turned to Alice. "What do you think?"

Alice scrunched up her face. "Don't be a silly. Carolyn doesn't want to listen to that old stuff."

Carolyn protested: "I do! I'd love to hear you two together."

Later that night, a humiliated Alice forced her way through "A Taste of Honey," as Dillard played the flute. Carolyn drummed her hand against her thigh in time to the music. "That was heaven," she said when they finished. "Can you do another?"

Alice demurred. "Honestly, we just play around with dopey old songs. We don't want to bore you with all that."

"It's hardly boring," said Carolyn. "It's beautiful."

Alice sang "Someone to Watch over Me," as Dillard reluctantly played the flute.

"Pretty," said Carolyn, when they finished. "That's the one your grandpa taught you, right?"

Alice could hear Grandpa Earle's thin, girlish voice. She wondered if they would still sound like the Andrews Sisters together. Geraldine must have seen the sadness flicker across Alice's face, because she suddenly got the same tight look of being caught unawares. Emilia Mae stared at the floor while Dillard placed his flute on the music stand and closed his eyes. Only moments ago, the room had been filled with bright notes but was now heavy with loss.

Geraldine snapped out of whatever she was in and clapped her hands. "Enough with the melancholy music. Time for Alberto's crème brûlée." (Was Emilia Mae imagining it, or did Geraldine purposely swallow her *r*s and stretch the *u*?)

As they started up the stairs, Dillard saw how Carolyn laughed when Alice rolled her eyes and mouthed the word *sorry*. He took the stairs two at a time. When he reached the top, he grabbed his hat, threw on his coat, and made for the front door.

"Where are you going?" asked Emilia Mae.

"Out. I need air. Feeling claustrophobic. Must have been those dopey old songs." Before he slammed the door, he looked at Alice, who was staring inconsolably at Carolyn.

Dillard got into his car, though he had no idea where he was going. *Anywhere but here*, he thought. He drove into town, up to the high school and down to the Sound, allowing his thoughts to flow. He'd lost Alice. She felt far away. He felt far away. Without Alice, Emilia Mae didn't work. Home didn't work. He didn't work.

He tried telling himself it was a temporary thing, that college kids always turned away from their parents and thought they knew better. But that wasn't the whole truth. It wasn't just Alice, he realized. I'm the one turning away. I'm the one who doesn't fit, never have. I need to get back to Skyville. Finish up the thing with Sharlene. Then what?

It was as if one chunk of the iceberg broke off, and the rest started to melt. *I'd be running away again, I know. This time, there'd be consequences. Emilia Mae. How can I do that to her? It's not her fault; she doesn't deserve this. What would I tell her?*

Dillard remembered that first dinner at the Wingos, how he'd stormed out. No one had known what to say except Reverend Klepper. He'd been very kind to him. Had invited him to walk with him after church, said he'd show him the town. They'd been walking after church for nearly seven years now. He was more comfortable with him than anyone else in New Rochelle. Reverend—Aloysius—was someone he could confide in. He would talk to him about all this on Sunday.

Dillard headed toward home. He wasn't calm, but he wasn't bound in fury, either. Sunday was only three days away. He could wait that long. By the time he got home, Alice and Carolyn were in the kitchen finishing the dishes, and the rest of them were sitting in the living room talking while Mantovani played on the record player. No one asked Dillard where he'd gone or why; they all laughed when he picked up the Mantovani album jacket and said, "Oh brother, I can't wait until Alice has to explain *this* to Carolyn."

Following Alice's orders, no one invited Carolyn to church on Sunday. Dillard went with Emilia Mae. After, as she always did, she went to Geraldine's house to help her and Alberto prepare Sunday lunch.

Dillard waited in the back pew of the church until the last parishioner had shaken hands with Aloysius. "I hope you're up for a good walk today, I could really use some advice."

Both men put on their coats and hats and headed outdoors. The sun was bright, and it was warm for December.

"How about we head to Twin Lakes?" said Aloysius, referring to the lakes in front of New Rochelle High School. "I find it so peaceful there."

They walked down a long hill. When they got to the bottom, Aloysius spotted an iron bench. "Mind if we sit for a while? Old man, old feet."

Aloysius pointed to a row of bare bushes in front of them. "It's amazing how something this nondescript can put on such a show in spring. Rhododendrons, these, as lurid a purple as you'll ever see. It's the thing I love most about nature. Nothing is as it seems."

Dillard nodded. "As a boy, I used to catch tadpoles at Lake Lure. I'd watch them over time as they turned into frogs. I suppose in our own way, we humans are chameleons, too. We just hide it better."

"Isn't that the truth," said Aloysius. "Take us, you and me. How many miles have we walked together in the last seven years, and still I know nothing about who you were before you came to New Rochelle."

"Funny. I could say the same about you."

Aloysius pulled off his shoes and massaged his stockinged feet. "Fair enough. I'm game to spill the beans if you are."

Dillard rubbed his eyes with his thumb and forefinger. He told Aloysius about all that came before Nick. Then he paused and said, "I'm about to tell you things I haven't told anyone else, things you're probably not going to want to know. So, tell me now if you'd rather I stop."

Aloysius slipped on his shoes. "I'm fifty-nine and have been living with my own secrets. If you're comfortable telling, I'm comfortable listening."

Dillard pressed his lips together and closed his eyes. Aloysius felt his discomfort. "Tell you what, why don't I go first? Would that be easier?"

Dillard shook his head yes. Aloysius cracked his knuckles. "Okay, here goes."

Aloysius told him about his childhood on the farm in Kingston, going to the seminary in Louisville, meeting Marguerite, and the baby, Linden. "When she was eight months old, Linden got diphtheria. This was before penicillin. She died. After that, I lost everything: my will, my faith. Marguerite went back to her family in Toronto, and I went home to Kingston. I was so angry and crazed, I tried to chop down an old linden tree on our farm. After a while, I got a job driving a delivery truck in the Bronx.

"About a year later, I met Cora. She's the one who urged me back to the church, got me to go to the Union Theological

Seminary, and introduced me to the pastor at First Baptist here. My life with Cora has been a blessing except for one thing. We've never been able to have a child of our own. Cora knows all about Marguerite, but I've never told her about Linden." He shook his head. "I've convinced myself it would be too hurtful for her, but in my heart, I don't think that's the real reason. Maybe I'm afraid that by telling Cora, Linden would become part of our lives. I don't think I could stand that. I pray for the courage to tell her someday. She deserves to know the truth.

"That's it. That's my story. Now you know everything. More than anyone else knows about me."

Dillard put his hand on Aloysius's shoulder. "Thank you for telling me. You know your secrets are safe with me."

"And yours with me," said Aloysius. "You and I are friends. Nothing's going to change that."

"I appreciate that," said Dillard. He took a deep breath.

"I loved a man once."

He told Aloysius about Nick, Sharlene, and the family, about the fateful visit to New York City. He watched Aloysius's face for signs of disapproval, and when he saw none, he continued up until the time he came to New Rochelle.

"I married Emilia Mae because I wanted a normal life. A home. I love Alice, and in my own way, I love Emilia Mae. It's just, now with Alice gone, it doesn't work for me. I don't know if I'm one of those men who likes other men, or if I was uniquely attracted to Nick. All I know is I can't stay here anymore. I want to go down to Skyville for a while. I want to start all over and find out who I really am, if that makes any sense. Emilia Mae's done nothing wrong, but I can't stay with her. It all seems very pretend, and I don't want to keep pretending. I don't want to hurt her, either. That's what I wanted to talk to you about. What do I say to her?"

Aloysius put his hands on his thighs, leaned forward, and with some effort, stood up. "That's a complicated story you have there. I have no idea if you're one of those men or not, but it hardly matters. Whatever in you is urging you to leave isn't going to quit until you do something about it. I think you have to tell Emilia Mae exactly what you just told me. She won't be happy about it, but I think she'd understand. Mind if we walk some more?"

As they headed up the hill, Dillard noticed how slowly Aloysius was walking. He was getting old. All the changes over the past few years must be hard on him. He'd talked often in the past year about the assassinations of Martin Luther King Jr. and Robert Kennedy. He'd exhorted the congregation to understand that hatred was the disease, love and compassion the cure. Lately, he'd even tried introducing some modern Christian music into the services to make them more contemporary. But really, how was someone Aloysius's age supposed to understand hippies, or protestors, much less men who liked men? Dillard worried he'd made a mistake dragging him into this and wanted to end the conversation. "Thanks for that advice. I'll have to think about it."

Aloysius stopped walking and grabbed Dillard's arm. "No, you *don't* have to think about it. You've been thinking about it for years. If it's men you prefer, then don't waste any more of Emilia Mae's life. She deserves to find someone to love her completely, as do you. Whatever you had with this Nick fellow is what you should have with whomever, and so should she. You don't have time to waste."

It took all of Dillard's self-control not to cry. "I don't want to hurt her."

"You're hurting her more by living a lie."

Dillard wiped the sweat from the back of his neck. "My father used to warn me not to tell people everything at once. Now I've blurted out everything, and you're stuck with my secrets. I'm sorry to burden you."

Aloysius smiled. "I guess we're even in the burdening department. In some ways, you and I are in the same boat, keeping secrets from our loved ones. God must have had his reasons for introducing us."

Dillard started to say something about how they could help each other, but Aloysius interrupted him by looking at his watch and exclaiming, "Good Lord, we've been gone so long, they've probably finished lunch and are preparing dinner by now."

They walked the rest of the way in silence. Aloysius seemed sad. Dillard felt exhausted. He wished he didn't know what he now knew about Aloysius. He thought telling his story to Aloysius would make him less anxious, but it only made him more so. It would take courage for Aloysius to tell Cora about the baby, just as it would take courage for him to tell Emilia Mae why he needed to leave. He wondered if both men confessed to one another so they could bear witness and give each other strength to do what they had to do. He resolved to tell Emilia Mae about Nick and Sharlene and why he needed to go to Skyville. He'd tell her next Sunday.

Chapter 29

Early on the next rainy Sunday morning, Dillard drove Alice and Carolyn to the Port Authority in Manhattan, where they would catch the bus to Boston. Alice sat in the passenger seat, Carolyn in the back. Dillard made it a point to drive by Birdland, where he hadn't been in all these years. "I once saw Ella Fitzgerald perform there," he said. Alice jerked her head toward him. "You did? You never told me that."

"There are lots of things I haven't told you."

Alice snuck Carolyn a confused look before asking, "What's that supposed to mean?"

"I don't know." Dillard shrugged. "Just that you never really know everything about a person, no matter how close you are."

Alice leaned in toward Dillard. "You know everything about me."

"Do I?"

Alice thought about the photograph and about the times she'd followed him to the Swan. "Do you think I know everything about you?"

"Obviously not," he laughed. "You never knew that I saw Ella

Fitzgerald live." Dillard looked at Carolyn in the rearview mirror. "What you think? Does Alice know everything about you?"

"I'm pretty certain no one knows everything about another person," said Carolyn. "There are always gaps in people's stories, intentional or otherwise, don't you think?"

"I do," said Dillard. He wondered why he'd brought up Ella in the first place. Was he trying to distance himself from Alice? Maybe that's why she'd been so odd. Maybe they were trying to distance themselves from each other. His jaw tightened. He distracted himself by worrying about where he would park. He found a spot a block away from the Port Authority and started to get out of the car.

"Stay here," said Alice. "You'll get soaked."

"Right," said Carolyn. "My umbrella's big enough for both of us. Thank you for your hospitality. It was a pleasure to get to know you." Before she opened the car door, she leaned forward and said, "I'll give you two a moment."

Alone in the car with Alice, ribbons of thoughts flowed through Dillard's head. He wanted to say, *I love you. I'm sorry. I miss you. I don't mean to hurt you.* But none of these words came. He turned to her and opened his arms. She moved closer and hugged him. He felt her tears against his cheek and wondered if she could feel his falling onto her hair.

Sunday night: linguine with clams. Dillard chopped parsley, boiled water, sautéed garlic. Emilia Mae set the table. The rain pounded the doors and windows while the spicy smell of garlic filled the house. It was cozy in here. Emilia Mae seemed happy, relieved, she said, to be free from Alice's scrutiny and Carolyn's judgment. "She's not a bad person. Obviously, comes from good stock. Smart. But holy cow, she drove my mother and Alberto crazy. She sure has Alice in her sway. She'll get over it, I suppose. But I've got to tell you, it's so nice to be you and me again, isn't it?"

Dillard smiled. They sat down to eat, this time at the Formica kitchen table, not the dining room table that they'd used while Carolyn was there. Paper napkins, not cloth. Dillard got up and pulled a bottle of Chablis from the refrigerator. He poured a glass for both of them. Emilia Mae raised hers and said, "To us."

Dillard raised his. "To you."

They talked about the visit, about Carolyn. "I feel as if she's stolen our girl," said Dillard.

"She'll be back," said Emilia Mae.

"I suppose, but in the meantime, it's weird to watch her trying to become a carbon copy of someone else."

"I know. It was strange how reluctant she was to sing with you the other night. I've never seen her behave like that."

"Really strange," said Dillard, pouring them each a second glass of wine.

"That night, when you left. Where did you go?"

"Nowhere, I just drove around."

"So, when you disappear for one of your head-clearing walks, do you just walk around?" Emilia's voice rose.

"Why are you interrogating me?"

"No need to get defensive. I just wonder where you go when you disappear from here?"

Dillard could feel the hot flush of wine. When he drank, he became looser. Now, with two glasses in him, he would choose his words carefully.

"Let me ask you something. We've known each other nearly eight years. Do you think I know everything about you?"

Emilia Mae looked surprised. He couldn't possibly know about all the men she'd slept with when she worked at the Neptune Inn all those years ago.

"Probably not. I mean, you can't know every thought that passes through my head, or what I was like when I was much younger. So, no, you don't. Do I know everything about you?"

"No, you really don't."

He put his fork down and bowed his head.

At first, Emilia Mae thought he might be praying, something she'd never seen him do at home. When more time went by, she stuck her face under his, and looked up at him. "Are you okay?"

He shook his head. That's when she saw he was crying.

"What's wrong? Are you okay? Did something happen with Alice? Tell me."

Dillard put his elbows on the table and rested his forehead on his hands. "Nothing like that," he mumbled. "It's just. I'm not. I'm not who you think I am."

Emilia Mae put her arm around his shoulder and waited for him to speak. She could feel his body heave.

"Have you been in prison?" she asked, thinking how it would answer so many unanswered questions.

"What? Why would you think I was in prison?" Dillard stopped crying and looked startled. "What a strange thing to say."

"It's okay if you were," said Emilia Mae, as if she were soothing a child. "We all have a past. Clearly you're not a criminal anymore."

Dillard had to laugh. "Really, Emilia Mae, sometimes your

263

imagination takes you to strange places." But when he thought about it, she was partly right. In the eyes of the law, he was a criminal. Sleeping with another man, when he did, had been against the law. He rested his head in his hands again. "I was with a man. I was in love with a man before I met you." He got up, took his brown tweed flat cap from the hall closet, and placed it on the table. "This was his hat."

Emilia Mae backed away as if a cockroach had crossed her plate.

Dillard continued: "Remember I told you I worked as a receptionist in a doctor's office in Skyville? It was the doctor. His name was Nick. He was a lot older than me, had a family with three kids. I got to know them and his wife. Nick and I went to New York one weekend and he died in our hotel room." He stopped talking and took a few deep breaths. No need to tell her how he died.

Emilia Mae heard the tightness in his voice. She reached out and held his wrist, but then quickly withdrew her hand. "So, what'd you do?"

"I was so numb and terrified, I snuck down to Skyville to get my father's car and instruments and came back to New York. I was scared the police would find me and accuse me of killing Nick. They could have arrested me anyway, for being with a man. I decided to get out of the city, which is how I ended up in this area."

He described his job at Freedomland and the other odd jobs he'd taken in Pelham, Yonkers, and Mamaroneck. "None of them lasted. I took a construction job here but had to quit because my Raynaud's was making it impossible to work with my hands in the cold. I was broke and staying in that dilapidated Neptune Inn when I saw your sign for free food. After that, well you know everything that happened after that."

Emilia Mae sat in her chair, her back hunched, her shoulders tensed as if fending off a blow. She was jiggling her leg, the way she did when she was nervous.

Dillard waited for her to cry or to lash out at him. But she sat staring at him as if she'd never seen him before.

"Are you going to say anything?" He fidgeted with the cap.

"I don't have any words."

After that, neither of them touched their food, though they did finish the bottle of Chablis. Emilia Mae got up to clear the table but sat back down again. "Are you telling me you like men?"

"I don't know what I'm telling you."

"Do you daydream about men? When you make love to me, are you thinking about men?"

"I don't know, Emilia Mae. I honestly don't know."

"Of course you know. Don't tell me you don't have fantasies. Everyone has them."

"Sometimes, yes, I do."

"When you go on those head-clearing walks, are you meeting men?"

"I swear, there's been no man since Nick. There was no man before him."

"Answer my question." Her voice was harsh. "When you go on those head-clearing walks, are you meeting men?"

"This is beginning to feel like police grilling."

"This is beginning to feel like a nightmare. Just answer my question."

"I go to a bar where men are, but I don't do anything. Just have a beer or two and come home."

"Are there women at this bar?"

Dillard looked down at his hat. "No, ma'am."

Emilia Mae suddenly remembered coming out of the ether after Alice was born. Everything spooled out in slow motion and coalesced into a piece, just as it was doing now: the reason why Dillard never looked at other women. Why a beautiful man like him picked an average-looking girl like her. How she must have made normal seem easy to him. How she gave him a ready-made family.

After that, her thoughts came more rapidly. *He has to leave. First Alice, now him. I'll be alone. I don't know how to be alone. How to be without him. He fills my world, all the mundane chores and conversation that come with it. I love his music. He knows how to fix everything. Picks out my clothes. Keeps the house in order. Makes our lives work. Who will take care of me? He's betrayed me. He's betrayed himself. What must it feel like to be him? To spend all these years pretending and wanting something very different from what he has. My life will stay the same. The house, the bakery, Mother, Alice. Alice will be heartbroken. Mother? I have no idea how she'll react. Where will he go? What will he do? Never mind, I can't think about that now. Right now, I don't give a crap.*

All she could think about was how every piece of her was in pain. Tears stuck in her throat. She put her hand over her heart and said in a strangled voice, "You've hurt me."

Dillard moved his chair next to hers and put his arm around her. "I'm so sorry. That's the last thing I wanted to do."

She shrugged his arm from her shoulder. "Don't try to comfort me. I have to get used to being without you."

"You don't have to do that right away."

He told her of his plan to go down to Skyville the following Friday and meet with Sharlene. "I need to tie up loose ends. I haven't spoken to her since Nick died, and she's agreed to see me."

"And then what?"

"Well, I thought I'd stay in Skyville for a while, then come back here and we'd figure something out. Now I've told you everything."

Emilia Mae's voice got stern. "I can't imagine how hard it must have been for you to pretend to love me. You need to figure this out and not let more time go by. And I need to get on with my life, find someone who doesn't love me because he has to. I seem to be cursed with people who are forced to love me, don't I?"

"Is that how it really feels to you?"

"Yes."

It was a mean thing to say, she knew. She felt for him, but he'd also caused her such pain that at this moment she wanted him to feel some, too.

"I do love you, you know."

Emilia Mae started to cry. "It doesn't matter. You need to go. Now."

"Can't we figure all that out when I get back from Skyville?"

"No, you're not hearing what I'm saying. You need to leave. Right now. I can't stand the sight of you."

"Where should I go?"

"I don't care. Go take one of your head-clearing walks. Go to that bar where all the men are. Surely, one of them would be happy to put you up."

"You want me to disappear, just like that? What about Alice? Your mother? What do we tell them?"

"I don't know," said Emilia Mae. "I guess we tell them the truth, that you like men. What else *can* we tell them?"

Dillard started to cry. "This is my family, my home. I can't just disappear like that."

"I can't talk about this anymore. Please go."

Emilia Mae walked out of the kitchen.

Left uneaten, linguine with clams congeals into pale yellow beads. The clams shrivel, and the sweet garlic smell goes acrid. Dillard figured that the least he could do was wash the dirty dishes, sponge down the sink and table. Take out the garbage. After that, he grabbed some clothes from the bedroom, got in the car, and started driving to Boston.

Three and a half hours alone on I-95, on the way to see Alice, Dillard thought about her. Little Alice, who was so kind to him when he started working in the bakery. He remembered when she took his hand for the first time, how he felt it a tiny miracle. Aside from Nick, the relationship he had with her was the only pure one he'd ever had. She was the first child to tell him she loved him, give him silly presents on Father's Day. People with children take these things for granted. To people without them, these gestures and words are gifts.

He took none of it for granted. What if Alice turned him away and wanted nothing to do with him? He had no claim on her. Emilia Mae was her mother. It would stand to reason that she'd choose blood over a stranger who wandered into her life when she was young. She wasn't that sweet little girl anymore. She was a college girl now who swore and listened to bad rock and roll. For now, she was under Carolyn's spell.

What if Carolyn told Alice to forget him? He couldn't bear it if Alice turned him away. How much would he tell her? Would he tell her about Nick? Sharlene? About what happened in New York? He remembered how angry he'd gotten at her when she'd asked him about that picture of him and Nick. He was so scared she'd figure it out. How much would she understand about all that? Would it burden her to know that she'd been the glue that held this marriage together?

Somewhere around Hartford, it occurred to him how important he was to Alice. She might think all those songs they sang together were dopey now, but they made her understand theory and harmony and that she had a voice worth nurturing. The many concerts he took her to must have counted for something. He'd taught her to ride a bicycle, to drive. He was the one she'd roll her eyes at when Alberto went into detail—in French—about one of his recipes or Geraldine made one of her embarrassing double entendres. Maybe he was as important to her as she was to him. Maybe he was even the glue that held *her* world together. Maybe they needed each other. He'd have to keep reassuring her he'd always be there for her, that she could tell him anything and everything. He'd never judge her. Ever. How could he?

By the time he got to Boston, it was well past one a.m. Hungry and tired, he fell into the first Holiday Inn he found. Normally, he scoffed at the idea of symbols, but the way a full moon had followed him from New Rochelle to Boston, might it be a beacon of hope? That and the smell of clams cooking in garlic would always bring him back to this time.

The next morning, he phoned Alice. She picked up on the first ring. "Hi," he said, trying to keep the nerves out of his voice.

"Dillard?" She sounded surprised to hear from him. "Everything okay? You're calling so early."

"Actually, I'm in town. I wondered if you could have breakfast with me."

"But is everything okay?"

"Sure."

"Should I bring Carolyn?"

"No honey, let's make it the two of us."

Alice said her first class was from nine to ten. She named a pancake place on Mass Avenue and said she'd see him at ten fifteen.

Dillard got to the restaurant at ten. He drank two cups of coffee and went over what he'd say to her. He decided he'd tell her everything. He went to the men's room to splash cold water on his face and studied his reflection in the mirror. He saw the bags under his eyes, the way his hair was receding. He looked old, felt older. By the time he came back, Alice was already seated. On this cold morning with only a faded sun whitening the sky, Alice looked radiant the way a happy person is radiant. Her dark eyes shone, and her smile was warm and unfettered with secrets. Her gold hoop earrings reflected her dark luminescent skin. In her black turtleneck and black jeans, with her long hair hanging beneath her shoulders, she looked like Joan Baez, only prettier. She reeked of that oil stuff.

Alice jumped up and kissed him on the cheek. "What are you doing in my town?"

He kissed her back. "We need to talk, and I wanted to do it in person."

She sat down. "Uh-oh, is everything okay? Are you mad at me?"

"No, of course I'm not mad at you." He sat down. "Things are sort of okay, but can we order first? I'm starving."

They talked about Alice's classes. She told him she was singing on weekends with a rock band in Boston. "I know you hate this, and you'll hate it even worse when I tell you the band's name. Ready?"

Dillard nodded.

"Electric Fruit."

"Whoa, that's horrible," said Dillard. "Are you having fun with it?"

"I really am. Carolyn says we sound a little bit like the Jefferson Airplane."

Dillard smiled. "I'll bet you sound beautiful."

Just then, the food came. Alice had eggs; Dillard, pancakes with bananas. When he finished slathering them with syrup, he looked Alice in the eye and said, "I'm here because I think your mother and I are going to split up."

Alice put down the piece of toast she was buttering. "What? Really? Did you have a big fight or something?"

"No," said Dillard. "Nothing like that. It's just that, you've probably noticed that we're very different people..."

Alice started to cry. "Yeah, so you've been very different people for a long time..."

"Don't cry, honey, please. It's just that, when you were around, it somehow made everything easier, made us better people. It's different now, and we both think it better if I leave."

Alice used her napkin to blow her nose. "Oh God, are you having an affair?"

Dillard smiled. "Oh, no. Neither is she." He took his time chewing his pancakes. Now would be the perfect time to tell her, but he couldn't. "It's just that sometimes when people are together for a long time, they grow apart for whatever reason. And if they both realize that, then it only seems fair—"

"Fair? Are we talking about fair?" She was crying harder. "I'll tell you what's not fair. What's not fair is you acting all lovey-dovey to my mom and making believe you're my father, and then walking out on us. That's what's not fair."

The legs of Dillard's chair made a squealing noise as he moved closer to her and put his arm around her. "It's not like that, Alice. I'll never leave you. I'll always be here for you. I swear it on everything I hold dear. You have to believe me."

She stared down at her eggs. "Where will you go?"

"I don't know. I'd like to be close to wherever you are."

"What about my mom? Do you want to be close to where she is?"

Dillard took his arm from around Alice and wiped the corners of his mouth with his napkin. "I want to make one thing very clear. Your mom has done nothing wrong. She's a wonderful wife and mother, and the best thing, aside from you, that's ever happened to me. I'm the one who's the problem. If anyone's to blame here, it's me."

He wished he had the nerve to tell Alice the truth, but he felt too vulnerable to risk feeling more so.

She wished she had the nerve to ask him about his trips to the Swan, but she couldn't bring herself to do it.

Alice clasped her hands together, put her elbows on the table, and leaned forward as if ready to make a confession. "When I was really young and first working at the bakery with my mother, Reverend Klepper said something to me one day that scared the bejeezus out of me. He told me I could light up death row, that my mother didn't have a natural bakery personality, but I did, and that the Lord had sent me to help her. So, I'm guessing she might not have a natural wife personality, either."

Dillard looked at her quizzically. "Aloysius really told you that you could light up death row? What a strange thing to say to a little kid."

"I know," said Alice. "It stayed in my head for years. You know how he always says stuff like that." She started laughing.

"He does, doesn't he?" Dillard laughed. "Death row, what a thing to say." They both laughed harder. They laughed the kind of laughter that swells into sobbing. The waiter came over and asked if there was something wrong with their food, which only made them laugh and cry more. That's how it went until just before eleven, when Alice had to be at her next class.

"Will you be okay?" she asked.

"I think so. Will you?"

"I'll try. Will you call me and let me know where you're going and what you're doing?"

"Of course."

Alice wiped her eyes, put on lipstick, and then got up and started to walk off. In a moment, she turned around, walked behind Dillard's chair, leaned down, and whispered in his ear.

This would be the other thing he'd always remember: how after everything, Alice had told him she loved him.

Chapter 30

I-95 headed toward Skyville: nearly sixteen hours ahead of him to think. Dillard replayed his conversation with Alice dozens of times. By the time he hit Philadelphia, he began to doubt the good feelings he'd had driving out of Boston. *Surely, Emilia Mae will tell Alice about Nick. Alice will remember how angry I got when she found the picture of me and Nick. She'll think I'm a liar and never trust me again. Emilia Mae's so angry with me, she'll only fuel Alice's distrust.* He told himself he would talk to Alice about Nick at another time, when she was calmer and he was less distraught.

By Roanoke, his thoughts drifted to Sharlene Moore. Would she still be as prim and formal as she was ten years ago? He pictured her in the same dark, shapeless clothes as when he last saw her, her tidy long hair held in place by two tortoiseshell barrettes. Why did she say yes to his visit so quickly? Did she want to tell him off in person?

Sharlene swung open the front door of the log cabin before Dillard even got out of the car. Her hair was gray and wavy and well below her shoulders. She wore a long flowing dress with a tie-dyed pattern and smelled of that godawful patchouli oil. A bunch of thin bangles wrapped around her wrist and sounded like jingle bells when she stuck out her arm to shake his hand. She studied him up and down. "Man, you've hardly changed at all. Hair's a bit darker and longer, but wow, those blue eyes. They don't quit, do they? You look great."

Dillard told her she looked great, too. "I like your hair."

"Thanks. When it started going gray, I thought I'm not going to do all that bullshit dyeing. This is me; I'm cool with it. Come on in."

Her face was still vase-shaped and her small brown eyes too close together, but that was pretty much all that remained of the Sharlene whom Dillard had known. The log house was the same on the outside. Inside, the once beige and neutral-colored walls were painted in bright greens, yellows, and oranges. There were batik prints on the wall, and on the mantel, a figurine with an engorged penis and another with pendulous breasts. A pair of large work boots sat by the front door. There were no pictures of Nick, only of the grown children, Zeke almost as tall as his father.

They settled on the couch across from the piano. She'd prepared some tea and pecan pie. "I remembered how much you liked this."

Christmas, the last time he'd seen her, she'd baked that pie. They'd all stood around the piano singing Christmas carols. It had been a happy time.

Now, they talked small talk: she about the children and her teaching job; he about Emilia Mae and Alice. This was no time to tell her about the separation. When they finally got to the subject of Nick, it was Sharlene who led the way.

"It took me a long time to get over Nicky. I was hurt and angry. I thought that was a cowardly and selfish thing for him to do. To me and the children. I quit teaching for a semester and just stayed around the house. Friends told me I should move, get away from the memories, but the memories kept me company. I left everything as it was, his clothes, his papers. I didn't move a thing, thinking he'd walk back in and it was all a big mistake. It took me more than a year until I was ready to get rid of it all."

Dillard didn't know that Sharlene called Nick Nicky. He felt jealous about the intimacy that that implied. Uncomfortable about what to say, he stuck to the platitudes: "Nick was very beloved by all of his patients."

"I know," she said, sounding slightly annoyed. "He was beloved by everyone. But tell me this, was he beloved by you?"

"Well, yes, I suppose so."

"I mean beloved in a carnal way. Was he beloved by you in a carnal way?"

"Why would you ask me that?"

"I'm not a child," she said. "I saw how you looked at him. At first, I told myself you probably idolized him, a doctor, an older man, and all that. We know what we want to know; we see what we want to see. Then one night, he came home with one cashmere sock missing...so unlike Nicky. At Christmas, you gave him a pair of cashmere socks. That's when I knew for sure. Right after that, he was gone. Were you with him when he died?"

Dillard remembered the note Nick had written. Sharlene knew about them, he'd said, but he'd made sure to remove any evidence that he was with Nick at the hotel in New York City.

"No," he lied.

Sharlene didn't ask any more about New York City. Dillard figured she knew what she wanted to know about that.

"Why didn't you come to the funeral? I was sure you'd be there."

"I didn't want to intrude."

"I wouldn't have minded," she said, twirling a piece of hair around her finger. "You're probably the only person, aside from my children, who understood what it was like to love and be loved by Nicky. At the time, I hated you for that, but in an odd way, it would have been a comfort knowing there was someone else there who was feeling what I was feeling."

"I'm really sorry. Where did you bury him?"

"We didn't bury him. He'd always said he wanted to be cremated, so that's what we did."

Dillard wanted to ask where the ashes were scattered but thought it too ghoulish. He felt like crying, but not now, not in front of Sharlene. She'd suffered enough. Clearly, she'd moved on. For all he knew, she had someone else, maybe the owner of the large work boots.

"I really wish I'd been there for you."

Sharlene bit down on the knuckle of her index finger. "I'm okay with it now, but can I ask you another question?"

"Sure. Anything." She deserved at least that.

"Does your wife know about you and Nicky?"

"As of a few days ago, yes."

She started to laugh, then put her hand over her mouth. "Sorry. How'd that go?"

"Not so well." He had to laugh, too. "She pretty much kicked me out."

"Is that why you're back in Skyville?"

"Not really. I came to see you."

"Well, now that you've seen me, what are you going to do?"

He shook his head and ran his hands through his hair. "I don't know. I don't know anything. Emilia Mae assumes I like men. I don't even know if that's true or if—you know—there was just that one, um—you know..."

"Here's what I know," she said, pouring more tea and cutting more pie. "When I first figured out about you and Nicky, I was furious and hurt. I threatened all kinds of horrible things, like telling the hospital about the two of you. For a long time, I blamed myself. I wasn't pretty enough, feminine enough, smart enough, domestic enough. All the crap that women heap on themselves when their husbands cheat on them. But after a long while, I started to think about things differently: how he must have loved me and the kids so much, he was willing to live a lie about who he was. He did his best, his very best. He was a wonderful father, and I couldn't have asked for a better husband. But in my heart, I always knew something was missing. He respected me, was grateful to me. I knew he loved me, but not in the way that a woman wants to be loved. He couldn't help it. It pains me to think he never got to live his true life. But you can. If you really loved him, then honor him by doing what he couldn't do. Go out and live your real life. Stop kidding yourself."

Dillard didn't deny anything, didn't try to argue with her. Nick had always said that she was smart and had her head on straight. He had been right.

"You're very kind," he said. "I just need time to think. Some quiet time, alone."

★ ★ ★

For the next six days, Dillard stayed in his father's old cabin, which he'd kept up, paying the taxes and fixing the leaking roof, with the dim hope that someday he'd return. Now, when he walked down to Lake Lure and stared at the floating dock, it looked abandoned in the flat winter sun. Emptied of its summer visitors, stores were boarded up and streets were empty. He had no friends here, no place to go day after day. Sharlene had been cordial but didn't invite him to drop by again. His father's cabin was small and held memories he'd just as soon forget: Aunt Denise, his father's absence, his mother's absence. He searched his father's closet for Lily Doucet's old shawl and handbag. The shawl was mostly moth-eaten, the bag had lost its peppermint Chiclet smell.

It was time, time to sell this old cabin and move on. There was nothing left for him here. He called Aloysius and asked about Emilia Mae.

"She's doing okay given the circumstance."

"How about Geraldine?"

"Strangely, okay. It seems that Emilia Mae confided in her about you, and she was very sympathetic. The Lord works in strange ways. How about you? How're you doing?"

Dillard told him about his meeting with Sharlene and how lonely he was in Skyville. "I'm ready to sell this cabin and come back to New Rochelle."

"Hmm, not a good idea right now," said Aloysius. "Too much speculation and gossip. It'll die down, I'm sure, but if you came back now, you'd be walking into a hornet's nest. Give it time."

PART 4

Was there anything more optimistic than a Skyville spring? Wildflowers dotted the mountains like pieces of a puzzle scattered on the floor. Canoers and kayakers churned the waters of Lake Lure, and Dillard said that when the cold air embraced the warm air, a soft mist settled over the place like Brigadoon.

Chapter 31

Alice's second pregnancy was so unlike her first. The first one—well, she could laugh about it now, but at the time it wasn't so funny.

At twenty-four, she had been singing in Quatro, a small expensive French restaurant on Beacon Hill that had the familiar smell of freshly baked bread. Alice had liked the quiet of it. She'd felt elegant in the black sheath and string of pearls she wore each night, and placed on top of the piano the jar that was always filled with dollar bills as the evening wore on. She'd sung the songs of the day, Dylan, Queen, Billy Joel, and some of the standards she learned with Dillard. One snowy night, when the restaurant was half empty, she played "A Taste of Honey." In the quiet, she could hear the whispers of his flute and feel his presence across from her. Although the melodies she learned from Grandpa Earle were mostly out of date, she'd squeeze one or two of those in a night and feel an old sadness wash over her. When the restaurant closed at eleven, she and the waitstaff were free to eat whatever was left over from that night's menu.

Quatro had four waiters. Most were young men from Harvard

or BU who never stayed long enough for her to learn their names, but there was one who'd been there as long as she had. He was slightly older and had a small space between his two front teeth, drooping eyes, and ears too big for his small head. He wasn't particularly handsome but had a quick smile and a laugh that rumbled up from his stomach. Every now and then, when Alice finished a song, he'd turn to her with a thumbs-up. Sometimes, he'd bring her water or something stronger when he saw her glass was empty, and though they'd only exchanged pleasantries, he felt like a friend. His name was Carl, and that's all she knew about him until an evening in the early spring when Alice hadn't eaten since breakfast and gulped down two or three gin and tonics. Midway through "Summertime," she felt lightheaded, not only dizzy but as if her own voice and the music were moving away from her. She was clammy and shivering and nauseous and sweaty and then she was gone. The next thing she knew, she was lying on the ground with people looking down on her. She heard a voice telling people to get out of the way. Carl. He knelt beside her and put a cold cloth on her head. "Don't get up until you're ready," he whispered. He put his arm around the back of her head and slowly fed her water. When she felt a little better, he helped her stand and walked her to the kitchen. He sat her down and told her to keep the cold cloth behind her neck.

"How do you know what to do with fainting women?"

"I don't," he said. "I'm a first-year med student, and we haven't gotten to that part yet."

It became an easy habit, the two of them going back to his apartment after work. It was a dark studio with a pullout couch, a desk, a stove, and a refrigerator, all in the living room. Alice would lie on the couch as Carl sat at his desk and studied. She liked how he pursed his lips as he read, as if he were drinking the words.

They began seeing each other in daylight. Long walks. Free concerts.

Alice and Carl. Everything about them fit naturally. They were the same height. When she wrote out their names, their letters circled each other gracefully. He knew the lyrics to most Broadway shows, and though he couldn't carry a tune they'd sing together while they did the dishes. She moved into his small apartment and within the year they were married. Nothing fancy. A ceremony with a justice of the peace and, later, a dinner in New Rochelle prepared by Alberto and Geraldine. Six months later, Alice became pregnant.

She was in the library at NEC when she had her first contractions. She called Carl, who said he'd meet her at home. They played Scrabble and drank ginger ale long into the night, until the contractions became more regular. "I think I'm ready," she said after a particularly harrowing one. Then came another and another, until it was clear that Alice was more than ready. They made it to the lobby of their building. "Now," she shouted as she collapsed against the wall. Her cries brought the first floor neighbors to the lobby. Carl yelled for them to bring towels and blankets and pots of hot water.

"It's coming."

Carl could see that her water had broken. "I can do this," he told her, and ordered another neighbor to bring out a pair of scissors and a book of matches. Meanwhile, the building's super had called an ambulance, which came just as Carl had gotten Alice settled by the mailboxes. The baby's head crowned in the ambulance, and they barely made it to the emergency room before Alice gave birth.

They considered calling their little boy Lobby, but decided he'd spend the rest of his life explaining his name. So they decided on Earle Jr. instead.

In his third-year rotations, Carl chose gynecology as his specialty.

By Alice's second pregnancy, she was teaching at Juilliard in New York City and she and Carl had a big apartment on a high floor that faced out to Central Park. From there, the greens of the trees and the glistening silver of the reservoir looked like something out of one of Earle Jr.'s storybooks.

Geraldine loved visiting them and called theirs "the happy house." One afternoon, when Geraldine came to the city to babysit for Earle Jr., Alice answered the door after the first ring. "Earle's been waiting all day for you." As if on cue, the boy came running into the foyer. Geraldine was always taken aback by his fine blond hair, so much like Earle Sr.'s. He also had his great-grandfather's sweet disposition. He threw his arms around Geraldine and nearly knocked her over. "What'd ya bring me?"

Sometimes it was donuts; other times, cookies.

"How about a bag of chocolate chips?" said Geraldine.

"Thanks, Grandma." Earle reached for the bag.

Geraldine dangled it above his head. "Uh-uh-uh, what did I tell you to call me?"

"Geraldine. Thanks, Geraldine," he said, grabbing the bag as she lowered it.

"Honestly, you spoil him," said Alice as she put on her sunglasses, getting ready to head over to Juilliard. Geraldine noticed her stomach. "You're gonna start to show soon."

"I know, another month. Carl's certain it's going to be a girl."

"Well, that's his business. I'll bet he's right." Geraldine liked Carl, and not just because he gave her free hormone pills.

"Yup, Carl's always right about stuff like that. Besides, he's dying to have a girl."

"I'll bet he's a great father."

"The best."

"Mind if I ask you a question?"

Alice looked at her watch.

"I'll make it quick," Geraldine continued. "I wasn't the best mother, was I?"

"I have to be at school in fifteen minutes," said Alice.

"Tell me the truth, how bad was I?"

This was so typical of Geraldine, asking a question that begged for the truth but demanded a lie. "You were fine," she answered. "It must have been tough, raising a kid on your own, and then helping raise me, too."

"You were a delight, but your mother—no picnic, that one. Me neither, I guess."

Was Alice imagining it or did Geraldine's nose turn red as if she might cry? She really couldn't be late to this rehearsal. She needed to snap Geraldine out of this mood quickly. "Look, my mom turned out fine. The bakery is a huge success, and I'm a happy woman. If you were such a terrible mother, none of that would be true."

Geraldine kissed Alice on the cheek. "You've always been the sweet one. You sure as hell didn't get that from me."

Chapter 32

On their second date at the Old South Barbecue in White Plains, Dave Turner and Emilia Mae sat across from one another in a red Naugahyde booth. She was saying how her old friends, Reverend Klepper and his wife, Cora, had celebrated their forty-fifth wedding anniversary camping in the Sinai Desert. "They're both around seventy—no spring chickens—as my mother likes to say. They've decided to travel as much as they can while they're still healthy. Pretty amazing."

Dave was chewing on the olive from his martini. His eyes widened, as he placed his elbows on the table. "How do you know them?"

Emilia Mae had just eaten three ribs. She wiped her mouth with her napkin, then reapplied her blood-orange lipstick; at fifty-two, she wasn't about to be seen without makeup. She told him about working at the Neptune Inn, Xena, switching churches, and getting pregnant with Alice, leaving out her experiences with the other men. "At the time, I thought I wanted to get rid of her. I was so young and scared. It turns out, she's the best thing that ever happened to all of us." Emilia Mae paused to sip her beer and gauge Dave's reaction.

"Is her father still in the picture?" he asked.

Emilia Mae laughed. "Oh no, there never was a picture."

He studied her face in a way that made her think there was barbecue sauce on it somewhere. "There's so much character and strength in your face," he said.

"Ha! A lot of good all that character and strength have done me."

"I'm serious," he said. "Your honesty, it's refreshing."

"Well, okay, I'll take that as a compliment."

"Please do."

Dave had recently moved to New Rochelle, where he opened a women's shoe store. They met when he came to the bakery for crullers. After he said he was new to town, she told him where to shop, where to eat. She liked his kind face; he liked her attention. On their first date, she took him on a walking tour of the prettiest parts of New Rochelle and showed him the landmarks of her life.

On their third date, he told her about his life. "My dad had polio, so our lives revolved around him. He was a quiet, modest man. Never complained or demanded anything. But because of his incapacity, my mother was our breadwinner. She worked as a bookkeeper for a printing plant in Newark. I'm the oldest of three, and my job was to take my dad into Manhattan to get his special shoes repaired or buy him new ones. I suppose that's what got me into the business in the first place. I own two stores in Jersey, this is my first in Westchester County. All three make customized shoes." Dave stopped talking and took Emilia Mae in with his big gray eyes. "Gosh, you look pretty today."

She plumped up her hair, high, wide, and auburn now, thanks

to hot rollers and Alberto. Earlier, she and Dave had gotten caught in a downpour, and Emilia Mae worried that the pouf had gone out of it.

"Anyway," he continued, "I finished community college and stayed near home to be close to my dad. I married Tina, my high school girlfriend, right after graduation. We scraped up enough money to open a shoe store in Newark that did custom work for people with orthopedic problems. I never had to drive my dad into Manhattan again."

On their fourth date, Emilia Mae told him about the bakery and her family. "My dad died when I was twenty-eight. He was very kind, but had trouble standing up to my mother. She's seventy-two now but has the body of a forty-year-old. She's had the same boyfriend for years. A piece of work, that woman. Alice is thirty-three, married with one kid, another on the way. How about you and Tina? Did you have any kids?"

Dave nodded. "Two, a boy and a girl. When she was forty-seven, Tina got breast cancer..." He looked away.

Emilia Mae took Dave's hand. "I'm sorry, that sounds horrible."

"It's the worst kind of loss."

"I know."

"Are you... Did you lose someone, too?"

"Yes, though not quite in that way. I was married for several years, and let's just say marriage and I ran out of luck."

Dave had his left leg crossed over his right thigh. He fiddled with the tassels on his Gucci loafer before taking a sip of his martini. He put down his glass and leaned across the table. "Emilia Mae, what if I told you that your luck just did an about-face. That you've found a man ready to give himself to you if you will have him."

Emilia Mae studied his face, a well-worn one with sadness in his shy smile. He was sympathetic in a straightforward way that made her feel understood. A big man, six-three, he had arms like cement. ("You would too if you'd been carrying stacks of shoeboxes your whole life," he told her.) His hair was gray, but he still had most of it. His nose was a bit crooked, but he had a lovely broad smile and his teeth seemed to be all his own.

"That's a mighty big statement, promising yourself to me. You know, you're talking to a grandma. We're no spring chickens, either of us."

Dave laughed. "You can't scare me. I've got three grandkids, two boys and a girl. At this stage of my life, I know what I want, and when I find it, well, why wait? Who knows how much more time any of us have? Are you willing to give us a chance?"

"Grandkids," said Emilia Mae. "I had no idea I'd like being called Grandma so much. My mother's so vain about her looks, she tells everyone *she's* the grandma. Even so, she keeps telling her grandson, 'Just call me Geraldine.' God, that woman never changes."

Dave smiled. "Are you avoiding my question? Are you willing to give us a chance?"

Emilia Mae jiggled her leg so much, she accidentally kicked Dave in the shin.

"Is that your answer?"

"Oh, no. I'm sorry."

She looked down at her hands, ringless for the past twelve years, and said tentatively, "I think maybe I am." Dave got out of his side of the booth and moved in beside her. He pulled her to him and kissed her. His lips tasted of gin, and she could feel his teeth against her own. Afterward, she saw how her lipstick had smeared his mouth. The sight of it rearranged things inside of her. She liked how dwarfed she was in his arms. For the first time since Dillard left, Emilia Mae felt safe.

She didn't tell anyone about Dave right away, waiting to see if this one would stick. Late one afternoon, as she and her mother were closing up, Geraldine watched Emilia Mae put on mascara and lipstick in front of the small mirror hanging outside the baking room. She was wearing a bright red blouse with pads that bulked up her shoulders, and an A-line black skirt that came just below her knees. "You getting all dolled up for a big date?" asked Geraldine.

"As a matter of fact, I am."

"Anyone I know?"

"No one you know, but someone you've probably seen. Dave Turner, that nice-looking big guy who always comes by for crullers. Tall, gray hair, a little older than me."

"I have noticed him," said Geraldine. "Very polite. Well dressed."

"Yup, that's the one." Emilia Mae blotted her lips.

"A word to the wise: He's very self-conscious about his looks. He could be another of your gay ones."

Emilia Mae swiveled away from the mirror and placed her hands on her hips. "You mean one of *our* gay ones."

The two women shared a guilty laugh. When Emilia Mae had told her mother about Dillard, Geraldine's immediate reaction had been relief. So that's why Dillard had rejected her. At the time, she told Emilia Mae about Alberto. "Everyone has forks in the road," she'd explained. "That's his. But it doesn't stop him from loving me completely, so what he does in his spare time is none of my business."

Emilia Mae defended Dave. "I'm sure he's not gay, Mother. I'm pretty sure there's not even a fork in his road, but thank you for your concern."

Geraldine couldn't figure if the tone in her daughter's voice was sarcastic or sincere.

It was a dazzling Indian summer afternoon, and Geraldine already had grapefruit-sized sweat stains under the arms of her green satin blouse. "I'm just looking out for your welfare. I don't want to ever see you that hurt again." She pulled out a handkerchief and blew her nose.

Geraldine was amazed how quickly tears seemed to come lately. She'd bawled watching *Coal Miner's Daughter* (Christ, she'd never been south of Atlantic City). Marching bands, the smell of lilies, commercials with dogs in them, they all made her weepy. Now that she worked at the bakery only three days a week, she had time to do whatever she wanted. Hell, she'd worked hard enough her whole life; she deserved to do whatever she wanted. She thought it would be different when she reached this age. She thought she'd feel satisfied and not expect any more from life than what she'd already been given. She had Alberto. She was part of the New Rochelle social scene. She was a grandmother and had a pretty happy family. But part of her felt like a failure, a fraud. She watched other women her age, the ones who had their hair done once a week, had subscriptions to the opera and ballet at Lincoln Center, went to matinees, took cruises to Bermuda. They had facelifts, manicures, pedicures, massages; took yoga; wore Armani; gave benefits; went to benefits; and they seemed pleased with themselves. She could afford to do those things (maybe not Armani). What was wrong with her? Why was she feeling so blue?

She often thought about Earle, about their early days, before Emilia Mae. She was so full of promise then, desirable and innocent. She'd taken it all for granted: her shiny hair, petite figure, the way men would look at her, Earle. If she'd only known that it would all disappear, what would she have done? Probably nothing. She was too flush with youth to believe it would ever disappear.

Then came Emilia Mae. Poor Emilia Mae. Geraldine had to admit she'd screwed up with that girl. Really, sending a child away at fifteen? What was she thinking? She knew what she was thinking. She'd wanted Earle for herself. She'd wanted things to be the way they had been. She'd wanted to be who she had been.

She stared at Emilia Mae, middle-aged now, and thought, *We're both getting older.* She dabbed the back of her neck with her handkerchief and said, "Look, I made mistakes. Big ones. I know sending you to the Neptune Inn was a bad idea. I was young and selfish, and I wanted things between your father and me to be as they were."

"You mean as they were before I came along?"

"Yes, exactly. Can you understand that?"

Emilia Mae saw the liver spots that stained the translucent skin on her mother's hands. Alberto had dyed her hair a little too red, and she still wore miniskirts despite the map of veins running down her legs. She looked frail and sad.

"I do," she said. "Dillard wanted to have kids, and I said no, for the same reason. I didn't want to share him." She wiped her eyes with the back of her hand. "I miss Dad. I miss Dillard."

"Me too," said Geraldine.

They fell into an awkward embrace until Geraldine looked up and caught sight of herself in the little mirror. "You need to get out of here and go on your date with that big guy, and I need to redo my makeup before I scare little children."

As they disentangled themselves, Geraldine said, "You know, that Dave fellow is lucky to find you."

Emilia Mae stared at her mother. "Gee, that's the nicest thing you've ever said to me."

Geraldine gave her one of her coy smiles. "Yeah, well don't get used to it. I still think you have the devil in you."

Chapter 33

As she did once or twice a month, Alice visited Dillard in his Greenwich Village apartment. She told him about her conversation with Geraldine, how she'd asked if she was a bad mother and seemed on the verge of tears. "Just because a person is old, do we have to rewrite history?"

"We all rewrite history," he said.

A stained-glass angel suncatcher hung from his living room window, and the houseplants on the sill were vibrant despite the cool fall weather. The radiator clanked as afternoon shadows lay across the parquet floors like fallen bodies.

"I don't think I do," said Alice. "Do I?"

Dillard smiled. "You tell me."

Often, their visits turned into truth-telling sessions, which is how Alice learned all about Nick, and how Dillard found out that Alice used to follow gap-toothed men, thinking that they might be her father.

"Are you asking if I ever lied about anything?" she asked.

"Not lied, exactly. You were kind of perfect. Did you ever do anything that was less than perfect?"

"You know I did," said Alice. "That time you found me wandering down the street without a purse, I'd ended up in a bar with one of those gap-toothed men and had a beer."

"Is that the worst of it?"

"Mmm, well, I also followed you to the Swan a couple of times."

Dillard ran his hand over his mouth. "Yeah, I used to sneak over there, just to look at the boys. Nothing more, I swear. You must have known about me before your mother did."

Alice said she hadn't wanted to think that until Carolyn met him. "She couldn't get over how handsome you were. She wondered if you liked men and said there was something about your manner that made her think that was so. I said, no, that couldn't be, but in the back of my mind I remembered finding that picture of you and Nick at the lake and how mad you got when I asked you about it."

"I was scared, that's all. She was smart, Carolyn. Are you still in touch with her?"

"Oh sure, we talk all the time and I see her about once a month. She's a fashion editor at *Vogue*, not something either of us could have predicted. Now, *there's* someone who probably never rewrote her own history. She always seems to live her truth."

"That's what I'm trying to do," said Dillard.

Dillard had spent the past three and a half years in the orchestra pit playing the flute eight times a week for *Annie*. It was numbing work; he didn't even call it music anymore. He was so bored he'd read books or do crossword puzzles during times the score didn't call for flute. He considered *Annie* his penance. Penance for what? For leaving Emilia Mae? Abandoning Alice? Loving Nick? Liking men? Here he was in New York City in 1981, where gay men unabashedly advertised themselves by the clothes they wore, the way they walked, where they went: the clubs, the baths, the bars, the shows, the Pines. Wasn't this why he'd come to New York City, to live his truth?

Yes, but not that way. It was no one's business what he was or who he loved. He wore a black suit and white shirt to work every day, and that became his uniform. Now at the beginning of his fifties, he kept his hair long enough so it curled at his collar. His blue eyes hadn't lost their blaze, and he was still fit and handsome enough to be called "pretty boy." Sure, he had lovers here and there. Mostly closeted gay men—a math professor at Rutgers, a young man who'd subbed for the trombone player at *Annie*. Occasionally he'd go to one of those clubs and end up leaving with some man whose last name he never knew. While those one-night stands satisfied an immediate urge, they left him feeling hungry—hungry for Nick, hungry for love, hungry for home. Sometimes the memories of those people and places were so palpable, he thought that if he would just dig a little deeper, he could crawl back into them. Visits with Alice were a high point; they brought him back to family and belonging. Greedily, he'd question her about her mother, her grandmother, the bakery, New Rochelle. He hadn't been there since the breakup, nor had he been back to Skyville since he'd sold his father's cabin.

When Alice visited him in early April, Dillard took her jacket as she plopped down on the couch and arched her stomach in his direction. "Look at this, a belly full of baby. It's a girl, we know for sure."

"That's wonderful. Do you know what you're going to call her?"

"I have no idea, though you want to hear something weird? You know how Aloysius always comes up with these strange things? Twice, out of nowhere, he's suggested I name the baby Linden. It's an odd name, but he thinks it's beautiful. Why does he care so much about what I name this baby?"

Dillard remembered the walk he'd taken with Aloysius right before he left New Rochelle. Dillard guessed that by wanting Alice to name her daughter Linden, he still hadn't told Cora.

"I have no idea," he said. "But I think we should celebrate your girl." He went into the kitchen, which, like everything else in his apartment, was immaculate. Plates were stacked up on the open shelves according to color, glasses lined up according to size. He brought out two yellow mugs and a plate full of sticky buns, Alice's favorite, and laid them out on the red dinette table in the nook off the living room.

The sun shot a rainbow through the stained-glass angel. The smell of cinnamon filled the apartment, and Dillard smiled as Alice licked her fingers and reached for another. She'd cut her hair into one of those Dorothy Hamill wedges, which Dillard thought accentuated her wide brown eyes and dazzling smile. Her gold hoop earrings played well against her high cheekbones.

"You still have a little Carolyn left in you, don't you?" asked Dillard.

"Oh yeah, the Carolyn in me will live forever. And speaking of Carolyn, she's giving me a shower two weeks from Saturday. I'd love it if you came and brought your flute."

Dillard took a deep breath and leaned back in his chair. She could hear the exhaustion in his sigh and see it in the dark rings around his eyes.

"But if it's too much, you don't have to . . ."

He smiled at her and stroked her chin. "You're more beautiful now than ever."

"I'll take that as a yes?"

"Of course, I'll be there."

This was life as he wished it. "You know, Aloysius and Cora think of you as their own. Linden's a pretty name. Why not? What does Carl think?"

Alice shook her head. "Carl says we can name her after a tampon company for all he cares, he's just so happy it's a girl."

They talked more about the baby, due in early June. Alice brought him up to date on Emilia Mae. "She's seeing this man who owns a shoe store in town. We've only just met him; he seems nice enough."

Dillard brightened. "That's great. She deserves the best."

Chapter 34

On the day of the shower, Dillard showed up at Carolyn's brownstone a little early, and out of breath after climbing the two flights to her apartment. She greeted Dillard with a hug. "I know, quite a trek, isn't it? What can I get you to drink?" She took his flute and coat and led him to a couch upholstered in a pale yellow chintz. "Water would be fine." Carolyn called for someone to bring out a glass of water and pointed at the couch. "Please, get comfortable. That's what this old thing is for."

Dillard studied her. She looked the same: tall, slim, long straight black hair. Her only concession to age was lip gloss tinged with coral and a bit of blush. Instead of her usual head-to-toe black, she was dressed in a creamy beige boatneck sweater, Siena-colored suede pants, and a pair of beige pumps. "You look very glamorous," he said.

She laughed. "Calvin, head to toe. I don't work at a fashion magazine for nothing. And you, you look pretty good for an old man."

"Old." Dillard closed his eyes. "You're not kidding, I feel like I'm a hundred and three."

She patted his arm. "Relax, no one will be here for another half hour. I'm going in the kitchen to help with the appetizers."

Dillard sat back on the couch, taking in the club chairs, the floor-to-ceiling silk curtains, and the angel-white carpeting. The room smelled of fresh cypress that seemed to be coming from the small green candles flickering on the mantelpiece. He must have nodded off because when he awoke, Alice, Carl, and Earle Jr. were whispering at the opposite end of the room. Dillard sat up and said, "It's okay, I had a little catnap." He got to his feet and went over to Earle. "Hey, buddy." He held up his hand for a high-five and waited for Earle to slap his. Instead, Earle backed away and stood between his parents.

"He's having a shy day," said Alice.

"I get it," said Dillard. Other guests started arriving, friends of Alice's whom Dillard had never met. Carolyn had made a mixtape and turned it up loud, which made it imperative to talk over "Baby Love" and "Having My Baby."

The room was filling with familiar faces. Aloysius, his hair as white as the carpeting, wearing big black glasses that magnified his already bulging eyes, and Cora, still a beauty, greeted Dillard with warm hugs. He'd last seen them two Christmases ago, when they'd come to Alice's for dinner. While they'd all promised to stay in touch, somehow none of them had. Dillard spotted Emilia Mae standing by the fireplace with a large man. He told Aloysius he'd talk to him later and went over to the two of them.

"Hi," he said.

She smiled and said, "Hi."

"You look nice," he said.

"So do you," she said. They came together in a hug. Emilia Mae had gotten so used to Dave Turner's massive arms that Dillard felt small by comparison; she could carry him if she had to. She stepped back and looked him up and down. "You've lost weight."

"It must be my fine home cooking."

"No, really, you seem thinner. Are you working out a lot?"

"Not really. I walk to and from the Alvin Theater every day. Must be about five miles. Otherwise, aside from swimming whenever I can, I haven't done much."

Emilia Mae stroked his cheek. "Well, eat more, walk less, or something like that. Don't lose any more weight."

She introduced him to Dave. His hand was still swathed in Dave's when Dillard felt a chill crawl up the back of his neck. He turned around in time to see Geraldine and Alberto enter the room.

This was the moment he'd dreaded. He hadn't seen them since the divorce and hadn't heard a word from them. Geraldine made a point of making eye contact with him as they each took a quiche canape from the waiter's tray.

"Good to see you again, Dillard. You're looking nice and trim."

"Thank you," said Dillard. "So are you."

Just then, Carolyn turned down the music and clinked her champagne glass with a knife. "You all are so kind to come and celebrate my friend Alice and the soon-to-be addition to the family. As most of you know, Alice is a music teacher. You may not know that she has a gorgeous voice. Another thing you may not know is that when we were at school in Boston, she was the lead vocalist of a group called Electric Fruit."

People clapped and laughed.

"Hey, it was the sixties, alright?" said Carolyn. "Anyway, Alice credits her stepfather, Dillard Fox, with nurturing her musically, and as a special request, she has asked if he would play the flute while she sang one of their favorite songs. So, Dillard, may we have the pleasure?"

The word *stepfather* hit Dillard like a stray bullet. He'd never heard himself described that way. Alice came over and whispered, "It's a sappy one, 'Someone to Watch over Me.' Are you up for it?"

"Yup, I can pull it together."

Carolyn had set up two facing chairs in front of the fireplace. While Dillard cleaned and pieced his flute together, Alice told the group, "This was the first song my grandpa, Earle Sr., ever taught me. Since then, I've sung it with Dillard dozens of times."

The crowd settled into chairs and the sofa, and some sat on the floor. Dillard played the four-bar introduction, and then Alice stood up and started to sing. Dillard hadn't heard Alice sing in many years. Her voice had gotten richer with age. The words came effortlessly, as if this was her story. Dillard tried to hold his concentration to the music and Alice, but his eyes rested on Emilia Mae. She was jiggling her leg the way she did when she was nervous. She was well dressed. Wearing pearls. Maybe the shoe guy gave her those. She'd aged. He'd aged. What did he expect? He smiled at her. She smiled back.

When the song ended, the group cheered and demanded an encore. "Just one more," Dillard whispered to Alice. They decided on "Fly Me to the Moon." When they finished, Dillard kissed Alice on the cheek and whispered, "I'll see you later." Carolyn stood up, clapped her hands, and shouted "Bravo!"

Dillard started to sneak out when Alice started opening presents, but stopped in his tracks as Alice held up the gift she'd received from the Kleppers: an antique yellow cashmere baby blanket with the letter L monogrammed onto it.

Chapter 35

Shortly after the baby shower, Dillard started running a fever. Over the phone, he told Alice, "I have a nasty flu that won't go away. Don't visit, that's the last thing you need."

The flu hadn't gone away by the middle of April, and still Dillard refused to see Alice. When she told Carl she was worried, he said he hadn't liked Dillard's coloring on the night of the shower. Emilia Mae had also commented that he looked gaunt that night, but what upset Alice the most was when she'd asked Earle Jr. why he hadn't high-fived Dillard that night, he answered, "I don't know, something about him was scary."

"Screw it," Alice said to Carl the last time Dillard refused to see her. "I'm going over there after my Thursday morning class."

That afternoon, she rang his bell and waited, and then rang the bell again. Even before Dillard opened the door, she smelled trouble, a sour odor: old food, sweat, excrement—it could have been a combination of those things or any one of them. A Dillard she didn't recognize opened the door. His face was unshaven and as ashen as an old newspaper, his hair long and unkempt. He didn't seem happy to see her, and even if he had been, his hollow cheeks and downturned mouth looked as if they'd been sculpted into a mask that held no smiles. "I told you not to come here," he said.

Alice stared past him to the rumpled blanket spread across the couch, the dirty dishes stacked in the sink, the dead plants on the windowsill. "Jeez, what the hell is going on here?"

"Nothing except this damn flu. I can't seem to kick it."

"Have you seen a doctor?"

"There's no point. Nick used to say the only thing to do about the flu is lie down and wait it out. That's what I'm doing."

Alice took Dillard's arm and led him back to the couch. He was wearing a long-sleeved oxford shirt over a baggy pair of gray jogging pants. She could feel how thin his arm was and saw how he walked, like a fragile old man. She got him settled on the couch. "First, I'm going to straighten this place up, then we'll talk about what's next. I don't know what you have, but I can tell you this much, it's not the flu."

After she opened the windows, washed the dishes, sponged off the crusty Formica table, threw out the dead plants, changed the sheets on his bed, and scrubbed the bathroom, she sat down on the green Naugahyde chair facing the couch.

"I feel so helpless," Dillard said softly. "What kind of a man lies on the couch and watches a very pregnant woman clean his house?"

"A very sick man," said Alice.

After a few minutes, she hoisted herself out of the chair and bent down to pick the cups off the floor.

"You're eight months pregnant," said Dillard. "You really shouldn't be doing this."

"I have an eight-year-old at home. Do you think I never get down on the floor to play with him?"

When she finished vacuuming and taking out the garbage, the place was neat and odor-free. Alice lay down at the opposite side of the couch from Dillard and put her legs up so that the two of them were lying head to toe.

"Are you eating?" she asked.

"When I can."

"How about drinking?"

"Tea, tea, tea, 'til it's coming out of my ears."

"How's it going with *Annie?*"

"Had to quit. Absent too many times."

"Money?"

"Some. Running out."

"Okay, we have to get you to a doctor. Do you have one?"

"Nope."

"Carl will find you one. In the meantime, you can't stay here alone."

"Right. Maybe I should check into the Plaza or the Waldorf."

Alice kicked his arm. "Very funny. I'm not kidding."

"Seriously. Where should I go?"

"Home with me?"

"Another great idea. I'm sick as a dog, so put me up with an eight-year-old and a baby about to be born. I'm sure Carl would love that."

"You know, Dillard, being sarcastic isn't helping either of us." She got up and headed toward the kitchen.

"Calling an ambulance?"

She turned around. "You're joking, right?"

"Sure," he said, reaching behind him for the glass of tea on the end table. Something thudded to the floor.

"Shit," he said.

"I'll get it." Alice came over and picked up the object. She rolled it around in her hand a few times then smiled. "I remember this." It was the rock with Dillard's name written in fading India ink that Alice had made as a place card the first time Dillard came to dinner.

"I know, it's funny, isn't it?" he asked.

"You mean that you saved it all these years?"

"That, and how you spelled my name."

Alice looked at it again. "D-i-l-l-e-r-d. Christ, what an idiot! Why didn't you tell me?"

"Because I was so touched, I didn't want to spoil it."

Alice kissed him on the forehead. "Even then, I loved you." His forehead was hot.

She went into the kitchen and called Emilia Mae. "Mom," she whispered. "I'm at Dillard's. He's sick. Really sick. He can't stay here alone...I don't know, he says it's the flu, but I'm pretty sure it isn't...I don't know what I want you to do about it...Okay, I get it, but I'm not leaving him alone here. He looks awful, exhausted. The place was a mess, and it stank. He's really sick...I guess I was thinking he could stay with you for a while. Just 'til he gets better. Carl will find him a doctor...No, I'm sure just a few days...I know it's asking a lot. I'll help out...Dave's a good guy, he'll understand...Aw, that's great, thanks. I'll call when we're ready to leave."

Alice walked back into the living room and stood over Dillard. "So, guess where we're going?"

Dillard shrugged.

"New Rochelle. You've heard of it, right? You're staying at my mom's house 'til you get a little better. She has an extra room, as you know, and there'll be people around to look after you."

Dillard was so tired he barely had the energy to resist. He waved a weak hand in her direction. "So much trouble. I'm sure Emilia Mae has better things to do."

"Please, don't even argue. She wants you to come and that's that. We'll pack a few things, then I'll call Carl and have him drive you to the house. Now, where's your suitcase?"

It was a strange homecoming. Everything was the same; everything was different. The walls he'd once painted in bright pastels were now tasteful yellows, mauves, and whites. There were new appliances in the kitchen, but the same old dining table and couch in the living room. Emilia Mae had gotten a new bed in place of their old one, and what used to be his and Alice's music room now held a washing machine, a dryer, and household supplies.

Emilia Mae didn't seem happy to see him, though she didn't seem unhappy, either. She was efficient. "I've made up the bed in Alice's room. I think you'll be most comfortable there." Alice helped him unpack and stacked his underwear, pajamas, jeans, shirts, and sweaters in her old closet. He hung his brown flap cap on the doorknob. Emilia Mae had turned the room into an office with a desk, a small bookshelf, and Alice's narrow bed. An Andrew Wyeth print hung over the bed, and travel posters of Taos, San Francisco, and Rome filled the other three walls. Dillard wondered if these were places Emilia Mae and Dave had visited or planned to visit.

When they finished unpacking, Alice told him to put on his pajamas and get into bed. Dillard was too exhausted to do anything else.

The sheets were cold. He pulled Alice's old comforter up to his chin. The floral scent of Tide, the same detergent he and Emilia Mae always used, brought him back to the nights he'd spent sitting at the foot of this bed, reading to Alice and tucking the comforter in around her. He closed his eyes. A warm feeling of being taken care of flowed through him. He must have fallen asleep, because when he awoke, it was dark outside. Alice was gone. He heard the thrum of a radio coming from the kitchen. He had the urge to cry out "Mommy." Which mommy? Lily Doucet? Emilia Mae? He lay in bed confused about where he was, who he wanted.

At some point, Emilia Mae appeared with a bowl of soup. She sat on the desk chair next to his bed and watched him eat. "Good to see you hungry. Are you up for company?"

"What kind of company?"

"Aloysius and Cora. They heard you were here and asked if they could drop by. Only for a few minutes."

Dillard started to get out of bed. "I'd better get dressed."

Emilia Mae gently pushed his shoulder. "No need. They know you're not feeling well."

Dillard went to the bathroom, brushed his teeth, and combed his hair. He looked in the mirror, something he'd been avoiding. He saw a hollowed-out version of himself. Dark circles under his eyes. Sallow skin. In a few days, he had an appointment with a doctor Carl had recommended. He told himself he couldn't face any doctor looking the way he looked. He'd shave tomorrow, maybe get Emilia Mae to cut his hair.

He was back in bed a half hour later when Aloysius and Cora came in on tiptoes. "How are you?" Cora whispered, as she sat next to him and took his hand.

"Stupid flu. I'll be better."

Cora's hand felt cool and smooth. She must have noticed that he held it tighter than he ought to because she rubbed his arm with her other hand.

"How've you been?" he asked.

"Oh, you know, the usual festivities, funerals, baptisms," she laughed. "I've started playing mah-jongg. Have you ever played? It's a fascinating game, addictive really. I'm trying to teach Ally, but I don't think he has the patience, do you Ally?"

Aloysius took off his glasses as Cora chatted about the women in her mah-jongg group. He blew onto the lenses and wiped them with his scarf. Cora had moved on to the trip they were planning in August. "Verona, it's supposed to be beautiful, and the food. Well, you know about Italian food. If we can, we'll go to Siena. Everyone says it's special—"

Aloysius interrupted: "Cora, we don't want to wear him out. Dillard, we just came by to say a quick hello."

Cora dropped Dillard's hand. "Goodness, I hope I haven't yakked your ear off." She stood up. "Why don't I go join Emilia Mae in the kitchen, and you two can talk." She kissed Dillard on the forehead. "You take care. We'll see you real soon."

Aloysius took Cora's place. "I adore that woman, but the older she gets the more loquacious she gets. Me? I'm the opposite. By now I feel I've said all I have to say."

"I miss you," said Dillard, sitting up. "I haven't found anyone to talk to the way I used to talk to you."

"Me neither," said Aloysius. "It's been a long time."

The two men stared at one another as if by doing so, they could fill each other up with what had not been spoken.

"Can I ask you a question?" said Dillard.

"Sure. Anything."

"Did you ever tell Cora about Linden?"

Aloysius shook his head. "We've planted ourselves in each other's lives, and to uproot us in that way doesn't make sense. At least that's what I tell myself. You, on the other hand, you are a stronger man than I. You told the truth and moved on. You'll never know what deep admiration I feel for you."

Dillard laughed. "Wow, for a man of few words, you've sure said a mouthful. But seriously, it takes courage to love someone deeply enough *not* to tell them something that could wound them forever. What's the point? I'm hardly courageous. I happened to blunder my way into a life I should have never had in the first place. I'm not sorry." He looked around the room. "I still have all this. But I hurt people along the way."

Aloysius shook his head. "Look at us, two old fools trying to sort out who we are. You're here. I'm here. That's all that matters."

Dillard lay back down. "I'm sort of here."

Aloysius stood up. "You're tired. Rest now, we'll be back."

Dillard slept until late morning. He bathed and shaved and made himself toast and jam. He was sitting at the kitchen table reading the newspaper when Emilia Mae walked in a little after noon. "Nice to see you eating," she said. "We need to fatten you up." She placed a box of shortbread in front of him and poured herself a cup of coffee. "My mother's been asking after you."

"Asking what, if I'm still alive?"

"Nice," she said. "She actually wanted to know how you were. It was her idea to bring the shortbread."

"Please thank her for me."

"How're you feeling?"

"Fine. Tired."

His jogging pants and shirt hung off him, much as his clothes had the first time she saw him. "You're looking a bit shaggy. How about that haircut you mentioned? Might perk you up."

Dillard saw the concern in her face, which did perk him up. "I'd love that."

She got a towel and wrapped it around his neck. He held the garbage pail under his chin as she started clipping. He remembered how her hands felt in his hair and how carefully she would measure each tuft between her fingers.

"Thanks for taking me in," he said.

"You're welcome. Alice said you were really sick."

"Just a stupid flu. Damn thing won't go away. It's really nice of you."

"I'm sure you'd do the same for me."

"I'd like to think I would. Though you have plenty of people to take care of you."

She smiled. "I suppose I do."

"Dave seems like a good man."

"He is. I'm lucky to have found him at this stage in my life."

"Yes, well imagine how he must feel. I mean, I know how it feels to be with you. Like he's the luckiest man alive."

"Did you really feel that way?"

"My life was in shambles, you know that. You saved me. Gave me a home, a family, a job. How much luckier could I have been?"

"Well, you could have been straight."

"God knows, I tried."

Emilia Mae plucked out one of his curls from the trash can.

"The first time I cut your hair, I saved one of these. Still have it somewhere. I couldn't believe a man with gorgeous thick blond hair like yours would choose someone like me. I was the one who felt lucky."

"I guess we were both lucky." He looked at the locks of hair that had fallen into the garbage and saw they were wispy, with no color at all. He wondered if Emilia Mae noticed. He stood up to wipe the stray hairs from the chair, and nearly toppled forward. Emilia Mae caught him by the elbow. "You okay?"

"Just a little dizzy."

"C'mon, let's get you back to bed." She guided him to the bed and tucked him in. "Get some rest. There's soup in the fridge and pralines in the cupboard above the sink. You know where everything is, so make yourself at home."

As the days went on, Dillard spent more time in bed. The doctor he'd seen was puzzled by Dillard's symptoms and put him on high doses of antibiotics. Despite that, he got weaker. Even getting out of bed to go to the bathroom was a chore. Alice visited whenever she could. On the day that Geraldine came to visit, the apple blossom tree outside his window put out its first petals. Dillard shaved and put on a clean shirt. He tried sitting up on a chair. They hadn't really spoken since he left New Rochelle, and he wondered what they'd have to say to one another.

He needn't have worried.

Geraldine darted into the room in a pair of blue jeans and a clingy turquoise sweater. He'd only caught a glimpse of her at Alice's shower. She was thinner than he remembered and wore so much makeup it was hard to see what was really going on with her face, particularly against the brassy color of her hair.

"Well, here you are," she said, studying him up and down. "A little less of you, but no less handsome."

"Thank you, ma'am," he said. "And look at you, age has made no claim on you."

Just like that, they were back in their old game.

"After all these years, I'm still ma'am?"

"Sorry, old habits."

She asked how he was feeling. He complained about the flu that wouldn't go away. She told him how chinless old Elaine Treaster's husband, Leon, of the ballroom fortune, had left her for a twenty-four-year-old event planner. He told her about the tedium of playing "Tomorrow" every night for nearly four years.

By now, his words were coming out barely above a whisper, and Geraldine could see by his strained face the effort it was costing him:

"Would you like me to help you back to bed?" she asked.

"Yes, please." He held out his arms like a child waiting to be picked up. Geraldine put her arm around his waist and slowly walked him to the bed. Once she tucked the covers in around him, she sat down by his side. "Alberto sends his best. He's still the wizard, busy as ever." She fluffed the hair around her ears. Dillard knew that was his cue to remark on her hair, but he was out of words.

He closed his eyes but could smell Geraldine's cigarette breath as she leaned in close. "Dillard, are you scared?"

He thought about Alice and the music, and Emilia Mae and the haircut, and the shortbread, and the Kleppers. He was home.

Everything was different, everything was the same. "No," he said. "Not really."

Chapter 36

Eighty-one degrees. The day foretold a hot New Rochelle summer, and it was only the second week in May. Dillard lay shivering under a comforter and wool blanket. Emilia Mae sat on his bed and took his icy hands in hers. "Raynaud's," she said, gently massaging his fingers. His skin was gray, and his fingers so thin she was afraid she'd break them. Not Raynaud's.

"Raynaud's," said Dillard, trying to smile. The eyes glowed. All the other features had sunk into his face. Beneath the blankets, Dillard wore one of Earle's ancient cashmere sweaters and a pair of sweatpants. Still cold.

Geraldine and Alberto came that afternoon, he with a Tupperware container filled with pureed lentils and squash, she with a bag full of shortbread. "I know you can't eat these, but I thought you might like to smell them." She'd held the bag under Dillard's nose. He'd made a smacking sound with his lips.

"I know," she said. "You've always loved them." She came closer and whispered, "You made Emilia Mae very happy for a while. Truth be told, I never got over that she snagged someone as handsome as you." She paused as something caught in her throat. "You know, you made me happy, too."

The Kleppers came two mornings later. Dillard's eyes were closed but he squeezed Cora's hand when she said, "We love you." Aloysius stood at the foot of the bed. "Rest easy, my friend," he said. Cora swore she saw Dillard nod.

The saying goodbye was beginning. Geraldine came every day. Sometimes, she told him gossip about people he might remember from the bakery; other times she sat next to his bed quietly. When Alice came, she'd sing to him, mostly songs they'd sung together. He opened his eyes for a moment when she said, "It looks as if I'm going to have this baby on May twenty-eighth, your birthday."

They all talked about these things—his hand squeezing, his nodding, his brief opening of the eyes—as if they were signs that Dillard was coming back. Geraldine swore he smiled when she told him that the old Neptune Inn had been turned into a whorehouse, and Alice thought she'd heard him hum a bit when she sang "Someone to Watch over Me." In his kind way, Carl tried to put them on a steady course: "Whatever is wrong with him doesn't have a name. I'm afraid it has no cure, either."

Whatever was wrong with him claimed him quickly and cruelly.

Dillard died surrounded by Emilia Mae, Alice, Geraldine, Cora, and Aloysius. When it was over, Aloysius spoke for all of them when he said, "I think he knew he died at home."

Dillard had left Alice an envelope labeled TO BE OPENED UPON MY DEATH. It was a single sheet. His Selmer flute and his father's antique instruments were to go to Alice. Whatever money he had left—

"it won't be much"—was to go toward an education for Alice's daughter: "NEC, maybe?" Emilia Mae would get the old Formica table he'd taken from their kitchen, and "anyone who wanted anything else should take it."

He wanted to be cremated. If there was a service, Aloysius should perform it, and he'd be "much obliged" if Alice would sing something. Otherwise, he wanted his ashes scattered in Skyville. He wrote down Sharlene Moore's phone number. "Call her, she'll know where to put me."

They waited until a month after Alice had her baby girl, Linden, and before dawn on a day in late June, Emilia Mae, Alice, and Geraldine left for Skyville. Alice had contacted Sharlene, who would meet them when they arrived. Emilia Mae got driving instructions from the AAA and borrowed Dave's Chevy Malibu wagon. After they settled in the car, with Emilia Mae behind the wheel, Geraldine in the front seat, and Alice in the back, Geraldine pulled the urn out of her shopping bag. Black metal, in the shape of a vase, it had a silver treble clef on one side, underneath which she'd had engraved DILLARD FOX MAY 28, 1931–MAY 16, 1981.

"Don't you think a simple urn would have done the trick?" asked Emilia Mae.

"He was a musician, after all," said Geraldine.

"Sure, but—"

Alice interrupted by poking her head between the two of them. "Mom, Grandma, we're on the way to bury Dillard, who happens to be right here." She tapped on the metal urn. "Can you at least lay off each other until we get the deed done?"

Emilia Mae and Geraldine smiled at each other, and Alice continued talking. "The way Dillard described Skyville, I'll bet it's gorgeous. He always talked about the mountains, the flowers, the way it smelled. I can't wait to see it."

Geraldine held the urn in her lap. "This was the right thing to do, bringing him here."

"It was," said Emilia Mae. "Thanks for coming with us."

They hit Skyville late in the afternoon. Sharlene Moore had told them to meet at her house and she'd take them to the appropriate place. They drove through town, expecting the smell of columbine and jasmine, the soft mists. Instead, the streets smelled of fried chicken and hamburgers and were dotted with Wendy's, Chick-fil-A, Hot Diggity Dawg, Sky's the Limit Souvenirs. Billboards were everywhere advertising God (I'VE BEEN HERE ALL ALONG), promising the messiah (JESUS: COMING SOON), and threatening damnation (HELL IS FOREVER. DON'T BE A FOOL, GET SAVED. 822-3344).

"This sure as hell doesn't look like Brigadoon to me," said Geraldine.

"It is pretty tacky," said Emilia Mae.

Alice noted that Dillard said the town had become more touristy than when he'd lived there.

As they drove up to the old log house, a woman in bare feet, a long floral skirt, and a man's shirt tied at the waist came out to the front porch. "Hey, welcome to Skyville," she said.

The three Wingo women squinted in the sun as they stepped out of the car. "You must be Sharlene," said Alice.

They introduced themselves and shook hands. Geraldine was still holding on to the urn, which she held out in front of Sharlene. "This is Dillard."

Sharlene stepped back. "Yes, we've met. Why don't you come in and have some iced tea?"

"I'd love some," said Alice. Emilia Mae shook her head. "Thank you, but I think we should do what we came to do now, before the sun sets, and if the offer still holds, iced tea after?"

"Sure thing," said Sharlene. "I'll run in and get my keys, then y'all follow me in your car."

Sharlene led them through some back roads where phlox were blazing and the coneflowers were bursting. They drove a little farther until they came to a lake. Lake Lure, the sign said. Sharlene parked in the lot and got out of her car, and the four of them walked to the lake's edge. The sun was low in the sky, and the water reflected magenta and orange. Canoers and kayakers churned the lake, and the air smelled like fresh, sweet summer, just as Dillard had said. Sharlene kept moving a few steps to the left, then a couple of feet to the right.

"Are you trying to find something in particular?" asked Emilia Mae.

"Gotta find the spot," said Sharlene.

Finally, she planted her feet on the muddy shoreline. "This is it."

They stood in a clump and looked to each other for what to do next. "We should say something," said Geraldine. "We can't just dump him here."

Emilia Mae remembered what Aloysius had said in the small service they'd held for him at the church. "Time takes and gives," she said softly, paraphrasing his words. "Time took Dillard, but not before he gave all he could to those around him. To me, he gave love and comfort when I most needed it. He became the father Alice never had and nourished her gift of music. He gave my mother...hmm, he gave my mother whatever the hell she wanted. Go in peace, Dillard."

They all stared at Geraldine, still holding the urn. "Uh–uh, I'm not doing this." She handed it to Emilia Mae, who handed it to Alice. They'd been told to bring a screwdriver and nail polish remover to unseal the urn. Alice worked the screwdriver around the hardened epoxy. When she finally got it open, she carefully removed the plastic bag filled with ashes. She thought to sing something, but why sing when the sound of the water lapping against the shore was as pretty as any song? Besides, this was Dillard's place, not hers.

Sharlene told her where to stand, then put her hands onto Alice's shoulder and turned her slightly to the left. "There, throw them in that direction."

Alice opened the bag and tossed its contents. The ashes fluttered over the water like a swarm of dragonflies and fell into the lake just in front of the floating dock.

Sharlene clasped her hands together and whispered, "Here he comes, Nicky"

Emilia Mae took Sharlene's hand and squeezed it. Alice rested her head on Emilia Mae's shoulder, and Geraldine linked her arm with Alice's. That's how they stood until the sun set and the color faded from the water.

Acknowledgments

I am one lucky soul to have had Millicent Bennett, editor and friend, guide me through this novel with her deft hand and generous heart. My fearless agent, Victoria Skurnick, has been an unfailing friend forever, and I would follow her anywhere.

Thank you, Ben Sevier, Karen Kosztolnyik, Brian McLendon, Matthew Ballast, Albert Tang, Jordan Rubinstein, Tiffany Porcelli, Kristen Lemire, and Carmel Shaka at Grand Central Publishing for making this such a painless pleasure. Seema Mahanian, with grace and passion, took this book through its final steps. I am so grateful for her care and dedication.

Stacey Reid and Lori Paximadis scoured the copy for errant punctuation and peculiar logic. Any mistakes in those areas are mine.

I'm grateful to Josh Deutsch, extraordinary musician, teacher, and friend, for the music.

My book group constantly reminds me why we write and how we read. Thank you: Meakin Armstrong, Catherine Chung, Alexandra Horowitz, Elizabeth Kadetsky, Sally Koslow, Aryn Kyle, and Jennifer Vanderbes.

The New York Society Library gave me refuge during the writing of this book. Thank you, Carolyn Waters and your gracious staff.

ACKNOWLEDGMENTS

My dear friend Lisa Grunwald spent almost as much time with these pages and characters as I have. They and I have all benefited from her brilliant insights and fine editing.

And always, Gary Hoenig. None of this would have happened without you.

About the Author

Betsy Carter is the author of the novels *Swim to Me*, *The Orange Blossom Special*, *The Puzzle King*, and *We Were Strangers Once*, as well as her best-selling memoir, *Nothing to Fall Back On*. She was the founding editor of *New York Woman* magazine and has worked at many other magazines, including *Newsweek*, *Harper's Bazaar*, and *Esquire*. She lives in New York City.